Driven

Other books by KaShamba Williams

Blinded—An Urban Tale
Grimey—The Sequel to Blinded

Driven

A Novel By
KaShamba Williams

URBAN BOOKS
www.urbanbooks.net

Urban Books
10 Brennan Place
Deer Park, NY 11729

ISBN-13: 978-1-893196-86-5
ISBN-10: 1-893196-21-6

First Mass Market Printing: April 2007
Printed in the United States of America

10   9   8   7   6   5   4   3   2   1

This is a work of fiction. Any references or similarites to actual events, real people, living, or dead, or to real locals are intended to give the novel a sense of reality. Any similarity in other names, characters, places, and incidents is entirely coincidental.

Submit Wholesale Orders to:
Kensington Publishing Corp.
c/o Penguin Group (USA) Inc.
Attention: Order Processing
405 Murray Hill Parkway
East Rutherford, NJ 07073
Phone: 1-800-526-0275
Fax: 1-800-227-9604

Editor: Joanie Smith
Cover Design/Graphics: *www.MarionDesigns.com*
Author photo courtesy of: Hope Rose, DBI, Inc.

Dedications

To my most precious angel resting above, my son, Robert Ross, Jr. *aka* Li'l Bobby. Not a day goes by . . . some days are worse than others, but I continue to press on.

To the rest of my supporting family members that have shared blood, sweat and tears while I was writing this book—I'm so sorry and *I'm so-sincere*! Mya, Mecca, Mehki and to my husband Lamotte that has suffered through extreme circumstances and substantial losses this year alone . . . the sun will continue to shine even in the midst.

R.I.P. to a dear friend who passed away recently—David "Doc" Chittum—a loving husband, father and brother to many.

To all of the dedicated fathers that have withstood the *'baby momma drama'* and continue to take care of their responsibilities—regardless of the situation(s)—stay strong! There are many that feel your pain.

To all the readers that have endorsed me in my projects. Thank you from the depths of my heart! Thank you for the emails, your honesty and your commitment to purchase a book with my name on it. I pray that I stay within the standards . . . if I don't, I'm quite sure you will let me know ☺. I'm keeping it green for you . . .

Acknowledgments

Lord, I thank you for humbling me everyday. Without you, where would I be? Of all the possibilities, I am most grateful that you pulled me in this direction!

Mom, thank you for the support and for taking care of the kids every weekend while I'm out on the road.

Kenyatta, nothing changes if nothing changes—the streets are waiting . . . on a novel that is.

Pop-Pop, Grandmom Portia, Dad, Dee, Leslie, Alexis, Toni, Bonita, Kashamba, Malik, Aunt Robin, Granddad, Kenny, Angie, Aunt Paulette, Kim, Steven, my step-daughter Jasmine, my stepson Lamotte, Kendra and baby Rhythm our newest member of the family, thank you for consistently advertising the name, KaShamba Williams.

Lois Moore, Teali, Brownsville, Hank, Bop, Nap, Aunt Tootie, Tuesday, Janice, Rhonda, Uncle Edward, Uncle David, Donald, Shontia, Cartilla, Trish, Ronnika, Kimyatta, Ms. Almethar, Uncle Mike, Aunt Ethel, Candy, Gibber, Carlton, Pete—thank you for holding ole' girl down, especially you Brown, only you know the real struggle!

To all my nieces and nephews.

To fellow Authors

To one of the realest authors I've met in this journey that offers endless support: When you said the wolves are out . . . damn if they weren't. I'm sticking and moving, and still holding the Heavy Weight Champion Belt! Al-Saadiq Banks, friends like you, are hard to come by. By the way . . . can I borrow Yusef? Just for a month! ☺

Vickie Stringer and Shannon Holmes thank you for "Paying it forward" . . . much respect to you for that. This comes directly from the heart.

K'wan, you have been a constant inspiration to me from the very first project and continue to keep it authentic. I have much respect for you.

Tracy Brown, tip ya hat to the side cause you put it down once again with a page-turning novel. I can't wait for *Criminal Minded*.

Arthur, you keep me laughing. I see why Tracy B. keeps you around. ☺

Nikki Turner, thank you for the plug. KaShamba still has love for you!

Joylynn Jossel, it's time to get them ready for *If I ruled the world*! Thank you for taking the time out of your busy schedule to help me in anyway you could.

T.N. Baker, watch what I tell you! It was already envisioned. Still, Sheisty is going to do superbly!

Trustice, you are a talented humble brotha. Many blessings sent your way!

Victor Martin, continue to keep the faith even when it looks bleak.

Carl Weber—Thank you for looking ahead. You've given me an opportunity that others wouldn't. It doesn't matter about all the whispers—I know what's true on my end—thank you! (I'm looking forward to the *Around The Way Girls 2* and *Girls In Da Hood 2*), Mark Anthony, Eric Gray, Reginald Hall, Hickson, Shamora Renee, Azarel, Brandon McCalla, Michael Baisden, Tony Rose, William Cooper, Heather Covington, J. Unique Shannon, Leondre Prince, Jo-Jo, Shahida Fennell, Anthony Whyte, Cho Woods, Freda Hazzard, Lenaise Meyeil (Your time is coming!), Lou Price, Jaa'mall Oglesby, Relentless Aaron, Crystal Winslow, Thomas Long, Tony Lindsey, Karen E. Quinones Miller, Shawna Grundy, Deborah Smith, Urb'n Anthony, Nishawnda, Rakeem Wilburn, Jessica Tilles, Petra, Ralph Johnson . . .

To the Literary Heads

Joanie, who said the Internet wasn't a useful source? For you and I, it was the connection. Thank you for joining with Precioustymes Entertainment in this journey.

Authors Helping Authors Group, Precioustymes Yahoo Group, TCP message board users, C2C Readers, Mejah Bookstore, my place away from home. Emlyn, Marilyn, Diane, Jewel and Carmen, thank you for making me feel welcomed. Ninth Street Books, Borders Express, B&Ns, Waldenbooks, Shrine of the Black Madonna, Darryl Harris, Source of Knowledge, Expressions, Urban Knowledge, Sepia & Sable, Truth, Tru, Karibu, NuExpression, A&B, Lushena, Culture Plus, Afrikan World, Hustleman Masaamba in Queens, Liquorous and many more.

Angie Henderson—Read In Color, Raw Sistazs Reviewers, Yasmine—APOOO, A Nu Twistaflavah, Forefront magazine, LIVE magazine, The Grits, Heather Covington—Disigold magazine, Amorous Sepia Readin' Sistahs, Ebony Expressions, Mahogany bookclub, Sister2Sister, Lloyd & Kevin— *www.theblacklibrary.com*, AALBC, Go On Girl, ARC, Sistah Circle, Nakea—As The Page Turns, Ebony Eyes, Between Friends and to all the other clubs that read any of my books—thank you!

Special Shouts

To all the females I've counseled in the community centers, detention centers, on the phone, email and in my home—much love to all of you! Armelvis Booker, Cindy, Ella, Autumn, Devon Chambers, Carla Banks (I got you next go 'round ma!), Liva—Dat's What's Up, Mil, Martina Gibbs, Shana, Shay, Donza, Cheryl, Shawnika, Tammy, Nicole, Tiffany, Shawn, Dawn, Cabrella, Russell, Ada, Michelle, Kita, Charmaine, Helen, Terrance, Keisha, Jimae, Red, Ronnie & Timmy, Ms. Francine, Buddha, Brian, Darren, Randy, Squirt, Rhonda, Renee, Chalary, Mrs. Lois, Ronnie, Gayle, Sheen, Karen, Dee-Dee, Shawn, Demar, Deartis, Shell, Bryon, Raven, Nina, Farren, Lori, Li'll, Professor Hurdle, Detective Mayfield, Detective Chapman, Nakea, Christine, Gary, Medina, Melissa, Kiana, Will, Rob Berry, Keith & Keisha, Spoony, Doug, Larae, Troy Stevens, Saundra, Kitty, Melanie, Verna, Wink, Tracy, Tilla, Roslyn, Elgin (Keep ya head up!), Duvowel, Picture That Productions, Crystal—All God's Children, OCJ Graphix, Foster's, Williams', Carrington's, Ross's Gibbs', Armstead's, Moore's, to everyone holding me down . . .

To anyone I missed, write your name here:

_____.

(I had to use that Jessica ☺.)

I'd love to hear your comments.
Visit me online at *www.KaShambaWilliams.com*
Or, email me at *precioustymesent@aol.com*.

Part I

WHEN SEEDS ARE PLANTED

IT'S IN THE BLOOD

"**T**urn this *shit* up! I know I gave a bitch at least six or seven babies off this song," Marv boasted to everyone in the car, gyrating to the beat. "What you talk'n 'bout? Nigga, pimpin' ain't easy. Stan, you can roll something on that!"

As Marv drove down the Jersey turnpike in a shiny black Cadillac Coupe Deville, his dark silky fingers barely touched the steering wheel while listening to a tune of The Isley Brothers, "Between the Sheets." The melody graced the car throughout. His lover and partner in crime, Loretta, smiled as if she'd hit the jackpot on Lucky Seven's at the Trump Casino in Atlantic City. His right hand-man, Stan, pulled on a freshly rolled joint that filled the car with smoke: from the burning of Arizona Red—the best marijuana around in the early 80s.

"*Shiittt,* I'll neva give a trick my sperm babies. I'll jerk my shit on they ass, on they stomach, and in they mouth. Wherever they want these babies to go," Stan joked.

Loretta hadn't joined in the conversation until she

heard Stan talking that shit. She could give a fuck about the last broad Marv gave pipe to, but her girl, Francine, would have a problem with it, for this was her husband who was popping that shit.

"Francine would whip your ass if she heard you bragging on those bitches," Loretta said, referring to Stan's wife and her best friend.

"Why?" Stan asked. "She'll never have to worry about a whore getting pregnant." Stan and Marv busted out laughing—both coughing up smoke.

"That's my nigga," Marv coaxed.

The windows fogged with density, thick as the morning meadow dew. Marv cracked the window for some of the smoke to clear.

"Loretta, play the back role and be glad I gave you this good dick, raw." Marv teased her. He was happier than a faggot with a bag of dicks that he and Loretta had a baby on the way.

No one seemed bothered or alarmed by the concealed twenty-five New York quarters of dope that they just copped from their Harlem connect. The three of them felt secure and comfortable leaning back, kicking the "willie bo-bo," on the ride home. Marv took two pulls off the Arizona Red then passed it on to Stan; each taking turns on a quest to get high. All of them were content riding down the New Jersey turnpike, which kept ambitious police officers stationed in the cut, anxiously waiting to make another black man a "Driving While Black Victim". With the fact that Loretta had half the stash of dope hidden between her legs and the other half beneath her largely inflated breasts, that covered her swollen motherly milk sacks that would nurture her unborn son, Marv, Jr., better known as Nasir, pronounced Nah-seer.

"Let me get a pull of that," Loretta craved.

"Are you dead-ass serious?" Marv asked, turning his head toward her.

"Yeah, why not? A little weed ain't gone hurt this baby."

Marv contemplated for a brief moment and figured what the fuck . . . his son was born from an O.G., why not teach him the game early on?

Marv and Loretta would share many road trip experiences like this one together, but the most noted memory they held dear to their hearts was of the natural-birth of their one and only son together, Nasir.

Nasir was conceived of a naïve young woman for a mother, with the genes of a pimp for a father, mixed with aged brandy and marijuana. This lethal combination would make or break him, as a young man.

During his birth, the tension in the labor room was building between Marv and Loretta.

"Push, Loretta. Come on, baby, push my li'l nigga out!"

Marv's eyes were bloodshot, glossy-red from getting high all night long.

Him and Stan hung out 'til the wee hours of the morning at the downtown titty bar, though neither one was a big tipper to the girls. They were there to get tore-down, free feels and to watch the pussy sellers.

Marv, yes indeed, he was quite the ladies choice. Signs he sent off to women would transmit like a female dog in heat. Women could never decipher whether his mating-call was perpetrated by money, or the lust of *them*. His mack-moves were much smoother than the average pimp. Women forced themselves upon him. He never had to recruit. The whores scouted him. Loretta, at first, wasn't any different from them. Her brother

Bucky was a stone cold junky, a big-time heroin user, toting drugs for Marv.

One particular off night, Bucky didn't have the energy to bring in customers because he needed a hit real bad—shaking, begging and jonezin' for that dream bag. Marv was known for having the "knock-out" that made you nod for what seemed like forever. Bucky, a rotten-tooth scoundrel, always wired and down to get high, was in a very bad way. He had to see Marv for a fix to get off E—empty. Without having any money to pay, he offered him his tender, young sister who was 17-years-old, in exchange for a bag. Marv had the best dope, and in desperation, Bucky gave up his little sister to get that feeling—from "knock-out." Loretta loved her older brother; doing anything asked of him. Bucky set it up for Marv to meet Loretta at the pool hall that same night, to get the fix he needed so desperately. Marv had checked around town and heard about one man that she'd been with. To him, she was hardly tainted—fresh meat for the team.

When Marv and Loretta met for the first time, it wasn't what either of them expected it to be. Marv couldn't take his deep, distinctive eyes off her. They were maxing out at Soldier's, an after hours club, shooting pool, alienating themselves from the crowd.

Marv sank the eight ball in the corner pocket, sucking his teeth; plotting to get some of that young tender pussy.

"You like what you see, don't you, girl?" he bragged with his golden tongue.

Loretta sat in the wooden chair next to the pool table, giving him her undivided attention, with her legs crossed. She had no idea that her big brother, the one she loved so much, used her as a pawn for dope. She felt special thinking Marv chose her over all the other females. It would never cross her mind that her own brother would set her up like this. She knew she was the shit tonight. She'd heard about the infamous suited-down, slender, chocolate-drop man in school in between classes, pep rallies and sporting events. He was even the number one topic of discussion in the girl's bathroom. The older girls, who were seniors, were always schemin' on a way to get Marv to notice them.

"It all depends daddy . . . what you gon' let me see?" she flirted back.

Neither Marv, nor Loretta, could care less if a bomb had gone off outside of the club the night they met. They shared a chemical bond like DNA chromosomes. Though Bucky's intentions were fiendish, he would never recognize the strong combination he'd put together.

If Marv could get any higher than he already was, his feet would be floating in mid air around the labor and delivery room. It was 3:47 in the morning and he was feeling the spirited nature, as if he'd smoked an ounce of that "sticky-icky" and drank a pint of Paul Mason—his favorite drink.

"I'm pushing his head out as hard as I can. His head is too goddamn big!" screamed Loretta in torturing pain.

Marv quietly laughed from the thought of his son having a big nugget that rest upon his shoulders. That head on Nasir would deposit solid wisdom and strong beliefs in his future. He knew from this point forward, though his son was Jr., they would call him Nasir—symbolizing a nurturer, warrior and a conqueror in life.

Loretta's blood rushed to her brain with every push, pulsating-the-veins that lodged in her temples.

"Aww, come on, baby. It can't be that bad; chuck that shit up like a real woman!"

Unsympathetic comments made by Marv without addressing Loretta's demanding needs during this time, was a bad move on his part. Loretta grabbed the hospital's brown water-pitcher full of ice chips, and threw it at him; scattering the ice with the bucket clunking around the hospital floor, just missing one of the nurses.

"What the fuck is the matter with you, Loretta? Are you out of your fuckin' mind?" Marv let that shit slide. At this point, he realized that she was in tremendous pain.

As if the coldness from the air conditioning in the room wasn't enough, she had the audacity to fling ice chips all over the semi-glossed white and beige tiled floor. The doctor sandwiched between the couple, requested that Loretta push long and hard one good time, in hopes to get this delivery over and done with. He was agitated beyond reason at the young couple. He hated to deliver babies for first time parents.

Loretta was seventeen and Marv was 23-years-old. He should have been prosecuted for indulging in having sex with a minor. However, Loretta lied to him about her age and told him she was 18-years-old, that night at the pool hall. He didn't find out until later by her mother, Mom Flossy, as everybody called her, that she had just turned seventeen.

Contractions were striking at an alarming speed, hitting Loretta's backside like the crackling of thunder and lightning during a ghastly storm.

"*Oonuch*! It hurts *sooo* bad," Loretta bawled, in distressing pain.

The stretching, tugging, and splitting of her vaginal lips could be felt by each pull. Marv convinced her to deliver naturally, without any pain stimulants. He was filled with tingling anxiety knowing he was seconds away from seeing his baby boy.

"You can do this shit, Loretta. You took in all of this shit here," he said holding onto his crotch.

The smell of tantalizing malt liquor and marijuana jumped off Marv's tongue after each magnified word, filling the room with his scent. Loretta screamed louder and louder as the pressure intensified until she felt an immediate release similar to the urgent need of taking a shit when it's at the tip ready to come out, whether you are in a position for it come out, or not. Sweat beaded on her forehead, while she lay on her back, sighing from the tremendous amount of force.

The weight of the head made her look up at the ceiling in the birthing room and scream out to God, *"Please don't let me die! I'm too young."*

She couldn't concentrate on one particular object. Her hands prickled, her eyes burned and she wasn't able to hear any sounds except humming noises. Using all her force, she pulled her knees back in cradle position. She pushed with all her power and finally a male child found his way out of the contracting canal. Head first, then his rugged shoulder frame. The rest of his body slid out with ease.

"Aaugh," she released; the load was finally lightened.

"It's a boy," Doctor Dworkin informed them.

"I know damn well it's a boy," Marv said confidently, assured that Loretta conceived a boy instead of a girl.

Faintly, Loretta spoke, exhausted from giving birth to their new baby boy. One would have thought this was Loretta's only child—but she had an older daughter.

She started screwing early at the age of fifteen, after the first time she felt that curious twitching between her legs. Her first child, a bubbly little girl named Sheena, had a father that was just as young as she was and didn't have a clue what a father was, let alone being one. He split the scene before Sheena was born. Loretta didn't really stress about having him around. Her mother was there to hold down the fort.

"I thought from the way I was carrying, it was going to be a girl. This is the same way I carried Sheena and the ultrasound man also told me, we were having a girl." She was a little disappointed, as her facial expression showed.

The look on Marv's face could automatically detect his disapproval of Loretta's comments. His jaw started to ache from clenching it so hard. His upper muscles tensed up, sore from the tightening. In a much-like-pimp manner, he responded to Loretta's conclusion.

"Like I told you before, Loretta, I don't make bitches, only pimps!"

Never did Marv imagine a dope fiend's hook up would lead to this—the best damn relationship he had in his life. The oneness he shared with Loretta was consummated through the birth of their son, Nasir.

It was a beautiful beginning for a small family. She gave him a son that bore his name. Marv was the happiest man, in a hospital full of sick and ailing patients, at that very moment.

Doctor Dworkin was about to tap on Nasir's buttocks to submerge him with his first sound—cries. An inch away, Marv puckered his thick, upper-lip looking at Doctor Dworkin positioning his hands to smack his namesake.

"What the fuck are you doing, doc? If anybody is

gon' smack my son for the first time, its damn sure going to be me. Slavery ended long ago, partna'." Marv pulled his hand back and smacked the left cheek layered with slimy white residue, and smeared it on Doctor Dworkin's white coat.

"Thanks, doc." Marv said to him, wiping his hands clean.

Doctor Dworkin lifted up immediately to change into a clean white overcoat. Nasir, startled from his traumatic birthing experience, cried out finally, peering through all the gook that was between his pupils and eyelids.

After Marvin cut the cord, the nurses scooped the baby up, and headed to the infant section of the room to clean him up. Relaxing for a few brief moments, Loretta finally looked up to see her son.

"Damn, that's an ugly-ass little boy with cracked-up skin, looking like a plucked-chicken running wild in the chicken sack!"

Marv came right back at her with his response. He took that comment very offensively.

"Loretta, when was the last time you looked in the mirror? You ain't a damn beauty queen yourself. He just came out of a nasty-ass corroded birth canal. He has an excuse, what's yours?"

Loretta laughed without regret; even Doctor Dworkin and the nurses in the room found his comment a little humorous.

The anticipation of holding Nasir was the only matter keeping Marv's spirit up. He was fighting, trying to stop his high from coming down.

"Doc, you can hand me my son now."

This was a moment he would never forget. When the nurse placed Nasir into Marv's arms, he held him tight,

rocking him back and forth: smelling of liquor and
weed.

Having never experienced a strong father and son
relationship with his own father, Marv was determined
to formulate a bond that no one, not even Loretta,
would be able to come between. He knew of his father
and had seen him only on occasion; bumping into him
at the number bank, when running numbers for his
mother. His father was like a team of investors backing
out of a bad deal, abandoning him, when shit got
rough. While love believed to grow inside of Marv, the
emotional feelings that occupied space in his mind was
full of hatred for the man that gave him life. No matter
how much effort his mother, Anna, put into raising him
to be a decent wage earning man, she could never fill
the void that only his father could in their son's life.
Unlike his father, Marv had an agenda: an agenda powered by the strong-will to be an influential factor in his
son's life.

Nasir forced his little chinky-eyes open to look at the
shadow of the man that held him so tight, he could feel
the unconditional love penetrating to his little heart.
Excited by Nasir opening his eyes and looking at him,
Marv hollered over to Loretta.

"Baby, this is my li'l man. Ain't this some shit? I'ma
father."

Loretta watched the connection that Marv built with
his son in a matter of minutes and felt slightly jealous
that he was more concerned about the baby than her
recovery. She was teary eyed, but praised her man for
the bond he began with his son.

In Marv, there were never reservations of abandoning his family and after seeing him as a proud father for
the first time, Loretta knew it would never happen.

Because of Marv's impressive jazzy-style, and creamy-black baby-soft-skin, young ladies practically threw their panties at him. On a number of occasions, females claimed to be pregnant with his child, trying to lock him down. As much as he expressed his desire to most of them that he wanted a son for his legacy to continue on, not so much as one of those hookers that claimed to be pregnant gave birth to Marvin Bundy's child. Though many lied and said they did. One went so far as to put an announcement in the local newspaper announcing the birth to the city, claiming that Marv was the father. When Marv went over to Lena's house, it was no way in hell that he was the father of the receding hairline, chubby-cheeked, high-yellow-skinned, baby boy. Especially, when the little boy's mother had a camel complexion. That didn't mix with a man that was a second away from being blue-black. He knew Lena had to be lying. For that, he beat her ass in front of her new man who sat back and watched his woman take an ass whooping—scared of jumping in, fearing he too would get his ass stomped. Lena made fun of Loretta the night before, telling everyone that Loretta was one of Marv's whores and that she was having a trick's baby. After that occurrence happened with Marv, she never peeped a word about Loretta again. That ass-whooping Marv gave her made Lena regretful months after it occurred, even though she still told people in the community that Marv was her son's father without it ever being proven.

Marv never contested Lena's accusations to people outside his clique, although he knew the only seed that his sperm produced into life was in his hands. The 6-pound 4-ounce baby had dark, creamy-chocolate complexion like his father. Nasir, with cracked-up, plucked-chicken-skin and all—this was his son.

Nasir's eyes focused on his father, blinking only twice as he stared.

"That's right, Nasir, its Daddy. Take a good look at me. I'm a pretty mothafucka, ain't I? Follow my lead and you will neva go wrong. You hear that, son?"

He conversed with his son like he understood what he was saying to him. Disappointed he had to hand Nasir over to the nurses, he knew it was time for his son to get the proper screenings and testing required of a newborn baby. He placed him into the arms of one of the nurses and told her to take extra precautions with him. Then, he bent over his woman, kissed her on the forehead and said, "We getting married when you settle in at home. I need my son branded with the Bundy name. I don't give a fuck how you do it, but you better work that shit out the best way you can."

He expected Loretta to pull it off somehow. Times weren't the same, today you can practically give your baby any last name, but during that era, you could only give the baby a mother's maiden name unless she was married with written documentation to follow. Marv was persistent with his request.

"If ya ass come home with a birth record that doesn't read, Marvin Bundy, Jr., I'ma beat the uterus out ya just to make sho' that you will *neeeva* make the same mistake twice." His bottom-lip hung after a delayed reaction from the extended sounds of *neeeva* coming from his mouth.

Loretta dozed off with the thought of becoming Mrs. Marvin Bundy. Marv had no idea of the initial reaction and feeling that consumed Loretta after hearing the big "M" word. Her body was flustered, which made her listen nimbly. She smiled for the first time in the birthing center. She didn't know how she would maneuver the changing of last names without legal documentation, but she was damn sure willing to try her luck at it. She would have Francine conjure up the marriage license, since she worked at the Office of Vital Statistics in the state building.

"Make it happen, Loretta. Make it happen, before you leave this here," dictated Marvin to his soon to be wife. "I'll be back later with your ring."

Loretta's mouth was dry as cotton, trying to respond. Had she not thrown the ice bucket at Marv, maybe she'd have something to wet the dryness that filled her mouth.

"Okay, baby," she said feeling the dryness.

She didn't want anything to slow up the process. She was trying to make sure everything was legitimate. It was not about to rain on her parade. Too many days she anticipated his hand in marriage, although she never guessed all it took was to have a baby by him. She would have had one sooner if she'd known he would propose to her.

Not in a romantic fancy kind of way, Marv proposed through general conversation. That was his formal presentation and offer of marriage. Actually, it was more like a demand. He wasn't going to take no for an answer. Loretta began to question herself. Was it only on the strength of Nasir that he proposed? Did he really love her, for her?

Loretta quickly looked at Nasir, who was bundled up in a nice warm blanket, and then over to her man she'd longed for—for years. Both of her men undoubtedly would consume her life.

For a minute, she forgot all about poor little Sheena, who was being raised by Mom Flossy. Her mother was concerned about the lifestyle Loretta and Marvin lived.

That's why she dared not to let Sheena be around them, but she knew there was no way in hell she would be able to take Marvin's only child away. She was pissed that he snatched up her fast-ass teenage daughter. Loretta had dropped out of school and everything. Hanging out with girlfriends was a thing of the past for her. Things were better for Marv this way. He didn't have to worry about the other females he fucked with approaching her at school. Yet, it was her mother that scolded her and tried hard to stagnate the love that Marv and Loretta shared.

Mom Flossy didn't particularly care for Marv, and neither did he for her, but he was taught to respect his elders. So, instead, he did things down-right under-handed: like the time when he greased down her rabbit fur with Vaseline. Or like the many times he would go to the supermarket and bring back white labeled brown bags that had *For Loretta & Sheena only* written on them. Mom Flossy never underestimated his deviant behaviors. She'd found out that Marv was pimping women one day after overhearing him talking on the phone, but in the same conversation, he confessed his love for Loretta to the person on the receiving end. Even with that, it still didn't change her opinion of him. Mom Flossy was a nosey woman, first; a concerned parent second; always up in their business. When she finally had enough of Marv, she forced Loretta out the house making her leave Sheena behind, pushing her daughter directly in the arms of the man she loved. Timing was perfect 'cause when she did that, Loretta didn't know how she was going to explain to her mother that she was pregnant—again.

A NEW BEGINNING

The cackling of the birds flapping their wings against the strong foundation of the hospital walls near the window made Loretta yawn, stretching her arms out to touch the ceiling. Soft rose petal colors surrounded the birthing room, which gave off an aura of peace. Loretta would remain tucked away in this room for three days—the maximum amount of days Medicaid would approve of. If she'd ever had a chance to reflect on her life, this was the time. She was feeling a bit antsy that Marv hadn't returned as planned, and it was already 10:00 a.m. He'd promised her that he'd be at the hospital first thing in the morning. Well, it was the first thing in the morning to *her*, and he was not there. She tried gently easing her legs off the bed to regulate the blood flow. She was tired of lying flat on her back. She'd spent the last 27 hours in labor and delivery, on her back. She'd be damned to spend the next 72 hours lying in the same position. To keep up with her man, her body best get back into shape, and fast.

The sounds of the television, in addition to the birds chirping and light cries from the newborns, were the only sounds she heard. That was of course, until she heard the loud voices that echoed through the A-unit that she was on. Everyone could hear the voices. Even the sleeping babies woke up from the ruckus.

"What room is Loretta Armstead in?" It was Marv; not asking anybody in general, but any person who would tend to his question.

The big baby-blue Mylar balloons flapping, with the writing "It's a boy" jolting up and down in the air covered his face. He questioned those in the area again. This time making sure they heard him.

"Excuse me, does anybody work in this *bitch*? What room is Loretta Armstead in? Anybody know? Or do I have to check all these mothafuckin' rooms myself to find out where she's at?"

Disturbed by his presence, one of the nurses pointed in the direction of Loretta's room. Marv was nonetheless thrilled.

"Something wrong with your mouth, bitch?"

Trailing behind him was his best-friend, Stan, and Francine, with a boatload of items for Nasir.

The open doorways to the rooms were easily accessible for anyone to come in and out of, freely. Loretta hadn't turned on the bright fluorescent lights due to the natural surge of daylight that poured through her room.

"Loretta, where you at?"

Marv walked past the first bed that was empty, searching for his woman. He hoped that the nurse hadn't sent them in the wrong room, for her sake. The curtain was pulled around the other bed, so he wasn't sure if she was on the opposite side of the curtain. He yanked the canary-yellow, flowery-looking separating-curtain back without fearing the response of a stranger greeting them. He looked back at Stan and Francine.

"She's not in this fuckin' room. I'm gonna cuss that bitch out."

Francine reached out to stop Marv from going to create a scene, which he was good at.

"Hold on, Marv. That's Loretta's overnight bag right there. This is her room."

Francine stepped in just in time, before Marv showed his natural color. The toilet could be heard flushing and that's when they knew, Loretta was in the bathroom. She walked out with her white, over-washed hospital gown on, taking baby-steps in her donated, white hospital slippers.

"Hey, baby. I heard y'all coming. I wanted to freshen up before you found me."

Marv kissed her on the cheek and helped her back onto the bed. Loretta loved when Marv showed his affectionate side. Stan and Francine extended there congrats and gave Loretta a warm welcome. With a strong emotional connection, simultaneously, Loretta knew what Marv's question would be as he looked around the room with searching eyes.

"Where's Nasir?" Marv asked.

"I just finished breast-feeding him, and sent him back to the nursery to rest."

The icy stare Marv gave her would instantly break Medusa to pieces.

"I don't trust these muthafuckas with my son like that. Haven't you heard about people snatching babies up from hospitals and shit? I want him in the room with you at all times."

Loretta wanted to let Marv have it one-good-time.

That day opened her eyes on just how protective Marv would be over his son. One of the questions hidden in the back of her mind was answered.

Francine held the marriage license so tight in her hands that the sweat print from her fingers dampened it. She shook it in front of Loretta's face.

"Girl, look what I'm holding in my hands!"

Had it not been for the stitches in her bottom, Loretta would have bounced around that room.

"Ooh, let me see it, Francine! Let me see it!" Every tooth in her mouth could be seen, as well as her gums.

Something about her name on the license with Marv's on it, filled every empty void in her body. Even without the preacher's signature validating the certificate, it felt like they were already a union.

Francine was a mutual friend of Marv and Loretta's. Their men formally introduced them; however, they knew each other because Francine went to school with Loretta's brother, Bucky. She would see Francine all the time walking home from school. Francine had a twig shape with huge, fluffy breasts. Her ass was nowhere to be found—she was in the family of flat-backs. Pancake was her nickname. Her glasses made her look very intellectual, and honestly, she was. She was the only person in high school to graduate with honors at the age of sixteen. She had a full scholarship to Temple University off of North Broad Street in Philadelphia. Her parents were so disappointed when she opted to accept a state job paying her a mere $18,000 a year. You couldn't tell Francine that because of her decision to skip college, she'd literally stopped her educational growth that may have provided for her a better job opportunity. She felt like she was on top of the world. She figured like this: how many other sixteen your olds were making that kind of money? She was hood-rich, loved by low-income neighbors, shunned upon by the middle class, and totally disregarded by those considered high class.

Her and Loretta eventually started being cordial to one another, and after the formal introduction, their friendship became tighter. Both of them were strictly about making money and pleasing their men. Francine didn't have any children, so it was easy for her to do extra special things for Loretta's children. To Francine, they were her niece and nephew, just not by blood.

WELCOME HOME BABY

Marv rearranged the furniture in the two-bedroom townhouse that he and Loretta shared. It was a small, yet snuggly townhouse. The second bedroom was small enough to fit a baby's crib in it and that was about it. The master bedroom wasn't that small, but it wasn't that big either. They were able to fit a queen size bed, one oak dresser and one oak TV stand in there. The closet was small enough to fit one person in it standing up; but it was their mofo' house and they were proud as hell of it, and the life they shared.

Marv was all prepared for his woman, and his son, to come home from the hospital. He wanted to make sure everything was perfect when his baby boy arrived home. He'd even spoke to Mom Flossy to check on Sheena to find out if she needed anything. Their conversation was everything but pleasant. Little shocks of spewing hatred and anger divulged back and forth between them.

"What the hell do you want, you low-life pimp?" Mom Flossy asked.

She hated his ways and wasn't the least bit afraid to let her emotions show how much she disliked him. Unlike the hoodlums on the street, she wasn't scared one bit. She'd cuss his ass out any chance she got.

"Is that any way for an old lady to talk to her son-in-law?" Marv asked, pressing his luck with her.

"Old lady, my ass. I'm well put together and better looking than half of those trashy women you got on the streets."

She was angry as the devil knowing he has to live an eternity in hell. Her daughter had to fall in love with a man, of all men, that was a pimp.

"You're not my goddamn son-in law. You ain't married to my daughter and you never will be!" she said very surely.

Marv couldn't wait to give her the news. His eyes darted around the room, scanning to see if anything else had to be rearranged in the house, and then he hit Mom Flossy with the news like she could visibly see him holding the marriage license.

"Well, what is this marriage license that I'm holding in my hands, then?"

Even though the marriage wasn't validated, he would use it to his advantage to make her mad. Mom Flossy jumped up from off the front porch of her house holding the cordless phone in her right hand, and screamed as loud as she could into the telephone.

"You mothafuckin' child molester! I'ma call the law. Loretta's only seventeen and I didn't sign a damn thing consenting for y'all to go and get married, negro!"

Marv smirked on the other end knowing he was getting under her skin.

"Flossy, Loretta turns eighteen in a few weeks. I don't care if we have your blessing or not. We are getting married and that's it. You either love me or leave me alone. You'd better get used to me 'cause I ain't going no-where!"

A raging bull snarling, kicking up dust, is what Marv was fighting against.

"Oh no, you low-life some-ma-ma-bitch, over my dead body—Loretta better not marry you. I'll kill that little huzzy!"

Outside of Marv's house, the horn could be heard inside from the sound echoing from the living room window. It was Stan, his main man, ready to pick up Loretta and Nasir from the hospital. The past few moments were full of disrespect, as Marv continued to rub it in her nose. Mom Flossy had finally sat back down on the front porch, rocking back and forth like a big baby that needed stimulation. After hearing the shocking news, she was convinced of just how much . . . she hated his ass.

"Mom Flossy, are you still there?"

Marv asked listening to nothing but dead-silence. He knew she was still lingering. That was one of her nosey tactics to try to catch someone slipping up and saying something that they shouldn't: by remaining silent, listening closely and acting like she wasn't on the phone.

"I know you're there, Flossy, but my time is precious. I got to go! I'm on my way to the hospital to pick up my wife and my son. Call me if Sheena needs anything."

He stood tall, standing upright, breathed in very deeply and let out a long unforced breath of air. The navy and white striped baby bag matched the navy blue Graco car-seat that he grabbed just before leaving the house. Stan was waiting patiently as Marv gathered the necessities for Nasir to come home, smoking a Newport cigarette that filled the car with a musty-lasting smell.

"Let's go, Stan, the man. They're waiting on us."

Marv then realized Stan was smoking in the car.

"Hold up, man. I know you're not chain-smoking knowing Nasir has to ride in this shit. Have a little respect for my young'n."

Stan plucked the butt of the cigarette out of the car ignoring Marv. His hand searched underneath his seat where he kept a can of spray deodorizer to kill odor. With one hand on the wheel and the other hand on the spray gun, Stan started spraying non-stop until Marv screamed at him. Marv was coughing uncontrollably between trying to cuss Stan out.

"What the fuck? . . ."

He gagged, trying to get a fresh breath of air from the outside. "Roll the window . . ." He gagged again, trying quickly to roll the windows down. His throat tickled from the chemicals.

Stan seemed to be fine, looking at Marv like he was the one blowing it out of proportion. Marv was finally able to clear his throat as the chemicals cleared the air.

"Nigga . . . you tryin' to kill me? Spraying that shit all in the car like that."

Stan attempted to light another cigarette, forgetting the reason he used the deodorizer in the first place. Seeing him pick up the lighter, Marv grabbed it out of his hand.

"I know this is your car nigga, but you won't be smoking another cigarette until Loretta and Nasir are out of this piece of shit."

"Fuck you, Marv. When you need to borrow my shit to creep in, you don't mind riding in this joint," Stan said.

Both Marv and Stan laughed at the comment.

"Ah nigga, I know you ain't pulling my card as many times as I bailed your ass out. You sloppy-ass, nigga!

"Get the fuck outta here!"

"You know if Flossy's ass didn't have my Cadillac impounded by the police, I would have my own transportation. I can get another car, but why should I when I have you as my driver?"

Stan laughed even harder. "Fuck you! Flossy hates your ass, doesn't she? What did you do to her?"

Marv looked over at Stan as if he didn't know. "Man, you know. I made her daughter fall in love with my fine ass, nigga!" he declared.

"You are one crazy nigga, Marv. That's why I fucks with you, man."

"Yeah, I'm that thoroughbred; I know. What you got to drink in this car? I know it's a fifth of something, hiding somewhere."

Stan reached under to the left and pulled out a fifth of Paul Mason. Marv's mouth watered.

"Hell yeah! Let me get my swig on."

His mouth was watering for the brandy. After he took a few mouthfuls, he passed the fifth over to Stan, who finished the rest of the bottle off. Now they were ready to deal with the world.

The Paul Mason worked its way directly into Marv's bloodstream, and the effects began to show as his eyes lowered lazily, and his speech began to slur.

"Where's Francine? I thought you said she was riding down with us?"

Stan answered, feeling the same effects as Marv, but drove his older model Cadillac with ease. He was a pro at driving, while drunk.

"Man, you know she's already there at Loretta's beck-'n-call. "

Marv nodded his head, acknowledging the comment. "Yeah, man, that's why I had the crib set up and the house spanked clean. I had one of the girls take care of that last night."

Stan let the thought ponder in his mind before responding.

"Let me get this right . . . you had one of the girls clean *Loretta's* house? Man, she's gon' kick your ass if she finds out."

Marv hadn't even thought about that.

"Who's gon' tell?"

Marv and Stan laughed at each other, once more. They'd become asshole tight since Stan took the rap during a prostitution sting. Never once did he implicate Marv in the ordeal, and took the rap by his lonesome. He knew Stan counted himself a trustworthy friend and he too, felt the same way in return. Although, Stan only received five years of probation after a completion of a drug rehabilitation program—that was time he wouldn't have to back up if he got caught out there again.

Weeks after Loretta came home from the hospital, she and Marv lived life like a newlywed couple—even though they still hadn't validated the marriage license. Marv was bringing all kind of money into the household, telling Loretta to save some of the money for Nasir's future. Loretta laughed at his gesture knowing they needed the money for today. *Why hold it for his future?* She thought. What she didn't realize was Marv had plans of letting go of the women, the heroin pushing, and his gambling habits—all to an end. He wanted to be a better role model for his son, or at least take the steps toward legitimizing his life. He even applied for jobs.

Nasir was two months old when Marv finally hit Loretta with the news that he was laying low from the street life. He saved enough money so they would be good financially for about one year. He figured the paycheck from his new place of employment, Amtrak, laboring rails and hauling materials was enough for them to make out.

Things were going as planned until Francine came over one day, hysterical because Stan was charged on a first-degree murder charge. Allegedly, one of the girls had a problem with a trick, and she called Stan to come assist her. Without a doubt, he went over to the motel to check it out. When he arrived the trick was beating the girl half-to-death. She was struggling, trying to get away from the man, but she had little to no energy to fight him off. At first, Stan pulled out his pistol to scare the dude off, but the scare tactic didn't work. The dude pulled out his own pistol trying to shoot back at Stan, but Stan shot at him first—shooting him one time. That one shot landed directly in the middle of the man's heart, and he died instantly. Stan tried to run, but the motel clerk had already alerted the police. The front entrance was barricaded with ten to fifteen police cars. It was impossible for him to escape. It was over for Stan—on the strength of a streetwalking prostitute. In the streets, the story was: Stan went out there, roughed up the unarmed trick and put a shot in his heart—straight gangsta. From his reputation, Marv liked the hood version better. That night Stan went to jail, Marv went over to comfort Francine.

While his road-dawg was in the pen, Marv settled down. He acted as if his family was a middle-class African-American household. He learned from Stan's mistakes to leave the whores alone. The only support he could

offer his partner was financial support, because of his
long-armed criminal history. He was held without bail
labeled as a flight-risk. Marv sent him $200 a week for
commissary items. In one month, Stan had over $1000
dollars, $800 from Marv and the excess from what
Francine could spare from time-to-time. Prison officials
made him send home $500 of it because they only al-
lowed a maximum of $500 on the books per month.

Marv was working hard, manning brutal labor, working the railroad lines, scuffing up his smooth hands that
now possessed hard calluses on the base of his palms,
leading to his four fingers. He promised Loretta that
his street hustle was over, but begged her to bear with
him on one last run. This run-to-cop would leave them
with sweet numbers in the bank. After that, he would be
completely finished with the game.

Nasir was coming up on his 3-month anniversary of
life. Marv and Loretta celebrated each month of his life
with a party. The way Marv analyzed, why wait an entire
year to celebrate a birthday annually, when you could
celebrate life everyday? However, everyday was a bit
much to celebrate a birthday, so he opted to celebrate
every month of his son's birthday. They sat down the
seventh of the month, as a family, to celebrate Nasir's
being with birthday cake, ice cream and once with a
Sesame Street character, Big Bird. Loretta thought he'd
gone too far, but was in seventh heaven with the fact
that Marv loved his son so much. After each party, they
would invite adult guests over for a few drinks. Loretta
had become quite the barmaid, learning how to pre-
pare mixed drinks like a professional. All of her friends
always called her to bartend when they hosted parties.

As this marked the third anniversary of Nasir's birth,
who was now fast asleep, it also was a live-ass party going

on. Friends and family gathered together to enjoy themselves at Marv and Loretta's. Loretta was behind the bar as usual, tossing the drinks from left to right of the table.

"One amaretto sour, one Hennessey and Coke, one vodka and orange juice, one whiskey sour, one Absolute and cranberry juice—who's next? The bar is hot tonight," Loretta said, handling her business.

"Who's the baddest bitch? I'm strapping these drinks with a little somethin', somethin' extra. One of you niggas has got to re-stock the bar tonight." The expression Loretta had on her face read, *pass them dollars!*

Mitzy, one of Loretta's acquaintances, came to request her favorite drink for the fifth time tonight: JB Whiskey on the rocks, the alcohol that made you pissy drunk.

"Girl, with all the money Marv's bringing into this house, why you need somebody else to re-stock the bar?"

Mitzy downed her drink like it was Kool-aid. By the sound of her voice, Loretta should of known Mitzy didn't mean any good by her statement. She wanted to be seen and heard. Wanting to be acknowledged wasn't bad in itself, but when it began to guide her emotions, it became a substitute for acting from the heart. What she really wanted to say was, "I can't afford to pay for this drink and I want another one. So, please don't ask for any money, 'cause I don't have none. I'm here to drink yo' shit up for free."

"I need people to stock the bar for drunks like you, Mitzy; guzzling down six to seven drinks at a time before you can even taste them. Swish it around your mouth a little bit. Enjoy the taste, damn it, before you ask for another. Niggas always freeloading off ya shit."

Loretta turned her head to serve yet another wanting customer which was an obvious incongruence between her gestures and true intent of her words. Tiny came out of nowhere and slapped Loretta five.

"I know that's right! She better pay-up, shut-up or get fucked-up in here." Tiny was the neighborhood trouble-maker.

Loretta kept her around just in case she needed someone to do her dirty work. She couldn't deal with her everyday, just on occasion.

Marv sat in the corner with his friends, Fat Al, Tom Cat and Bucky, his soon to be brother in law. He didn't know why Bucky's doped-out-ass was all up in the mix of things. Most likely it was to scheme on how he could get a free high. He was made up of a cesspool of lies and deceit, trying to act like he was really on Marvin's side, knowing he was full of trickery.

Marv talked intimately with all three of the men, about his plans of leaving the game and making one last run. Fat Al and Tom were down with him, but Bucky decided he would fall back on his involvement, which was a good move. Marv gave Bucky the job of letting all the hustler's that coped from him know to pay-up any outstanding money, or risk the repercussions.

Talking with friends only made Marv sad thinking about his boy and his circumstances. Stan was in a bad situation and wasn't a thing he could do to save him— not this time. Stan was sure to get life, or the death penalty. To avoid the same outcome as Stan, Marv knew he had to plan very carefully to execute his last run, without any mess involved. His intentions weren't to involve Loretta, but she insisted—they were in this thing together—no matter what. If something were to go down—both of them were going-down together.

When the night ended and all the alcoholics drank up the last bottle of liquor, everyone, including Mitzy's drunken ass, had to be escorted to the door. Mitzy stumbled a few steps to the right, a few steps back, then back to the right—but still had to go the hell home. They didn't care where the people were going—but they had to get the fuck-out-of-there. Francine was the last to leave out. Loretta noticed the hesitation in her.

"What's wrong, Pancake?"

Francine was fucked-up. She looked at Marv and for a second, envied Loretta. Marv stood back from the door, coolly observing her.

"Ain't nothing wrong with her. Shell be all right. Won't you, Francine?"

"I *guess* I will," she wavered before leaving.

Loretta locked up the house and started cleaning up the trash left behind. That was the only problem she had with inviting guests over—she always had to clean up after them. Marv lay back on the couch with his feet propped up watching Loretta's curves sway from side-to-side.

"Come over here," he called out to her.

Loretta looked at Marv with his lustful-looking eyes, knowing what he wanted. She smiled at him with a smile that lit up her whole face. The dirty napkins, used cups, unfinished slices of birthday cake could remain right where they were; even the aluminum pan on the dining room table, with a few pieces of chicken left over in it. It was mostly crumbs, but it was enough to snack on later that morning.

Marv turned on the stereo player, now winding his groin from side-to-side listening to Marvin Gaye's "Sexual Healing" classic. Loretta danced around the room, holding her hands out for her man to join her in a little bump-and-grind. Accepting her mating call, Marv rolled off the couch taking her hands slowly. He thrust her body around so that her backside was lodged against his protruding groin. Their bodies painted together as if they were the only lover's in the world. Loretta lay her head on the left-side of Marv's shoulder with her eyes closed, enjoying each second with him. The sweet melody bounced gently off the walls, caressing their thoughts and enticing their minds. Both of them feeling like they'd spent an eternity together, yet realizing they'd only been together for one year. Nine months of that year, Loretta was expecting. Marv finally throttled Loretta around to face him, placing his hands on her face.

"Loretta, I love ya funky-ass." He was as sincere as ever as he slow-gazed in her eyes. He placed on her finger a one-carat princess-cut diamond ring.

Tears of joy skipped down Loretta's face as she showed her deepest admiration toward him.

"Marvin Bundy, I love your funky-ass too!"

Her lips met his as they passionately embraced with a long, slobbery French kiss, tongues battling each other in-between each breath. Loretta knew how Marv disliked being stared at while kissing, but she couldn't help it. She couldn't believe that this man loved her so; and to think, she doubted his love. For each second she had, it had to be a lasting memory—even kissing.

Just as Marv began to tug away at Loretta's blouse, he thought he heard a faint cry from upstairs. At first, he passed it off and continued to remove the fabric from Loretta's upper-body, but when the cries became louder, he knew it was Nasir.

Damn, Loretta thought to herself, toying with her

new ring. She thought for sure they were getting ready to get it on. She used all the reserves she could to keep Marv sexually enticed.

"He'll be okay. Let him cry a little," she tried to convince him. She was into the foreplay and nothing was going to come between her session. When she stopped getting a response from Marv, feeling his hard-on going down, she knew the foreplay was over.

"I'm not going to let him cry, and bitch, neither should you," he said loosely.

Him calling her a bitch didn't bother her at all. Bitch was a word he used often to refer to women.

"So you're just gonna stand there and act like you don't even hear him crying, huh?"

Loretta turned her face in the opposite direction like she didn't hear him. It didn't register in Marv's mind that Loretta was inexperienced as a mother.

He reached the top of the stairs, grazing his hands up the dark gray-painted wall, while his feet stepped down on the feather-gray carpet, until he reached out to open Nasir's bedroom door. Nasir was stretching out some-kind-of-bad in his crib, kicking his little legs, with his hands moving about wildly. He had one little tear in the corner of both eyes, which were so tiny they couldn't drop.

"Stop that crying!" Marv demanded of him. "You're a fighter like ya daddy. You have to fight that shit! Crying is for pussies."

The 4-ounce bottle was resting inside the crib, untouched. He picked Nasir up and fed him. All the ranting and raving stopped when the large rubber nipple was placed in his mouth.

"You like big nipples, huh? So do I," he smiled.

Nasir started sucking madly on it; like he hadn't

eaten in days. He was crying from little hunger pains. He drank every drop of the 4-ounce bottle, burping on his own without assistance. He was no different than his father when it came to eating—he was downright greedy.

Marv held him, stroking his back to lead him back to sleep. The night-light dimmed the room while Marv talked to his son.

"Nasir, I will always love you, son. You hear me? I need you to grow up to be a strong man like ya daddy, not a fuckin' dope-fiend like your faggot-ass, Uncle Bucky. Ya hear me!"

Nasir shifted his head from side to side making Marv believe that he was really understanding him. He unintentionally revealed the information about his last run to his son. Why? He didn't know. If his heart ever skipped a beat from fear, this was the time.

GUT INSTINCTS

When daylight hit, Marv contacted Fat Al and Tom Cat to find out if they were ready to go. He was ready to get this last run over and done with. Loretta had already arranged with Mom Flossy to tend to Nasir while she supposedly cleaned up around the house from the party last night. Of course, she was lying; her ass wasn't letting Marv go on this last run without her. He tried to influence her to stay back, but it didn't work. Since she was determined to go, both of them plotted, just as before, that she would be the scapegoat. The police hardly ever suspected a woman of carrying the drugs in their time. It would be a little harder now that she couldn't hide the weight in between her breasts. Since she'd given birth to Nasir, her stomach had gone back down tremendously so, she didn't have the coverage she once had. She wouldn't be able to stabilize the drugs like she did before.

Fat Al and Tom Cat pulled up in a dark gray Monte

Carlo. It was ugly as hell, but when someone was behind the wheel, that bad-boy drove smoothly. If it were running, you'd never know it was turned on. That's how quiet it was. Marv and Loretta were ready to go as soon as Fat Al opened the driver's-side door for both of them to get in. They both hurried in like someone was watching their every move. Loretta ducked her head inside, greeting both of them, with startled faces. Marv followed behind her, noticing the look that Fat Al and Tom Cat gave her.

"What's wrong?" questioned Marv as he looked in, turning to both of them to get an answer.

Neither one of them uttered a word, but both were thinking *why did he bring her along?* as they remained still, not saying a word.

"That's what the fuck I thought."

Marv, stared waiting to see if either one of them were going to say something. When they remained silent, he grabbed Loretta's head to rest underneath his arm and pulled her body close to his.

The ride to the city went smooth, as did the transaction. Loretta had everything tucked under her girdle. The maternity top she wore would have thrown anyone off. Because she had so much weight—drugs—on her, Fat Al and Tom Cat were skeptical to ride back home with her in the car.

Fat Al got to arguing with Tom Cat. He thought they made a wrong decision getting involved with Marv this time. Then they started thinking about what if they got caught—acting all paranoid. Easily, they would get 10 to 15 years mandatory, for the dope. Tom Cat finally got up the nerve to tell Marv about his gut instinct. They were all standing alongside the car in the parking lot near the distribution house.

"We need to get out of here. It's hot as a bitch!" Marv said to them looking around.

Tom Cat, with his little frail being and scared-ass, responded, "That's what I wanted to talk to you about, Marv." Hoping Marv would understand. "Why don't we use your Amtrak discount and catch the train back home? Loretta can drive the car back by herself. No need for us all to get jammed up. I-I-I mean, if something were to happen, of course."

The thought of 10 to 15 years kept buzzin' in his ears. It was no way in hell he was going to do time for no man. Marv frowned and little droplets of water formed on his upper-lip. He wiped the sweat clean with his index finger.

"I can't let my woman drive back alone with all the shit."

Loretta heard them going back and forth with who should drive and who should catch the train. The conversation was loud and clear, and so was the sound of the po-po coming down the street. With the keys already in the car, Loretta jumped from the back to the driver's seat and took off. She wasn't about to get caught while they contemplated on how they were going to get the shit home. They never had this problem before when it was her, Marv, and Stan. Marv had to throw salt in the game and get two sucka's who were scared-stiff, and had no balls to grab on. They wasted too much valuable time going back and forth about transporting the drugs, and now, a decision had to be made. Loretta wasn't afraid to chance it but she wanted to make sure Marv was going to be okay, to hell with Fat Al and Tom Cat. She tried circling around the block, but when she saw the vice squad had all three of them against the brick building, she took-off for home. Marv was an experienced man; he knew how to get back.

Marv looked down the block in disbelief that they were being frisked. He knew Loretta was smart enough to get ghost—take her ass far away from that scene. She was just as crazy and swift as him. He just hoped Fat Al and Tom Cat didn't start singing like two fucking snitches.

"Well, I guess that solves everything," Tom Cat whispered under his breath in a very charismatic way. He was glad that he didn't have any drugs or paraphernalia on him, of any kind.

"Shut the fuck up you, bitch-ass, nigga!"

Marv was pissed. He didn't have anything on him. He was clean. He knew they would be let go once their names were run-in.

They shouted down a taxi just as soon as they were free. They were ready to catch the next thing moving back home. Marv was worried sick the entire time riding home, hoping and praying Loretta would make it back safely.

After the long ride, he couldn't wait to check up on Loretta, and Nasir for that matter. Especially Loretta, since she had the drugs in her possession. When he finally made it to the house, he looked around for Fat Al's car. No sign of it anywhere. He walked down to the corner to scan the parallel blocks to see if she parked the car somewhere around there.

"Where the hell is she?" he mouthed to himself very concerned. "She should've been back by now."

His steps paced across the wooden floor, wishing Loretta were there, left a note or something. His heart was beating fast and his hands started to shake uncontrollably. Inside the house, things were left just as they

were before they left out that morning. His stomach
began to rumble. He didn't like the way he was feeling
at all. He immediately picked up the telephone to find
out if Mom Flossy had heard from her. If anybody knew
where she was, it would definitely be her. He was more
than disappointed when she informed him that she
hadn't heard from Loretta since they'd dropped off
Nasir, and instead of getting smart with him, she asked
if everything was okay. He didn't want to frighten her,
so he told her things were cool. Mom Flossy knew better, something wasn't right. She could sense it.

   Loretta drove very cautiously to avoid any unnecessary contact with the police, even obeying the "no speed-
ing" laws. Normally, she would have been driving 80 to
85 miles per hour, but today, she was driving strictly by
the rules—precisely at the local speed limit—55 miles
per hour. She hadn't quite made it halfway through her
journey to her final destination. She popped the cas-
sette in the player—Harold Melvin and the Blue Notes.
"Let The Side Show Begin" swarmed the car. Loretta
snapped her fingers after each melody, singing along
with the chorus. She thought about Sheena and Nasir
and how she was going to be a better mother to them.
Since she knew she displayed signs of emotional insta-
bility, it was time she stepped-up her role as a mother.
She had the perfect little family. A damn good man and
two beautiful kids. She couldn't ask for a better father
for her kids. Marv was the epitome of a loving, depend-
able father. She smiled on the inside—her heart was
warm as if she sipped on a glass of brandy. Just then, a
loud pop could be heard that sounded like a loud bal-
loon burst. The car wobbled from side-to-side, and

Loretta just barely had any control to steer the vehicle straight. The back tire of the Monty Carlo blew out!

"FUCK!" she screamed out.

"Don't fuckin' panic!" she repeated to herself. *"Get control of the wheel and don't fuckin' panic!"*

For a moment, Loretta silently prayed to God that she did not end up in an accident. She grabbed hold of the wheel with force, without fear, steering it to the side of the road.

When the vehicle finally came to a complete stop, she yelled out, *"Thank you Lord."* Then spoke out loud. "Damn. What the fuck am I going to do?" She didn't know how to fix a flat tire, and didn't know if Fat Al had a spare, anyhow. Even if he did have a spare or a donut, she wondered who in the hell was going to put it on. Marv handled all the maintenance on his car. She hadn't a clue what to do, and Marv wasn't around to bail her out of this one. If she had paid attention when he changed the tire on several occasions before, instead of acting like it was a man's job, she would have known how to handle this shit with ease and not be dependent on someone else. Too late for independence now. A quick assessment had to be made to continue to avoid a police encounter.

Loretta began to sweat profusely. Very discretely, she removed the dope from her girdle and placed in underneath the passengers-side seat. At this moment, she'd wished the vice squad never had stopped on that block, because if they didn't, Marv would be with her to correct this situation. It was only a flat tire, something very easy to correct. She needed him more than ever, as she watched cars rolling past without even glancing in her direction. Hopelessly, she began waving down drivers that passed her by, hoping this time, a Good Samaritan would stop to assist. After ten cars or more passed by without stopping, Loretta's worst fear was becoming a reality. Either somebody called the cops to help her out, or the bastards were making routine stops. What was she to do? It felt like her heart was jumping out of her chest the way she was breathing. Tossing the dope would be a sure giveaway and besides, what would Marv think of her if she did that, being paranoid? He hated when muthafuckas cracked under pressure.

"Try to stay calm, Loretta."

This tactic wasn't working for her. She was having an uncontrollable panic attack.

Opening the trunk, she began pulling out all kinds of shit. Fat Al had old newspapers, a filthy blanket that God knows what or who squirted cum juices on it, dirty clothes, old sneakers and a box of opened soap powder with its contents sprinkled all over everything. If Fat Al was supposed to be washing his clothes, he was a little behind. His clothes smelled like ass that hadn't been washed in a few weeks, maybe months. Not wanting to touch any of the contents, she lifted up the trunk-board to search for the spare. When she lifted it up, the filthy blanket began to unfold. She couldn't believe her misfortune. There was a sawed-off shotgun wrapped up in it. She turned around to see how close the police were to her. The car had just pulled up. With the quickness, she shut the hood of the trunk. With her pressure rising every second, the final blow came when the "good-old-boy" got out of his K-9 unit vehicle.

"FUCK! I'm going down," she said nervously.

Using her best wit she tried her damnest to play it off with the officer before he started asking for her driver's license and registration information. For one, she didn't possess a driver's license and two, she didn't have a clue if the car was registered legally. So her efforts to sway him off had to be damn good.

As the officer situated himself to get out of the car, the German Sheppard barked out of control with his strong sense of narcotics.

The veteran officer allowed the German Shepherd to accompany him on this stop as he did, addressing motor vehicle violations. Soon as they were close enough, the German Sheppard's bark became increasingly loud. The officer knew what that meant. Before he even began to read her her rights, he had her with her hands behind her back in handcuffs.

Fat Al and Tom Cat would be relieved that they weren't with her. She was going down with a kilo of pure uncut heroin, and an unregistered firearm that wasn't even hers. Usually, Marv could be relied upon in times of uncertainty—but this time, he could not.

Marv stood at the front entrance of the door pacing back and forth. It was late and Loretta hadn't shown up or called. He knew for sure things didn't go down as planned. He'd already called Mom Flossy about twenty times, who after the third call had started cussing him out from worrying about Loretta's whereabouts. He wanted to leave the house, and then again, he wanted to stay just in case she called or so happened to come home.

Damn! I hope my baby is all right. Shit just don't seem right, he said over and over in his mind.

By 11:00 p.m., Marv knew that either Loretta was arrested, or more horridly: someone killed her. You couldn't convince him of anything different. This was unlike her, not to at least call home. Not being able to face what lie ahead, Marv sat back on the couch and drank a pint of Paul Mason. He felt like crying, not on the outside, but internally, knowing Loretta had no business going on this last trip.

At 1:17 a.m., the telephone rang. Marv had dozed off in a drunken sleep. He almost missed the call. One ring too late and he would have.

"Hello?" he asked anxiously waiting to find out who was on the other end.

When the operator responded, "You have a collect call from. . . ." he knew his baby had been snagged, but with how much shit, he didn't know.

Before the operator could finish, he was hollering in the phone, "Yes, yes, I'll accept the call."

Loretta was ashamed of how she got herself into this mess. All she could think about was Marv and her babies.

"Marv, please don't be mad with me." Those were the first words that she pleaded.

Marv couldn't believe she would think he was angry with her, and she was locked-up behind bars technically over his shit. Even behind bars, she still remained loyal to her man. The man in him wouldn't allow her to feel like she let him down.

"Baby, I'm the one that should be apologizing, not you. It's my fault you're in this mess. This is the reason why I didn't want to involve you in this in the first place."

The line went dead for a second.

"Marv, my bail has been set . . . it's $500,000—cash," she nervously stated.

The little bit of heart Marv had left, was shattered into pieces. He closed his eyes and dropped his head back.

"Did you hear me, baby?" Loretta asked, uncertain if he heard her.

"Damn, this is your first drug-charge, isn't it?" he questioned, figuring at least her bail would be secured and he could get a bail bondsman to get her out with $50,000, cash.

He knew they had that much, but with bail set at $500,000 straight cash, and a kilo worth of heroin down the drain, how would he maneuver this? He had to think, quick-witted and sensibly. Just that day, he cleaned out his stash to make his last run, his last re-up, his last cop. If all had gone well, he knew his family would be set.

"Loretta, do you remember when I told you to put away cash for Nasir's security?"

"Yes, I remember."

For her sake, he hoped that she put that money away for a time such as this.

"Where is it?"

Loretta had no choice but to tell him about her hidden-stash spot. Every woman had at least one that she kept hidden from her man—just in case.

"Look into Nasir's closet, behind the panel board. Inside you'll find a black lock-box. The key to open it is in my panties drawer, underneath the last bra folded on the bottom, in a red wallet."

Marv wanted to laugh at how far she went just to keep the money hidden from him. "That's my girl," he said under his breath.

"Alright; how much is there?"

Loretta had to think. She'd been skimming-off-the-top just a bit, but was sure it was a good amount in there.

"It should be around $50,000 cash. I had to use a few dollars a while back, but it was only a few," she revealed.

"That's not even going to put a dent in your bail. I'll see what I can do okay, baby? I'm going to get you out of there, if it's the last thing that I do. So, don't you worry about a thing."

To give him some hope, she informed him about new possibilities. "Don't worry baby, I'll be alright. I have a preliminary hearing scheduled some time soon. It's my guess that they will reduce my bail after they drop the firearms charge."

Marv couldn't believe his ears. "Did you say a firearms charge?" He shook his head again. "A fat mothafucka!"

Fat Al was known for carrying a sawed-off shotgun, but Marv asked him not to bring it with him.

"Yes, I did. That fat bastard had a sawed-off shotgun in the trunk of the car. Not only that, they're saying it had a body on it. I'm not sweating that because I know I wasn't involved. Good for me that my fingerprints aren't on it. For all I care, they can arrest Fat Al for that shit."

Marv's next response was his concern. What, if any, did Loretta tell the police? Even though she was his ride-or-die woman, under pressure he knew that most of the time, they started snitching.

"Baby, what did you tell them?"

Loretta knew better not to run-off the mouth too much, fearing the phones might be tapped.

"Don't worry, I'm straight. The only problem that we will have is whoever's fingerprints is on that gun. Whoever's prints are on it, that's whose shit this is!"

Marv had to think back if there was a chance that his fingerprints were on it. He couldn't remember if they were or not.

"You have one minute remaining," the operator interrupted their call.

"Well, baby, my time is up. Do what you need to do to get me out of here. Nasir and Sheena need me."

With her few seconds remaining, she managed to get this out, "And, don't have no bitches in my shit!"

She didn't need to lose sleep about that, Marv was on a straight mission to get his woman out of jail. He couldn't concentrate on anything but how to get up the money needed to bail Loretta out. He called any and everybody that owed him, or that he did a favor for with his connections. This was one situation that he was incapable of taking control of. He knew he had to contact Mom Flossy, sooner or later, but needed her to be cordial to him during this trying time. His perspiring brows filled with a salty content, dropped down to his lips, causing him to accidentally taste the fluid. Picking up the phone to call Mom Flossy, he quickly hung it back up, not ready to deal with her shit. The best thing she could do for him was shut the fuck up and tend to the kids. He sat back down on the loveseat with the phone placed in his lap.

"Time is money," he analyzed.

He dialed the telephone number again and this time with enough heart to remain on the line.

"Hello? Who is this at this hour of the morning?" Mom Flossy asked in a very nasty tone.

She had on a short, loud-pink nightgown, showing what once were nice and thick thighs, only now they were old and saggy, with a head full of pink rollers. The kids were resting quietly in her bed.

"Yeah, it's me again," Marv answered, knowing he called her one to many times tonight.

"I told you eighty times, I haven't heard from Loretta—so stop calling my damn house. Her fast ass is probably laid-up in a motel with another man and don't want to come home." She'd hope to hurt his feelings by that comment. However, Marv knew the real deal. "She'll be home in the morning, right after check-out time," she teased.

Marv made every attempt to keep the peace.

"That's bullshit and you know it. I called to tell you that Loretta is in jail on weapon and drug charges. I need you to keep an eye on the kids until I can get this shit under control. Can you handle that?"

Mom Flossy threw a damn tantrum on the phone, screaming like she didn't have any sense. Sheena shifted in the bed almost awakened by her grandmom's loud voice. Marv wasn't trying to hear what she had to say and he wasn't willing to argue endlessly with her, so he let her hear the dial-tone this time. He had to choose his tactics very carefully as he took it to the streets to get money owed to him. The first stop was to see Bucky's slick ass.

Bucky had followed through as instructed by not only telling the debtors, but he collected any money owed to Marv on the streets. What Marv didn't know was that the money Bucky collected, he spent already on dope. He didn't have one silver dime of the money left to give to Marv. He wasn't about to inform Marv of that though. He would lead Marv to believe that every-body totally disrespected him when he approached them to get Marv's money. When really, none of them wanted trouble with Marv, so they paid Bucky off what they owed.

Marv walked a few blocks down to where everyone hung out, asking if anyone had seen Bucky. None of the dudes could pinpoint one particular spot, but told

Marv that he'd been through the block several times that day. Marv decided that he would hang around a bit and wait for the chance to see Bucky come back through. While waiting, he used the corner payphone to contact Francine to let her know what had transpired with Loretta. She offered the little bit of funds that she could, and of course, assistance with the kids until Loretta came home. She would do anything for them.

After a brief stint on the block, Bucky's doped-out ass came cruising around the corner looking for another bag. Bucky's eyes lit up like a flying lightning bug and he took off running when he spotted Marv. Mom Flossy had already made her rounds calling everybody to inform them that Marv got Loretta locked up on drug and weapon charges, so he knew Marv needed bail money. Marv thought he was tripping when he saw Bucky try to dip away, but when Bucky started to haul ass down the street, he knew his ass messed up by telling him to hit the streets for him. The way Bucky was running for his life, he knew money had to be involved.

Marv chased Bucky for blocks, until his legs cramped and he could no longer keep up with him. Bucky was quick on his feet and was used to being chased. Marv was long overdue at the gym—he was out of shape, heaving strongly to take in some oxygen. "I'm going to beat the shit out of Bucky when I catch him." Marv could hardly breathe, let alone utter the words. He had to pull-up his awareness when dealing with people, period. He took his time walking back down the block, so he could catch his breathe and to see if he could catch some of the other fiends who owed him money.

Tawny, a nice, grey-haired older man found his way to the bootleg liquor store, right across the street from where Marv was standing. Tawny saw Marv, but didn't go out his way to speak. Marv was posted-up with one of the girls named Tessa, who was wearing little to nothing, exposing body parts that should have been covered.

"Hey, daddy! What can I do you for?" smiled Tessa, displaying her wide gap between her teeth that complimented the large gap between her legs.

Marv didn't dig her at all and she continued to overlook that. However, he had to be sharp and on point to get the money from her, since he hadn't been around for a while.

"Maybe later on, baby. You looking good enough to eat!"

He was setting her up for the kill. Tessa twirled around in front of Marv to show him all of her.

"Tell me how bad you want it. Maybe we can work something out."

He smoothed his tongue over his thick-juicy lips. Tessa began to shake with lust.

"We can leave right *now*, daddy!"

Marv had her where he wanted her.

"Nah, baby, maybe I wasn't clear."

This time he just barely touched her erect nipples when he went to place his arms around her, sliding a few fingers in her mouth.

"If you want this dick, you have to pay for it."

The anticipation built up in Tessa. This would be her first time with Marv. Never before did he give her the time of day.

"You ain't said nothin', daddy. You can have all of this!" she said sucking his fingers for dear life.

Tessa slightly touched Marv's face with her pinky-finger that was accented by a silverfish costume jewelry ring. She placed her other hand inside her brassiere and handed the knot of money to Marv. It was a knot full of twenties all throughout. Not the fake-me-out knot that some men carry around with mostly ones, wrapped around with one twenty.

"You did say we would hook up later, right?" She wanted to be sure not to line up dates around that time.

Fuck no, was his mental response. She would be stood up, but he wasn't going to tell her that.

"Yeah, baby; later on tonight."

Once he spotted Tawny, Tessa was a longtime memory. He left her standing there not knowing what time or place she should meet him.

"Tawny! What's up, baby? Let me holla at you for a moment."

Tawny was oblivious to what Marv wanted. He'd already paid off his debts to Bucky.

"What's good old-timer?" Tawny responded.

Marv cut straight through the chase.

"I need that dough. That's what's good, old head."

Marv had a distant stare as he spoke, giving Tawny direct eye contact. Tessa was across the street bending inside a vehicle talking to a trick and everybody else on the block was doing his or her own thing.

"I gave what I owed you to Bucky. He said you sent him out to collect the money, so I gave mine up. Listen, man, I don't want no trouble, but I don't have your money. I gave what I owed to Bucky. You know how under-handed Bucky is." Tawny's suspicion was accurate. There was noway in hell he should have given the money to Bucky.

Marv honestly believed Tawny, but he had to raise the money some way. He had to make an example out of someone . . . why not Tawny? He wasn't trying to hear that bullshit line all night. Mothafuckas were going to pay up twice if they had too!

Without a word, Marv cold-blasted Tawny in the nose with the butt of a blunt object he picked up on the street. Blood streamed down his face. Now everybody was paying attention to Marv and Tawny. Tessa dashed inside the car of the man she was soliciting and told him to pull off. She knew how vicious Marv could get. Poor Tawny, he didn't deserve that at all. He was at the right place—wrong time.

Marv's venom rose. "Any of you mothafucka's that owe me money, get ya ducks in order! I'm coming for my shit!"

He searched Tawny's pockets, finding his wallet, cleaning it out of all green. Tawny had just got paid a $1,500 paycheck from the car plant where he assembled parts together for Chrysler vehicles.

Everybody started buzzing about what Marv did to innocent, little Tawny, and those that did owe him money and didn't have it to pay knew they would get into a rumble with Marv tonight.

With his pockets $3,500 heavier from Tessa's and Tawny's keep, Marv made way to the local bar as the late-night hours drew wanton spirits where anybody and everybody hung-out at, to collect what was owed to him.

WHAT HAPPENS IN
THE DARK

The blinking red and white sign lit up a three mile radius reading brightly, CAS BAR. The marketing technique of buying the largest, hanging sign in the area certainly paid off for the owner. When the sign was lit, everyone knew the Cas Bar was open, and when the sign was off everyone knew it was closed, because of the midnight-darkness in the area. Heaps of men and women filled the interior of the Cas Bar, and dozens more loitered on the outside of the bar. The scene created an illusion that most of the frequenters dreamed of—having money, power and respect. The Cas Bar was the place people went to see the moneymakers, beautiful women, pimped-out mobiles, or to buy hot clothes and hot electronics off the street. All of the moneymakers gained respect and power, even the women who stayed on their grind. Marv was in that limelight of moneymakers, so whenever he came around he was received with love. This was one of his recurrent pit-stops. The only aspect he hated about this spot was the fact that too many of Loretta's underage, ear-whispering girlfriends were fond of the club also.

Marv remembered one night when Loretta was around six or seven months pregnant with Nasir, he was down at the bar balling-out. He was posted-up at the bar, eyeing fat ass Marie. Marie had an ass that *shit* was proud to be in. Add that with her tender light skin, grey eyes, beautiful black tresses of hair and you had a top model chick.

When Marv positioned his eyes on Marie, he knew he had to have her—at least, for one night. Hoping that by sending drinks her way all night long, after a while, she would be ready for him. At first, Marie wasn't pressed about the drinks coming her way. Anytime she hung around the Cas Bar, men were sliding drinks to her. Also, she'd heard about Marv and his way with the ladies from her sister, who was an associate of Loretta's. Marv, on the other hand, was persistent. Much like an addict, he wanted what he wanted, when he wanted it. It was a must that he get with her. While he loved Loretta to death, he figured a little extra trim wouldn't hurt, at least, not once in a while. It worked in his favor, not his woman's.

After he finished playing eye-tag with Marie, he was feeling real nice from his one-after-the-other shots of alcohol. His pressure was rising from his internal lust. When he had enough and was ready to leave, he slithered down off the barstool. He'd seen ten or more men trying to hit up on Marie, and watched how she politely refused them all. The unceasing exchange of eye contact assured him that she wanted him just as bad as he wanted to fuck her.

Marie noticed Marv coming her way. Opening her

purse very promptly, she looked to admire herself with her small mirror pack before she made direct exchange with him. Everything was in tact. She was ready for her intimate encounter with him. Walking with a serious pimp-strut, with his black pantsuit, topped off by his slick-ass black brim, Marv was looking too damn good that night. He glided his way pass other women interested in him, letting them down easy as he continued to stride by. "Not tonight, baby," he would tell them, as he focused solely on Marie. A broke-ass buster that couldn't afford to buy him or his momma a drink, let alone Marie, occupied the seat next to her. Marv excused the man from the barstool he was sitting on, and propped his elbow on the seat. He turned directly to face Marie, whose beauty was stunning as the disco barlights skimmed past her face.

It didn't matter if everyone at the bar was eyeing them. It was about Marv and Marie that night. Taking his right hand with his white-gold diamond pinky ring glistening, and his black leather-banded, big-face silver watch, he placed his hand over her soft tanned coconut skin.

"Did you get my message?" he asked her in a very smooth tone.

"What message?" she replied, unsure of what he was talking about.

"The message I've been sending you across the bar all night."

Marv's confidence and slight arrogance started turning Marie on, intensifying what she already felt. She couldn't portray that she was an easy target, so she came right back with a witty response.

"Nobody sent me any messages. All I've been receiving is drinks handed to me all night from the bartender. I thought maybe he was the one sweet on me," she replied, with tinges of red showing on her cheeks.

Marv already knew he'd bagged her from the steady case of stares he acknowledged from her. It was now time for them to get past stage one.

"The bartender? Baby, don't insult me like that. You knew the drinks were coming from me. Besides, I had to make sure that before we left out together, your mood was set right for what we're about to get into for the rest of the night."

He fondled her hand as he spoke gently to her. It was written. She was leaving with him. That was without question.

"What are you talking about?"

Marie's approval and lust could be read by her direct body language. Her signals were strong and persistent. Marv didn't have any more time to waste playing this cat and mouse game. He already informed Loretta that he'd be touching base around 3:00 am, and it was a little past midnight and they hadn't left yet.

"Look around the bar, baby. Do you see these folk looking in our direction?" Both of their eyes scanned the room.

Marie nodded in agreement, "Yes, I see them."

"Well, baby, they're not looking at *us*. They're looking at me. I'm the "Don" of the room. They even named the bar after me. That should let you know, I'm not usually the one who picks. I'm hand-picked. The women elect *me*. I don't choose *them*. Pimps-up; ho's-down! Now, baby . . . let's roll. . . . By the way, what's your name?"

Marie was mesmerized by Marv's poise—his pearly straight white teeth, the smoothness of his tone, and the way he took control of that situation.

"Marie Don Juan. That's my name. It's a pleasure to meet you, Mr. Marvin Bundy."

She didn't have to ask Marv his name. She came to the bar specifically in hopes that he would recognize her anyway. Tonight was her lucky night. Not once, did she have a man confront her in such a way. She was always the center of attention—just not this time. All eyes were in fact centered in on Marv. Maybe not so much for his good looks though—the men were focusing in on him because he picked up the bar's finest female of the night. The women were focused in on him because they couldn't believe that he was out in the open, openly flirting with another woman with Loretta's friends sitting right inside the bar.

Marv walked hand in hand with Marie, out to his shiny black Cadillac Coupe Deville. He escorted her to the passenger's side and opened the door for her. After she was sitting pretty, he shut the door and proceeded to the driver's side. They rode around for about a half an hour before pulling into Lover's Lane, an overnight bed and breakfast spot. It was elegantly designed and smelled sweet throughout the place from the red rose fragrance. Marv tipped the girl at the check in desk as he usually did, when he stayed a night with a female acquaintance. Being with Marv almost made Marie feel withdrawn, and shy. He had that approach of influence over people. Marie didn't know how to act.

Inside the room was a woven wicker basket, full of fresh fruit—strawberries, blueberries, seedless grapes, oranges and apples. The outer area of the basket was garnished pretty with fresh water crescent. The bed was dressed by a female's touch. The diamond shaped sauna tub greeted her. Marv sensed that Marie was swept away by his ladies' charm, though he had to make sure she was okay with their arrangement. He didn't need any woman hollering rape.

"Marie?" he said, hoping he'd remembered her name correctly.

"Yes," she responded in a passive voice.

"Marie, you are okay with this, right?"

"Of course, I am or I wouldn't be here," she emphasized trying to build up her stolen courage.

"Come here, then."

Marv embraced Marie's sweet smelling skin, gently kissing her forearms with wet moist kisses. Her erect nipples touched his swollen chest filled with ego. He looked over her shoulder, down to her buttocks and lusted, *"Yeah! I'm about to tear this ass up, bend that shit over and hit it from the back!"* The low cut black dress came in handy for that night for both of them—it was easy access.

Marv slipped Marie out of her black dress into the rising hot water in the sauna. He undressed, pulling each layer of clothing off of himself, enticingly. Marie's eyes fixated all over his body. When he finally arrived to remove his boxer's, Marie filled with lustful anticipation. She sighed a little when she saw his average seven inches. But, she thought *larger is not necessarily better, it's how a man works with the size he's blessed with.* And, that indeed, was the case. Marv showed her tricks that a man with twelve inches couldn't possibly have done with her.

One thing for sure, she thought, she didn't have to wake up the next morning worrying about having braised and ripped vaginal skin when she went to use the bathroom. The contact with the urine and the open flesh was a sensation that was not a good feeling for her.

She'd be able to wake up with a smile on her face, ready for rounds four and five.

They lay in the bed after the third session of good fucking, sleeping like babies. Marv wasn't like most guys his age, trying to damage and beat down a woman, screwing like a rabbit—all fast. He was into caressing and loving the natural essence of a woman leaving her with memories of a good fuck.

The loud knock on the door interrupted both of them out of their peaceful sleep. The door shook from all the banging.

"What the fuck?" Marv lifted up his head quickly. Marie was scared to death.

"Do you know who that is?" she asked, wiping cold from her eyes.

"I might have a wild guess," Marv stated, stepping over their clothing on the floor, over to open the door with his boxer shorts on.

Just as he guessed, Loretta's extended stomach came awkwardly, busting through the door. Loretta knew better to create a real scene, fearing what Marv might do. She cursed a few times, but after Marv gave her that deep look of sincerity, she did as instructed.

"Calm down Loretta," Marv said trying to keep the peace.

Loretta went over to the bedside where Marie had covered herself up completely and snatched up the covers to reveal Marie's bare essence.

"No the fuck you didn't, Marvin Bundy! You got this nasty whore up in the bed. How could you do me like that? I'm pregnant with your baby."

Marie still didn't look up. Loretta was in a state of tears. Marie was Mitzy's older sister. Mitzy had been telling

Marie about Marv for a long time. However, Marv never had an encounter with Marie at all. In fact, she looked nothing like Mitzy. It was obvious they came from different seeds. Marv scratched his head and looked at Loretta with regretful eyes.

"What do you want me to say, Loretta? What the fuck, I'm busted."

Somebody had to follow them to know where they were staying. He walked over to the window, pulled back the curtains and saw Bucky and Mitzy standing by Mitzy's beat down buggy.

"No, those two bitch-ass niggas didn't," he vexed.

Marie didn't move. She remained butt ass naked, coverless. Marv looked back over to Loretta, who was still searching for answers.

"It's too late for this bullshit, Loretta. Now either, you're going back home with Mitzy and Bucky, or you're going to join us, 'cause I'm going back to sleep. The damage has already been done."

As crazy as it seemed, Loretta wasn't about to leave and give them more time together. She was staying right there—not to indulge in a threesome, but to interrupt their intimate party.

"Well, you better tell your whore to move the fuck over, 'cause I ain't leaving! Where's that bitches pocketbook? She's paying for this shit!"

Marv had Marie move over, and he lay sandwiched in-between both women. He was *big pimpin!*

This was one of Marv's fondest moments that started at the Cas Bar. Tonight, he was there on another mission.

ALL IS WELL . . .
THAT ENDS WELL

Bucky was sitting on a bar stool in the Cas Bar, taking in his last shot of Crown Royale, talking much junk to Freeze. Freeze was an old friend of Bucky's, but a new associate to Marv. He was also one of the individuals that owed Marv money.

"What it be like, Freeze?" Bucky asked, nodding his head in the middle of every other word.

Freeze looked at Bucky in pity. Bucky didn't use to be like this. Bucky was a straight up-and-up guy, dumped by one of the prettiest girls in the neighborhood. After getting dumped, he went home to crying to his mom like a baby. His father James, Mom Flossy's boyfriend at the time, beat the softness up out of him. James didn't believe a man should cry, let alone cry over some woman. Women he thought, came a dime a dozen. He didn't understand why his son only had one girlfriend anyway. To him, all boys and men should have three and four girlfriends at a time—just in case one acts up, there was always another pussy to get into. Mom Flossy watched as

James beat Bucky, not stopping the physical abuse at all. Something tainted Bucky after that. He started dogging women, stealing from everyone, drinking, smoking and lastly shooting heroin, trying to live up to who his father wanted him to be . . . "The Man."

Bucky's behaviors were off-balance. He drove himself crazy trying to follow his own moves, trying too hard to control his nods while sitting at the bar. Over an hour ago, he was running for his life. Now he was nodding out without a care in the world, like Marv still wasn't after him. Going to the bar was a bold move, because he knew sooner or later, Marv would show up there. Freeze continued to gulp down his shots of Gordon's Gin.

"Man, I asked you a question." Bucky's glossed-out, "lazy eyes were covered mid-way by his lazy eyelids. Seeing the state Bucky was in, Freeze wanted to avoid the dramatization.

"Go the fuck home, Bucky. You look like shit."

Bucky leaned back causing his rear end to slide off the stool. His legs were wobbly as he dropped them down on the floor, causing his back to slam against the brown paneled wall.

"Just look at you," Freeze responded in sympathy. "Let me give you a ride home, because if I don't, one of these niggas in here are going to kick your ass for looking so fucking stupid."

Bucky didn't hesitate and allowed Freeze to escort him from the bar. "I hear Marv's is looking you."

Confused by Bucky's muffled words, Freeze repeated what he *thought* Bucky said.

"Did you just say Marv is looking for me?"

Bucky shook his head up and down. "That's what I said, nigga."

The bluff was apparently working.

"Looking for me, for what? I don't owe him jack!"

Bucky puckered out his lips. "Yeah, that's what your mouth says."

His response caused Freeze to be in an emotional state of confusion. "Man, stop playing with me. You're drunk and doped up; talking out your ass."

Just as sure as the night falls, so did Bucky walking outside of the bar. Freeze bent over to pick him up.

Marv was in front of the Cas Bar screaming on Fat Al from a distance.

"Fat Al, you fat black son of a bitch! You got my woman sitting in a cell 'bout to rot out on carrying a concealed deadly weapon. You knew when you purchased the mothafuckin' sawed-off shotgun from down south, that it was dirty. Now they talking about adding a murder one charge 'cause it had a body on it. Mothafucka, you dead tonight."

Marv was losing his mind. Everything he was trying to do was fucking up. He wasn't in arms reach but moved closer and closer as he mouthed each word to Fat Al. The closer Marv came, the faster Fat Al moved to his woman's vehicle that he left running. He was making a quick stop to the bar to pick her up. He saw the distance between them as an opportunity to grill Marv about his loss.

"Come on, Marv, you knew the odds were against us. I took my shit in case shit didn't go right. I didn't know those dudes. They ya peoples, so of course, I took my security. I'm sorry that Loretta got jammed up with it, but that's the risk of the game. Nigga, what about my car? I took a loss too. I told you I wasn't feeling that shit when we were up there. Don't blame her slip-up on me. Best I can do is send the bitch a money order."

Fat Al made it to the car with his woman sitting in the

passenger seat before Marv could catch up to him and sped away. He wasn't worried about the car because it was registered in his uncle's name—who was dead. They could trace back the owner and still come up with cobwebs.

Marv had just gotten to the Cas Bar. Already, he was creating chaos. This was the second time tonight someone got away from him. In rage, he pushed his way through the crowded block, trying to slide inside the side entrance of the Cas Bar. He was going to kill Bucky and Fat Al when he caught up to them.

Freeze was lifting Bucky up off the ground. When he rose, Marv completely weakened his manhood, staring at Freeze with his cold black eyes.

"What, nigga?" Freeze asked.

From the way Marv stared at him, he knew Bucky's comments were right. Bucky continued to pull himself off the dirty gum stained cement pavement. This couldn't be a better time and place for Marv.

"Two in one," Marv stated. He was happy that he could get two of them, with the effort of dealing with one.

He should have never let Bucky get away earlier. He knew that an enemy wounded nursed back to health would come back stronger than they did before.

Bucky was damn near blacked-out, as he staggered down the street, holding on tight to Freeze's forearm. Marv stood directly in the pathway of both of them. When Bucky got in hands reach of Marv, he felt a strong powered kick, straight to his mid section.

"Aaagh," Bucky moaned.

Freeze dropped Bucky to the wayside and prepared for an all out brawl. The bull face Marv displayed wasn't to be taken for granted. He continued to stomp the guts out of Bucky. Freeze tried pulling Marv off, but Marv had a strong force behind him. Marv wanted to leave Bucky with nothing to negotiate—no hope of reason, and no room to maneuver him out of this situation. He wildly pounced on Bucky until blood oozed out of his mouth. Freeze tugged and tugged at Marv with all his might, finally pulling him off of Bucky. Marv was thrown a few steps, but quickly recovered on his feet.

"Stay the fuck out of this, Freeze. This here is family business."

All of the anger and resentment from today's events caused Marv's nose to snarl with flame.

"Family business or not, I'm not going to stand here while you stomp the life out of him."

Freeze wasn't going to let it go down that easy. Once again, Bucky had stirred up a rivalry, creating new enemies for Marv.

The height of the beating had reached its peak and soon everything started working unfavorably against Marv. Friend's of Bucky's gathered around him, while someone went inside the bar to get a cold pack, hopefully to bring the life back into him. Bucky's arms were heavy and sprawled out loosely.

Unfortunately, for misperception, Freeze was ready to battle Marv next. Freeze was a dirty fighter. He pulled out his hunter's blade, ready to stick it straight through Marv. Freeze was taught early on, to win his battles through his actions, not by his words—never through argument. He refused to argue with Marv; his actions would explain it all.

Marv's impulsive behaviors stripped his mind naked and nothing was left but the thought of defeat—defeat of failing Loretta, defeat of failing Nasir, defeat of failing his mother and defeat of living life in the wicked streets.

Marv dove into Freeze trying to scoop him into a bear hug to slam him onto the ground. Freeze took three steps back, dodging out of Marv's way. Marv stumbled to the ground but hurriedly got back on his feet. The Cas Bar sign lights started blinking, dimming the streets after each blink. Someone in the crowd hollered, *"Watch out, Marv! . . . He has a knife!"* Marv looked around hopelessly for an object to use. Freeze had him where he wanted him. Marv would regret that being hostile made him nervous—causing him to make costly mistakes, reacting in anger. Freeze stretched forward; just missing Marv's neck. Marv leaned his head back in-the-nick-of-time. He ducked, grabbing one of Freeze's legs. Freeze hobbled, but managed to stay steady. With strong force, Freeze plunged the knife in the upper modular of Marv's back. Marv felt the plunge and loosened Freeze's leg to pull out the 8-inch steel knife that continued to dig into his skin. Just as a *caution* sign is placed on a lifted curb, subconsciously, one is made to look down so they don't trip, but at the same time, they ignore other signs that may be detrimental to their health.

Marv didn't expect Freeze to overtake him; all he really wanted was his money to bail his woman out of prison. With all his resources nearly exhausted, he did what most men would do, fight for their existence. Marv fought the pain that rammed over and over in his flesh, even grabbing the knife with his bare hand. The sharpness of the knife sliced easily between Marv's ring and middle fingers. He tried pulling his body far away from each stab of the knife, but his legs were heavy and numb. Freeze continued to stab Marv multiple times and at Marv's weakness point, Freeze kicked him over and plunged Marv three more times in the heart.

All Marv could picture is the day Nasir was born and that long gaze Nasir gave him while he was in his arms. It was then, he shed tears for his son.

Mostly everyone in the surrounding scattered after they witnessed the severity of Marv's injuries. It was only two people left on the scene when Freeze fled: Bucky and Marv. Though, Bucky had come to, Marv was dead and gone, stabbed thirty-one times. The consequences of his death were immediate and stood against everything his heart stood for—to be a loving father. Bucky's hopeless ambition to scheme and connive caused Marv his life, and his nephew Nasir, to be fatherless.

BEHIND THESE WALLS

The large steel bars that shut behind each guard entering and existing, marred Loretta's thought process. Forty-eight hours passed and she was already throwing a fit about the-less-than-comfortable thin–ass mattress and steel bed frame. She was reminded each time as she looked out the two by four, bulletproof glass window by the lettering *Welcome to the Federal Correctional Institute* that she was in jail. Loretta cried inside from the reality of being away from Marv and the kids. She was hoping everything was grand with everyone, even with her gone. All night long, she tossed and turned, wiping off droplets of sweat. Each time she engaged in a tranquil bit of sleep, it always ended up with a nightmare, causing her to sweat excessively.

The restless sleep didn't help her situation one bit. She was already stressing about her case and the well-being of her loved ones. She thought about Marv, and how stupid she was not to get the marriage certificate validated. If it was left up to Marv, they could have gone to Justice of the Peace Court to get married, but no;

Loretta wanted a real wedding. This, too, was part the reason why Marv had to come up with more money. Now, she wished she went ahead and got married at the Justice of the Peace and then and had a wedding afterwards. It was a little too late for that now.

When the morning came, Loretta, uninformed as to what occurred with Marv, was escorted out the cell to the eating area. The white prison jumpsuit with big black letters that held the initials FCI on them were an injustice to all women. Every suit worn by them was two sizes too big. Even skinny women looked rather chunky in them. Prison was a strange world to Loretta. She didn't know anybody. When, around her neighborhood, everybody knew her. She'd gained much notoriety as Marv's woman.

Since certain pods were assigned to breakfast at different times, other women still caged-up, banged on the glass to get the attention of those heading to chow. Loretta tried to stay focused, but it was hard; hearing stuff like "Come over here, bitch," "Fresh meat on the block," "Eh baby, you got a man?" Not all women were curiously- satisfied by another woman's touch, but those that were, were plentiful in number.

"Armstead, move ahead."

Loretta was surprised that the woman guard dressed in dark blue, carrying a black jack and mace, named Kita, remembered her name. She moved in swift motion to the line grabbing a white styrofoam tray, a white styrofoam four ounce cup for juice and a plastic fork to eat with. Her eyes squinted to see what was being served for breakfast. On the menu this morning was S.O.S.— Shit on shingle: A dark-gray cream sauce with ground-up hamburger meat, served on square white bread, looking unfit for a dog to eat.

"Who is going to eat that nasty looking shit?" Loretta asked Tonya, the girl standing next to her in line.

"You are, if you know what's best for you. Shit, this is a prison luxury meal. It's the prison's version of creamed chipped beef. So, eat up!"

Judging by the cornrow rolls going straight to the back of Tonya's head and her deep voice, she was a little butchy, but seemed to be cool. Loretta received her two-scoop portion of S.O.S. from a missing-tooth, less-than-healthy-looking female inmate about twice Loretta's age. Just then, she wanted to cry. She had just turned eighteen and placed with seasoned criminals.

Loretta never acted her age. She always hung around older men and women. Getting with Marv, made her act even older. The streets made both of them old before their time. She sat down at chow, picking over her food. Tonya sat next to her, trying to get Loretta to run down the four-one-one on why she was incarcerated. Loretta wasn't quick to share any information. Marv taught her best—temporary withdrawal would make you more talked about and admired by your peers; always say little as possible, until you earn your respect. These were rules she had to live by, especially being in prison.

When chow was just about over, Guard Kita pulled Loretta to the side.

"You. Armstead. Over here."

Loretta did a double take to make sure Guard Kita was calling her. The women guards in the prison talked and walked, harder than men on the streets.

"Yes, you. Let's get moving."

Loretta stepped over to the side waiting to find out why she'd been singled out. She smiled as she thought, *"I knew my baby was coming through."*

Instead of being taken back to the booking area as Loretta thought, she was escorted to the chapel where the grand chaplain, a small frame, white man, with pale-skin and very thin lips, met her. Loretta frowned up her face as the chaplain asked her to have a seat. Guard Kita, accompanied by two other guards, guard Misha and guard Lateefah, stood at the entrance door with their hands folded Indian style. Loretta sat down, unsure what they were going to do to her.

When faced with adversity, never show your fear; another one of Marv's valuable lessons.

Loretta fixed the frown from her face to a peaceful look and tried to remain calm. The chaplain read a scripture from the bible. One that Loretta wasn't famil-iar with. The only scripture she knew was the one with the Lord's Prayer, and she still couldn't tell you where to find it in the bible, then, the chaplain gave praise to Hail Mary and formed a cross with his hands in front of his face. Loretta still hadn't a clue what was going on. The chaplain stood facing Loretta as she sat so very pa-tiently.

"Loretta Armstead."

Before the chaplain could get finished, Loretta inter-rupted him.

"Yeah, that's me," she answered worriedly.

The look on the chaplain's face wasn't any indication that Loretta should be alarmed. She looked intently at him, still patiently waiting for him to continue. The chaplain prolonged his words, ignoring the advice of those who recommended that he tell her from the very beginning of the morning. He was too familiar with the delivery of this kind of news. He knew the aftermath would be melodramatic, over the top and sentimental.

"Ms. Armstead, there's been a terrible accident."

Loretta looked puzzled. "What do you mean a terrible accident?"

Her heart instantly started beating at her chest. Was it Nasir? Was it Sheena? Was it Mom Flossy? Or the inevitable, was it Marv? Her thoughts panicked in question. If the chaplain had said Bucky, she would have been hurt but she'd survive, but if he said it was Marv, Sheena, Nasir or even, Mom Flossy, she was going to literally lose her mind. She stood up from the seat and the three guards came forward. The chaplain waved them back.

"I'll handle this." He reassured them, telling them not to worry. "Ms. Armstead, I don't know how to tell you this any other way."

Loretta fixed her eyes on him with fear, not wanting to know who it was, but she knew she had to find out.

"Marvin Bundy, the father of your children, was murdered last night—stabbed thirty-one times."

He didn't have to tell her stabbed thirty-one times. Loretta screamed and screamed and screamed. Everyone in the prison heard the heartfelt screeching. She dropped to her knees trying to pick up her heart that just fell out, holding her stomach to lessen the in depth pain. *This* was the reason she couldn't sleep last night and kept having horrible nightmares. Her best friend, her partner, her lover, her confidant, the Clyde to her Bonnie was taken from her—just like that.

"*Nooooo*! How could he leave me like this? Marv Bundy," she screamed. "I thought we were in this shit together. Why would you do this to me? I can't live without you. Baby, *why*?" she cried in misery.

The memories she had of him would last a lifetime but she wasn't ready to live her lifetime without him. She would never be the same from this day forward.

They had to medicate her with high doses of valium everyday.

Much to the dismay of Ms. Anna, Marv's mother, Loretta wasn't able to attend Marv's funeral and she had to beg Mom Flossy to bring Nasir. Mom Flossy was sick beyond medication. Here she was at 54-years-old raising two kids, a 2 year old and a 3-month old baby. Her daughter was behind bars, and the only father the kids knew, had been murdered. She didn't like Marv, but she loved and respected the genuine concern he had for her grandbabies. She was saddened that they had to grow up without a father.

In a way, Mom Flossy was glad that Loretta wasn't able to come to the funeral. How would she react to all the women crying-out, saying Marv was their man? It was a madhouse full of shamelessly crying females, as another black man bit the dust from a black-on-black crime.

Weeks after the funeral, Loretta still medicated and on suicide watch, was taken to court. Her hair was all over her head and her eyes were big as light bulbs. She didn't even notice Mom Flossy as she waved with love to her. Her body was numb and comatose. If they'd given her an overdose of valium that would have been okay with her—she wanted to die—anytime, anyplace. This was supposed to be a preliminary hearing; instead, they sped up her trial. The prosecutor in the case worked with the Feds to get Loretta to drop-a-dime on the "big man" that was really behind the drug operation. They knew she was just a pawn. In no way was she going to give up Marv. She couldn't see ratting on a deceased man; especially for a man she loved and honored so

much. It was death before dishonoring her man's name.
Surprising though, the Feds were willing to cut back the
time she was facing, if Loretta informed them about the
owner of the sawed-off shotgun. Her prints weren't on
it, so they had to suppress the evidence in her case.
They wanted the culprit that owned the vehicle. If they
could get to him, they could wrap up a ten-year murder-
case and move up in the ranks. They did their research
and found that the owner was a dead man. To get further information to crack the case, they needed Loretta
to cooperate. The problem was Loretta only knew Fat
Al by his street name. She never knew where he lived,
his woman, or any other information. He was Marv's
friend who he rarely talked about. So, she gave up what
she knew. Sadly, that wasn't good enough. The Feds believed she was being dishonest by withholding information, and withdrew their help. Though her fingerprints
weren't on the gun, she was penalized and sentenced to
the max they could give her. She was ordered to serve
18 years in a federal prison.

Not only were Nasir and Sheena without a father, but
now they were also without a mother and left in the
hands of Mom Flossy, who passed-out cold when she
heard the verdict.

Part II

ONLY THE
STRONG SURVIVE

OUT OF CONTROL

Many years passed the Armstead family. Mom Flossy at seventy-two now, was at her wit's end with the responsibility of her grandchildren. Nasir had just turned eighteen and Sheena was 20-years-old; both of them still living in her household.

Sheena was fucking up a storm, and on the brink of becoming a parent. Nasir was looking for ways to make extra money. Loretta was at the bitter-end of her 18 year sentence getting ready to come home and Bucky was M.I.A.—missing in action.

Nasir was getting older and with age came maturity—but for some—idiocy. He had grown to be a fine young man at 6'1", 175 pounds of pure solid flesh and dark skin, silky smooth like his fathers. His lips, full and thick and his thick eyebrows made his facial features a triple threat. He was making chump change, selling bootleg CDs and DVDs. The money wasn't nearly enough to contribute to the bills, feed him, clothe him and allow him a few extra dollars in his pockets to trick with the females. The money just didn't stretch that long for a wanting young man that had to keep up with the next man. Instead of taking on a job, he figured he would try his hand with the neighborhood crew called the Horsemen.

The Horsemen were a group of older boys who made money illegally by selling heroine and cocaine. Nasir would see them in passing everyday, going to the basketball court at the local park. Normally they taunted the younger inquisitive boys until eventually, they too, became a member. Every time Nasir passed Chauncey, the leader of the group, he would catch Nasir checking them out—their gear, their jewelry and their cars—giving them his undivided attention. Chauncey knew that just as quickly as a gas lighter spit out fire, so would the transition be to get Nasir to join the squad. Through Chauncey's eyes, Nasir was too curious, waiting for the open invitation to arise. The inquisitive boys were easy to attract, for most of the boys knew about the struggle early on and wanted to find an exit from poverty, even if it was a negative way out. Fast money and popularity were what most of them desired. They knew with that, they would finally gain the respect of a man; respect that every boy or man considered necessary. If only Marv were alive to school Nasir on the outcome of this illusional game—jail or death. It was possible he could have guided his son in another direction; but sorry to say, he wasn't.

Sheena had been dipping out every night for the past two weeks, creepin' with Alex, her new boyfriend, over his mom's crib. She had filled out thickly. She was not the skinny, long faced, sad girl anymore. Nowadays, her long face dressed up her mid length hair, brown skin and her alluring smile. Alex's mom worked the night shift and countless overtime hours throughout the week. The house was always empty for them to run around and have fun in. Alex was her savior during her troubling teens. He was the comforter that overwhelmed her with unbroken interest, unlike others that couldn't focus in on her for more than five minutes. They were sexually active and never used protection. In a way, Sheena wanted to get pregnant, so she could spoil her baby to death. Her and Alex would be the perfect parents, she often thought. She was becoming more and more interested in the courtship she shared with him. She was happy that her mother was on her way home, but she was grown, what could her mother do for her? Her needing years were over now. Mom Flossy tended to them the best way she knew how.

Loretta was serving her last few months at FCI. Her situation just barely changed over the course of eighteen long years. She'd still been a patient and a dedicated pill popper of valiums, isolating herself from other female prisoners. The only time life entered her carnal body was when Mom Flossy and the kids visited her. She cried before each visit and after each visit ended. She was emotionally-slapped, and still hadn't come to the conclusion that she caged her mind by depression. Reality was a distant semblance in her mind that was harnessed by a chemical imbalance, subdued with a stronghold of drugs to help her ease her pain away. Would a man ever fill the shoes of her fallen comrade? She'd given up hope in most family members, friends and certainly in herself.

Each time Nasir came to visit, he felt like he contributed to his mother's loneliness and bouts of depression because he was the spitting image of his father. They shared the same characteristics and this often reminded Loretta that he was just like his father. He wondered if this was the reason why she cried at each visit, because he reminded her of their substantial loss.

Losing Marv affected Loretta, but it also affected Nasir in ways that only another fatherless young man could identify with. Besides, Nasir hardly ever talked about how his father's death affected him. He tried to stand tall as a man and handle his feelings most times alone. He had to be strong for all the women in his life—Loretta, Mom Flossy and Sheena—trying to be the man of the household. Especially since, every old man Mom Flossy made friends with, mysteriously disappeared without saying goodbye, to anyone.

Nasir's act of love for his family was overrated by those on the outside, looking in. For he was only the shell-of-a-man pretending to be the man. Nobody had to even ask who the most favored in Mom Flossy's household of the children was. That would be an insult, if asked. Nasir held that position without a doubt. Sheena would never disagree with this fact.

Loretta started noticing a detectable change in Nasir's appearance and noticed his attitude was changing as well. He wasn't disrespectful or anything like that, but he was always checking for time on his watch like he had other places to go and other people to see. He'd grown tired of watching his mother in the same condition for years and wanted to visit less frequently, if he had to continue to see her this way. However, Mom Flossy wasn't having that. She knew the key to Loretta coming back to reality was through the strength of her children, chiefly Nasir.

Mom Flossy's influence on her grandkids was an influence that many parents wished they had over their children. So, out of respect for his grandmother and caretaker, Nasir never missed a visit, but his mind wasn't always there with them. As soon as Loretta started with the "same" opening line—they all knew things hadn't changed.

"Mom, doesn't Nasir look just like his handsome daddy?"

Mom Flossy agreed on the account of her daughter's well-being, but prayed that one of these days, her opening-line would change. Sheena was still getting the short end of the stick while her mother was incarcerated. It was sad.

"You know Mom, I often wonder what Marv would be like today if he were alive."

That was Loretta's next response after her question. After that, the conversation would open up by Loretta singling Nasir out, asking him most of the questions; like the visit was made just for the two of them.

At the brink of each hour and a half visit, Sheena would get minimum opportunity to talk about all of her positive endeavors. However, Loretta never seemed interested in what Sheena had to say.

Time and time again, Sheena would try to stand out for her mother to notice her, but decided she was in a no win situation. So, she rebelled against everyone except, Nasir. Perhaps she was tired of chasing behind the attention that Nasir received naturally. Typically, this would have caused sibling rivalry, but in their case, they bonded together. Both were bothered by their mother's imprisonment and the absence of their fathers. Sheena always became further agitated when her and Nasir discussed their fathers because her father was still living and not once did he show a bit of concern for her. Sometimes he would walk past her and not say a thing to her; like she wasn't even his child. She never understood why Nasir got so mad at her for never opening up her big mouth when they saw him. She treated her father the same way he treated her—like a close enemy.

Nasir would tell her all the time, "At least you have a father living to talk to. All you have to do is open your mouth to speak. Then, maybe, you can get answers from him. I'll never have that chance to talk to my father."

This is when the big sister in Sheena would feel it necessary to go over and hug the life out of her little brother. She gave him hugs that were filled with love. Mostly everyone felt sorry for Nasir: his family, the neighbors, his friends, and people in general who found out that his father was murdered when he was only 3 months old. They were even sadder when they found out his killer, Freeze, only served 3-years in prison, because jurors felt as though he acted in self-defense. In spite of this, in a weird twist of fate for Freeze, the day he was released from prison, he was killed in a motorcycle accident. He too, left behind a teenage son.

The Horsemen were an outlet for Nasir—a way he could help support the family. Besides, his mother was coming home soon and would need a place to reside. Mom Flossy didn't have a problem with Loretta coming back to live with her, but Nasir wanted a new start for his mother.

He started hanging around Chauncey daily. Chauncey introduced him to all the members of the Horsemen and especially the "drug world". He used Nasir for his personal gain by giving him a job right off the bat of making drug deliveries. It was coolly high with Nasir, because it was a part of his "come-up." He was now able to buy a few luxuries he couldn't afford without having leftover money from his side hustle. Having clothing and staying in the latest gear wasn't a problem. Francine, Loretta's best friend, made sure they had at least two or three new outfits a month. It wasn't much, but it was more than anyone else was offering. When Francine and Stan took a vow at the hospital the day Nasir was born to help Loretta, that's just what they did—through good and bad times. Even after Stan got locked-up and was serving a life-sentence for murder, Francine definitely kept up her end of the bargain. She was there when Mom Flossy was handed down the news of Marv's death. She was there when Ms. Anna and Mom Flossy went down to the city morgue to identify Marv's body. She was there frequently, on visits to the prison to see her friend. If the rolls were reversed, Francine was sure that Loretta would reciprocate the same love and concern for her. Francine was included as a family member. In fact, she was closer to Mom Flossy than her own son Bucky was, who kept his distance after Marv's death. Really, he was ousted when Mom Flossy found out the truth behind Marv's murder.

Meanwhile, Nasir started making a name for himself out in the streets due to the affiliation he had with the Horsemen. Internally, Nasir felt in his spirit that there wasn't longevity in the Russian roulette game of narcotics. His short-term goal was to make some quick cash and disembark on a legal gig.

Mom Flossy's house was only blocks away from the park where the Horsemen dealt drugs, which meant Nasir never had to go far. She never forced them into anything. They had to want for themselves as much as she wanted for them. Nasir spent late nights down the Henrietta Johnson Park with his friends, waiting to hear the whistling call from one of the Horsemen to make a delivery. Henrietta Johnson was a notable community

warrior that fought with blood, tears and years of hard
labor to keep drugs out of her community. With the
sight of the events that took place by Nasir and other
young men and women in the park, Mrs. Johnson was
turning in her grave.

The park was the happening spot for all the ballers.
Nasir's tolerance for his surroundings gave him the window to peace. He loved being in the hood, not to mention he felt a closer spiritual connection with his father.
This was the same park his father spent time at, when
alive. Not only that, not too far away was the bar that his
father was killed in front of. He felt his father was always
around, protecting him. The park was the only place in
the hood where youngsters were free to express themselves, positively or negatively—there were no rules.
Once they stepped outside of the hood, everything they
did or said was judged; or at least tried to be controlled
by someone not accustomed to the lifestyle. The park
was the only place Nasir could go to yell out, scream
out, or act out when he needed to release.

Seeing his mother in her state of mind was enough
not to let him stay with a one-track mind. It was also
enough for him not to be down about his father.
Although, not a soul would ever let him forget about
them. He heard stories every night in the park from old
heads, old flings and people who knew Marv and
Loretta. The women who had a side thing going with
his father when he was alive, even tried to kick it to him
from time to time, offering him more than conversation. They figured if they couldn't have Marv, they'd get
the next best version—his son. Some stories were new,
some repetitive. Like the presence of Marvin Gaye in
this present day, so was the memories of Marv—they
would always live on.

Outside the relationship he built with the Horsemen, Nasir befriended Brian years back while in high school. Both young men shared the same commonality of losing a father in the streets to a violent crime. Relating to each other would come easy and second nature for them. Days when Brian was down, Nasir lifted him up. Days when Nasir was down, Brian did the same in return. Days when both of them were down, they paid a visit to the cemetery that embodied both of their father's remains. Lately, the visits to the cemetery were more frequent than usual. Puberty probably triggered the increase in emotions for both of them.

Nasir's first experience with a female was with his sister's friend. One night, Mom Flossy allowed Sheena to invite a friend over. Simone Nutbutter was her name. Mom Flossy was a little suspicious at all the attention Simone was giving to Nasir, who was eleven, than to Sheena, who was around Simone's age. Nasir was into playing with racecar tracks, army soldiers and toy guns. The hide-and-seek game that Simone played with him seemed all too fun, especially when Simone would catch him. He thought it was extremely funny when Simone pulled down his pants, and put his little chicken in her mouth and fondled his ball sacks. He thought it was all in sync of the game.

At the end of the game when Simone finally let Nasir catch her, she would make him touch her breasts first, put his fingers in her hairy spot next. Then for the grand finale, she showed him how to put his member into her stretched out hole. Nasir never told anyone about this little hide-and-seek game that he played with Simone, 'cause if he did, she promised never to play it again. He couldn't have "Ms. Nut-Tin-But-Butter," not feeling him out like she did the first time. They played that game a number of times when she came to stay, until Nasir got tired of her trying to control him. He was no longer a virgin. "Ms. Nut-Tin-But-Butter" popped his cherry, introducing him to the world of sexual intercourse.

When he was 13-years-old and having a rough time trying to understand the changes that were occurring in his body, he went to Mom Flossy trying to get advice about his changing body. She tried her best to explain the changes to him, but she would never be able to physically understand. She was not a man. Nasir's voice was changing, his body was growing, his facial hair was starting to sprout out and to top that off, his hormones were doing things he couldn't handle. He didn't have a positive male influence in his life to share with him his growing pains. His Uncle Bucky would sneak through once in awhile but never faced Nasir, and he was oblivious to his Uncle's reasons why.

Now at eighteen, he was starting to get attention from him selling. He began to learn how the drug trade went down and he was building his clientele by personally delivering to them to make the sale. The Horsemen thought they were getting over but Nasir was playing this out to reach his short-term goal. He knew how the business ran. The only thing he didn't know about was, who the main source supplier was. That information he didn't need to know. He concentrated on mastering the game. This flocked the interest of the older, shapely, pretty females that came around the park. All he wanted to do was get his paper—money—up to their level. He wanted to be included in the circle to get with the fly chicks. For now, he had to settle for the girls that were his age.

Nakea was an around the way fast-ass teenage girl.

She had a young hustle' getting a little cash that showered her with gifts, put her on a pedestal and adored
the ground that touched her feet. Nasir heard all the
rumors about Nakea boning, giving up much ass and
giving the best blowjob for a girl her age. Of course, for
a young man wanting notches on his belt, he was willing
to take his chances at getting some. Mainly one of those
outstanding blowjobs all the other boys his age were
talking about.

Nakea's personality sent off an emotional alarm system warning Nasir not to mess with her. Instead of listening to his inner-voice, he avoided the detrimental
signs that evidently were screaming out to him—*DON'T
MESS WITH THIS ONE!*

While Nakea's little boyfriend-hustle' hustled, in-
between his deliveries Nasir would make small talk with
her in the park. The first time he tried to converse with
her, she brushed him off. But the second time he approached her, he broke the ice with a humorous comment and a compliment about her new sneaks. That
did the trick because she came back with a teasing response. From then on they were buddies. He knew she
had a boyfriend, and his weight (position) wasn't heavy
enough to invade her man's space just yet. What he did
was make sure when her man was gone, to slide in his
place. Nakea stayed outside all hours of the night. Nasir
didn't know the story behind that. Really he didn't care,
as long as he was able to make his moves on her. The
less supervision she had, the greater the chance for him
to get in her panties.

His reputation with the Horsemen boosted his self-
esteem up with the females. All the older girls the
Horsemen were involved with, considered Nasir to be
their "little brother." Anytime one of them greeted him,

they did so with a sisterly hug, letting him get free feels. He loved when they came around. A few of them were lining up to get fucked.

The Horsemen put Nasir down to getting a motel room if he really was trying to get some from a girl. Before then it never crossed his mind to get a room. They explained to him, that it wasn't cool to try and sneak girls in your mom's or your grandmom's house. That was played out. Plus, it wasn't worth taking the risk of him looking over his shoulder. Chauncey was getting some on the regular, and Nasir wanted to be just like him, in the same position he was in—getting much play.

Every night for two months straight, he'd asked Nakea to go to the motel with him—every time she refused. Instead of this making him change his mind, this made him more persistent in wanting her. Not for her looks, 'cause she wasn't the cutest young girl around the park. She kept her hair in cornrows or in long weaves to conceal her natural-length. Her teeth weren't the whitest; they could use a little whitening. Her shape was *a'ight,* but no way in hell could she compete with the older girls. Her skin tone was borderline dark-skinned. The best physical attribute about her was her flawless skin. She had no reason to have pimpled up skin—she fucked enough. Her clear skin was a mad give away.

Material items brought about shine to her. She kept a new sneak and a new outfit, courtesy of her boyfriend, Sean. His family had a history of getting money. His mother was the ringleader. He followed behind her steps and started hustling at the mere age of 11 years old. He was sixteen years old and getting real cash flow.

Nasir was still getting it in with other females in the midst of his pursuit to conquer Nakea. She didn't hinder his one-night stands. If boundaries were the only issue, he'd set them for everyone including Nakea. Everyone was fair play. When Nakea started noticing the interest and play Nasir was getting from other females, she thought twice about his offer. With his pockets starting to weigh heavy, Nasir knew eventually, he'd have his day. The thought of making her his main girl was never in his mind. She simply didn't have the potential of a first class pick—not even a second class pick, more like a third round, fiftieth pick in the last part of the draft when scouts were getting the scraps.

Nakea started spending the night with Nasir at motels, but still tried to play hard to get. Nasir knew he was getting beneath her skin when she started ducking her boyfriend. He knew she was acting like that because her boyfriend caught a case (criminal charge) and was on his way to Juvenile Hall. Nakea needed another sponsor to fill his shoes. Once Sean went away she planned out for that shoe-filler to be Nasir. When her boyfriend got arrested a second time, she knew she made the right decision to be with Nasir; it was that night she asked Nasir if he was getting a room. This time, Nasir knew—she was going to give it up. He wanted to make the night extra special, by buying two bottles of cheap imitation wine, Boones Farm—lemonade and peach flavored. Neither really drank and that was what the old head that was outside bumming change recommended. He put both bottles on ice in the white bucket left in the room by the motel clerk. He carried his tape player and his homemade slow jams tape he made late night while listening to the Quiet Storm on WDAS, 105.3 FM dial.

Once again, he borrowed Chauncey's car for means of transportation. He stopped home to tell Mom Flossy he wouldn't be home again tonight. She was sick and tired and sick of being sick and tired. She couldn't wait for Loretta's day of release. For her children's sake, Loretta had to snap back to realism. If she didn't, Mom Flossy was going to make this world real to her. Nasir was into doing his own thing, not what Mom Flossy wanted him to do.

Just like his father's smooth ways, Nasir had the room set up and prepared for Nakea when they would arrive at the motel. He ordered Chinese takeout and timed them, one hour before they'd arrive. That was plenty of time for him to pick Nakea up from the block. He acted as if this was a first time experience the way he carried on, but it wasn't. He had the romance of his father embedded in him. His emotions were rhythmatic, just like Marv's. Nasir even stopped by the drugstore to purchase a sentimental card and a single chocolate rose, decorated creatively with red and silver aluminum.

He pulled up to the park where Nakea was sitting with two other hot-ass hood rats, both with mad faces because Nasir chose Nakea instead of them. Nakea tried to act all hard, not moving from her space until Nasir blew the horn, and then rolled down the window to call her name, trying to make it seem like he was sweating her. That's when she decided to get up from the concrete steps, wipe off her pink and white jumper and her new pink and white Nike's, that her man paid for before going to jail.

"I'll check y'all later," Nakea said to her friends and got into the passenger's side of the blue Mazda 929. Where in the hell was her mother when she needed to be around?

The radio station in the car was locked on 101.7 KISS FM, expressively playing the throwback song, "It's On Tonight" by Mary J. Blige, featuring R. Kelly. If Nasir

DRIVEN 105

had his way, this night would last forever, pleasurably, not regretfully. He nurtured his lust with her that night. Nakea did all the things that the rumors entailed. She was a hot mama ready for action.

The motel scene increased with Nakea and Nasir from one night on the weekend, to three nights—once during the week, and then on Friday and Saturday. Nakea hadn't even completed the 9th grade and with the school year at the end, it was apparent that she wasn't going to complete it this year either.

It was a game to Nasir. After so many rounds with Nakea, like he had with Simone, it became boring. He played along with it for a little while to let her know he was the winner.

Nakea had an older sister named Shonda, who was dumber and frisker than she was. Shonda gave birth to her first child at sixteen, not knowing who her daughter's father was because she'd boned so many different guys without protection. Nakea followed right behind Shonda's nasty trifling ways, but both believed that by sending off excessively low voice tones to guys, they were coming off as the shy type. That was all a role to manipulate attention. Their mother was a homebody stuck on stupid—always getting downplayed by a man. She let both girls do any and everything their little minds wandered for them to do. Neither Nakea or Shonda had a relationship with their fathers. The reason could have been because their fathers were brothers. They were blood related from the same birthing canal. Both of the fathers stayed away from crazy Daisy, their mother. Both men were shamed by sharing the same woman and for the fruits of their labor that produced two fast-ass daughter/niece combinations.

Nasir had pushed Nakea to the side and set his eyes on the newest prospect on the block, Sonya. Sonya was four years his senior, but she was still considered up for grabs by the older boys. *Let the best man win* was their motto in the park. Nasir, Brian and two other friends, Cal and Donny, watched from the park as Sonya's family unloaded into their townhouse.

It was broad daylight, hot, but not that humid for a June day. Sonya had on shorts, hugging her ass and a shirt cut so low, her breasts bulged out of it.

"Who is that?" questioned Brian looking like he just lucked up on a centerfold picture from a Playboy magazine.

"That's Sonya. She's a friend to my girl, Stacia. She told me that Sonya and her family were moving around the way, but I didn't know it was this soon," answered Cal with handed down information from his girlfriend.

"Bet twenty dollars I'll be the first to break her in!" Brian blurted out.

"Nigga, please. She's too old for you," Cal responded in return.

Nasir monitored every move Sonya made. He even thought he caught a glimpse of eye contact with her when she looked down the street at them sitting in the park.

"Bet that twenty dollars," Nasir challenged him.

"I can do better than that, cuz. I'll give you forty dollars, if you can hit that by next Saturday."

Nasir looked over to Cal and responded, "It's a deal then."

They gave each other a handshake; known to the brothas as some dap.

Nasir knew he had to work hard to pull this off since

she was four years his senior. Nakea was a distant memory to him and all week his was trying to brush her off, so he could fuck Sonya. Money for the mall was the only way to get Nakea's young-acting ass out of his face. He gave her $150 dollars, and basically told her to get lost for the week.

Sonya lived one block away from Nakea. In fact, if you walked around the corner on the same square-shaped block, the only space separating their houses was the back yard space. Sonya started sitting on the steps, just like the other girls did when they first moved into the park area to find out who the breadwinners were. Like an eagle sitting in a tree, Sonya watched all movement. When she wasn't scoping out the scene, she was carrying loads of laundry enroute to wash clothes. That was the avenue for Nasir to make his move.

On the way to the laundromat on Saturday, the last day to get paid on his bet with the fellas, Nasir asked Sonya if she could use some help with the baskets. Sonya was much too eager to accept his call for help. Later, he found out that it was her birthday through conversation. That entire week before Nasir rapped to her, she wore tight-ass shorts with her butt cheeks showing, and shirts that exposed her titties—like she was begging to be seen. Nasir gave her all the eye contact she needed that day, to get what he wanted—a piece of ass. Brian was sitting in the park, blinking his eyes to make sure it was his boy that he seen carrying the dirty clothesbasket.

"Nasir," Brian yelled out. "I see you making big moves, homey."

Nasir kept walking with Sonya as she blushed from ear to ear hearing Brian's comment. The joke was on her and she didn't even know it. When Nasir and Sonya reached the end of the block where Nakea's house was, Nasir positioned the basket on the side of his face to conceal his identity just in case Nakea was sitting on the steps. He didn't feel like answering twenty-one questions about whom he was with. Sonya didn't even catch on to what he was doing. Nasir spent the entire afternoon with her helping her wash clothes. She was impressed so much, that she invited him over later to her house. Her mother was in and out. She wanted Nasir to chill with her on her birthday.

Sonya was a tad bit different then Nakea. Sonya was very experienced; she was like a used car you bought from an auction with high mileage and many owners. Her freedom of expression through her skimpy clothing gave off an, *I'ma slut, nothing but a fuck message.* She was a head-hunter, much like college students—not due to the advancement in education, but due to the fact that she loved giving up brain. Sonya didn't prove Nasir wrong when she sat on the couch pretending to be watching television. She was waiting on who would make the first move. Her hands ended up right in his lap, making his joint rise. The couch was oversized—there was ample space for two bodies to bump and grind.

"Let's see what you have here."

She almost made Nasir feel the same way Simone made him feel. She pushed his back against the couch to ease the tension she'd seen building up in him and straddled herself on top of him. Her oversized breasts in need of a serious breast reduction, smacked him right in the lips.

"Put 'em in your mouth," she lusted, laughing while pulling off her shirt.

Her bra was far from the dirty holey bras that Nakea

wore. It was just too damn small for those big, oversized breasts of hers. They needed extra support or something, because for a young woman, her breast sagged to her stomach. She thought she was putting on a show for Nasir, but in the back of his mind, he knew she was giving this up too easy. He didn't even have to do nothing but carry a basket to the laundry mat to hit it. He kept checking around the unorganized room to see if anyone else would appear.

"What are you looking around for?" Sonya asked him. "I told you my mother wouldn't be home until late tonight. We're all alone, don't be *scur-red*!"

"I'm not scared, just cautious," he stated.

Sonya unbuckled his pants, grabbing at his dick. "Anybody ever give you head before?"

Immediately, Nasir came back with the response, "Nope," hoping she would be as good as Simone and Nakea. Just his luck, she was better than them all. Her blowjob blew him right out of his mind.

He found out what a multiple orgasm was for a man with his joint in Sonya's mouth. Sonya was the best that had ever done it. He left out her house, feeling like he graduated from high school straight to receiving a PhD. She made him feel like a real man, but he knew that she was nothing more to him than another piece of free ass.

ONE HAPPY FAMILY

"Nasir and Sheena get your shit and let's go!" Mom Flossy yelled at both of them. She made sure the night before both of them knew what time to come home. For today, Loretta was being released from prison.

"*Damn Grandmom*, it's too early." Nasir responded, placing the pillow over his head.

"Watch your damn mouth boy. Ever since you've been sniffing up those hot-ass girls asses, you've been feeling yourself."

Sheena walked past Mom Flossy to the bathroom, shaking her head in agreement.

"He sure has," she added.

Mom Flossy noticed her breast filling out and the changes in Sheena's eating habits. Her assumption of Sheena being pregnant had to be true. Almost every night she was dreaming of fish. She'd wait though to pop the question when Loretta was home, thinking that would be the right time.

"Hurry up, you two. You know we need to be at the

prison by 9:00 am to pick your mother up. Let's go! Neither one of you seem excited about her coming home."

By this time Nasir was sitting on the side of his bed with his hands cupping his face. Sheena was walking back and forth from the bathroom to her bedroom like she had left something.

"Don't the both of you talk at once!" Mom Flossy said with one hand on her hip and one hand on the banister.

"I'm straight, Grandmom. I'm glad she's coming home, it's just. . . ." Nasir stopped airing out his concern before he struck a nerve with Mom Flossy.

It was too late. Mom Flossy needed him to clean up his statement.

"It's just what? What is going on in yo' mind?"

Nasir looked up at his grandmother with a frank look of bother.

"Nah, I'm just saying, I hope she can survive out here. It's been eighteen years. Things changed; we've changed," he said profoundly.

"*I heard that!*" Sheena yelled out from the bathroom.

Mom Flossy shook her head. Out of all the year's she raised them from infants to young adults, never did she believe this day would come and they not be on cloud nine about their mother coming home.

"Both of you done lost your damn minds. You should be thankful that your mother's time is up. Had it not been for that no good ass. . . ." She stopped midway in her comments as she witnessed Nasir's neck stiffen up.

Sheena came out the bathroom patting her face with her hand towel.

"It's not nice to speak bad about the dead, Grandmom."

Mom Flossy cut her eyes at Sheena. "What the hell can he do to me dead? Come get me? He's already haunted me since he's been gone. Every time I look at that big-head boy sitting right there, I'm reminded of him."

Nasir started humming as if he was in a séance. "*Mmmmm, Mmmmm, sshh! I* feel a connection."

Sheena and Mom Flossy gaped at him oddly. Nasir held his fingers to his temples.

"Its coming through, hold on."

Both of them continued to stare.

"Grandmom, my dad is sending a message to you. He says he loves you, too!"

They all laughed together and made way to get dressed to pick up Loretta from the prison.

While in the car on the ride to pick Loretta up, Mom Flossy told her grandkids about the surprise welcome-home party she had planned for their mother.

"I've planned this big shindig for your mother tonight, and I don't want neither one of you spoiling it." She waited for a response of agreement. "That means don't open your big mouths."

Sheena gazed out the back seat passenger's window.

"Can Eric come to the party?" The courtship Sheena had with Alex had been over when she got caught slippin' with Eric.

Nasir responded before Mom Flossy had the opportunity to.

"If she can bring Eric, then I'm inviting both my girls," he proudly boasted.

To Mom Flossy, this would be an excellent gateway for Loretta to witness first hand how far gone her children were. The changes in both of them were prevalent. There were also other signs. Like when Francine would come over with clothing—none of the things she brought for Nasir were fashionable to him. He stopped accepting handouts. She knew he was into something else, but never pressed him about it.

After five minutes of silence, Mom Flossy decided to speak.

"I don't know if it's right to bring your little friends around your mother on her first day home. Let her get settled in first before you start introducing her to them."

Sheena smacked her lips. At age twenty, she felt she had paid her dues. She didn't need to explain to a damn soul.

"Well, mom is going to have to understand—this is who I am and Eric is my man now, not just my *little friend*. If she can't accept that, I won't be at the party tonight. If she wants to see me, she can find me at Eric's house."

"You mean to tell me, you done got that grown, that a wet-ass means more to you then welcoming your mother home?" As Mom Flossy spoke, the car swerved and hit a big pothole in the street.

"Grandmom, watch where you're going. You gonna kill us, getting all upset with Sheena," Nasir said, now focusing on his grandmom's driving skills.

"Shut up, boy. You ain't no different. You think I don't know what you out there doing. Since when did you start to wear all that jewelry? I ain't never bought you a watch, necklace, nor a ring, but I seen like three or four watches in your bedroom, two pinky rings and a lynx chain. Tell me why you don't have them on today? What? You scared your mother gone find out?"

Nasir started laughing, playing it cool. He was eighteen years old. What could Loretta say or do to make him change? By far, he knew his Grandmom wasn't a dummy. She was hip to the game. Her son was a junkie and her only daughter's deceased lover was a pimp and a hustler. He responded to her as sincerely as possible.

"You know what, Grandmom? Times were hard for all of us, especially for Sheena and I. Not having a mom or a dad around really fuc . . . well excuse me, messed us up. We love and appreciate all you've done for us, but it's time to let us go, Grandmom. We're grown. Let us be Mom's worry now. She shouldn't have a problem accepting us for who were are. We were made to accept her and the fact that she sacrificed her life, and had to do time in jail—leaving us. We were the ones getting laughed at when we were in school and outside playing with other kids, because the kids knew she was locked up. She didn't go through that. My only memories of mom, is going to visit her at prison, and you expect us to change because she coming home? Nah, Grandmom. I can't do that. I'll be at the party later, but like I said, my shorty's gonna come through."

Mom Flossy had a blank expression on her face.

"Well kids, with that said, and you feelin' that way, I'm going to do like I did when your mother got out of control—turn my plate over. I'll let both of you, since you think you are grown, handle yo' own affairs. I love both of you dearly, but it's been time for you to get out there on your own. I'll be damn if I'm going to have three generations living with me."

Sheena and Nasir peeped at each other and were like, *"Damn!"*

*   *   *

"Armstead," C.O. Kita called out, thirty-five pounds heavier than she was the first day she met Loretta. *"Bag and baggage!"*

Loretta already was prepared. The last six months, she had to wean herself off of valiums and antidepressants. She wanted to face reality and now, the day had finally come. She'd feared that things weren't going to work but was anxious as hell to get home and find out if they were.

This day was anticipated. Over and over, day after day, she practiced what she was going to do. When they finally called, *bag and baggage,* she was ready to face her challenges head on.

If it were raining or a blizzard on the outside, it would have been a sunny day to her. She was so happy to be going home. By chance, it was sunny. With her pictures and letters that she'd accumulated over all the years, she was prepared to get the hell out of the prison facility. The loud clinking of the metal door opening or closing, for once, didn't bother her as she walked out the door onto the tier. Envious and jealous female prisoners shared their opinions as Loretta paced with a smile on her face.

"I don't know what you're smiling for. You'll do something dumb and be right back," one cellmate believed.

"The girl been high since the day she arrived, now all a sudden, she the happiest women in the world," another inmate shouted.

Tonya, her only friend yelled. "Shut the fuck up. Y'all just jealous! Loretta girl, go get some good dick for me and you, both."

Nothing anybody yelled at Loretta broke her level of concentration until Tonya had made the comment about good lovin'. She would never get the lovin' that

Marv used to give her. At least, that's what she thought. That walk down the tier seemed like it took three hours to reach the existing doors.

After spending the last eighteen years of her life behind bars, Loretta was finally free. She was getting out of jail today. Her fears couldn't override the feeling of joy she had. Mom Flossy, Sheena and Nasir, waited outside in Mom Flossy's Buick Regal waiting for Loretta to step foot out of those prison walls. Loretta had no prewarning for what she was about to face . . . reality.

Soon as Loretta was let free, she ran straight into the arms of her son. Jealous prisoners gawked from their cells wishing it were them.

"It figures," Sheena mumbled.

Mom Flossy stood with her, arms open; waiting to be greeted, with reciprocating love. Loretta's looks had aged quite a bit. She wasn't that same young, vibrant teenager anymore. Her shape had disappeared in the weight that she gained and her face was riddled with worry wrinkles. Loretta faced the sky and breathed in for ten long seconds.

"Thank you, Lord. I know *you* and Marv are watching over me." She grabbed Sheena in a bear hug and made a mental note to herself. *Sheena has really filled out.*

Tears of joy rolled down Loretta and Mom Flossy's face.

"Alright, let's get you home," Mom Flossy said, wiping tears from her eyes. Loretta sat in the front seat of the car, but turned her body to face both of her children.

"So, how are you two?"

"Just fine," Sheena whispered.

"I'm straight," Nasir responded without shying away. "The question is, how are you?" he asked, trying to get a feel on how she was going to react now that she was home.

"I presume I'm doing as expected. Guess what?" Loretta responded gaining everyone's attention. "My medicine was cut back!" She said that as if they should be excited.

"Is that a good thing?" Sheena asked very sarcastically.

"It could be." Nasir answered back on his mother's behalf. "That's good mom."

"What do we have planned today?" Loretta queried, energized as a kid in a candy store.

"Nothing," Sheena answered back, hoping her mother understood how she really felt on the inside. "I have plans already with Eric."

Sheena had to start a negative buzz. Mom Flossy sensed that Sheena would be the initiator of the vibe.

"Who's Eric?" Loretta wanted to find out. "I thought his name was Alex?"

"No, that's another boy she been screwing," Mom Flossy interjected.

Loretta had an, *okay* expression come across her face. "Since when were you allowed to have a boyfriend?" she asked jokingly.

"I didn't know I had to ask. I'm grown, remember? Or, has time slipped you by?"

Loretta blew out some hot air from her mouth. "Whew! I deserved that, I guess."

Mom Flossy couldn't pull the car over fast enough. "No, you didn't."

Mom Flossy's five-finger imprint landed across Sheena's mouth. Nasir watched the women of his family react over-dramatically.

"Women," he whispered.

Sheena started crying loudly. "I don't care! Hit me all you want. I'm still going to do what I want to do and nobody is going to stop me!"

Mom Flossy directed her comments directly at Loretta.

"I'm glad you're home. Now you can deal with these hardheaded young adults. They think they know it all."

Loretta hadn't a chance to get transitioned back into the household and was faced with conflict already.

"And while we're gathered as one happy family," Sheena stated cynically, "I might as well tell everyone now. . . ."

Everyone waited for the obvious.

"I'm pregnant with Eric's baby and I'm keeping it."

Loretta had a feeling she was, but wasn't ready to deal with it.

"I knew it," Mom Flossy wailed out.

"That's why A-Rock, (Alex) left you after all these years—you was creepin' with dat nigga!" Nasir stated in revelation.

When they finally made it to the house, they parted, going separate ways. The ride back created a cloud of stress, raining over their happy reunion, if they were supposed to have a pleasurable one.

Francine had already planned to take Loretta out for the day to get her hair done, a manicure, pedicure and a professional massage. Shortly after, they would go wardrobe shopping. In the time that Loretta had been away, Francine had advanced on her job and was now the supervisor of the Vital Statistics Division. Her annual salary increased to $33,000. What an increase from the measly $18,000 she started with. She'd purchased a home under the 1st time Home Owner's program on the north side and had a nice Subaru Legacy as means of transportation.

Loretta was in the house changing her clothes into something more comfortable. Mom Flossy handed her a homely white short set that had not one feature that would make the set stand out.

"Here, wear this," she said giving it to her.

Loretta wasn't up on the latest styles, so she accepted with much appreciation.

"Thanks, Mom." She leaned over and hugged her mother for the fifteenth time today. "Thanks for every-thing, mom."

Mom Flossy knew her daughter had sustained a great ordeal over the years. Though she didn't want to put too much pressure on her, she knew that she had to do what was best for Loretta to survive. This was a second opportunity for her to guide her in the right direction, since she felt she failed her in the past.

"Stop getting all mushy with me, Loretta. Just be-cause you're home don't mean you can depend on me. Tomorrow, you can carry yo' grown-ass around the cor-ner to the Social Service building and get a little assis-tance for yourself until you can get a job. I've done my job of raising your children. I'm not about to take on another responsibility. You hear me!" she said, openly admitting she was worn-out.

"Thank God that Sheena graduated. I don't know how she did it . . . stuck up under Alex, night and day. Too bad for him now She done moved on to the next man—Eric!" Her head hung low, which showed her em-barrassment for her next comment. "I was very disap-pointed when Nasir stopped going."

Loretta tuned in with genuine concern. "He dropped out? Why didn't someone tell me this sooner?"

Mom Flossy's head popped back up like a tentative rabbit in fear. "Don't start asking me questions like that. Had I told you while you were in prison that the boy dropped-out, you were liable to be a damn zombie, worse than you already were. I did my best with those kids but they needed more than I could give them—love from their mother and fathers. I watched these kids damn near kill their spirits, hopes and dreams crying after you. Anna helped out when she could, but in case no one informed you—she's bedridden and in need of care herself."

She had to bring Loretta up to date, on how the problems escalated over the years.

"I begged Nasir to go over to visit his Grandmom. At least to develop a relationship with that side of his family—he never listened. He's too busy chasing them hot little girls that he can't see straight. These kids have been screwing up something for a *looong* time. I'm surprised Sheena wasn't a teenage parent. I noticed the change, but what could I do?"

Loretta's heart sank. "You could have gotten them counseling. Put them in programs to occupy their time, Mom."

Mom Flossy looked fiercely at Loretta like she'd lost her mind. "What the hell you think I've been doing all these years, whistling Dixie? They've been in counseling three or four times. They were members of the Boys & Girls Club, but there comes a time when they want to learn from experience. Just like you did, when you were younger!" she said, gut punching Loretta. "Remember those days, huh? My kids are grown. I was forced to raise yours. Now, it's my time to enjoy life. My hands are washed up." She clapped her hands together as to say, *I'm done.* "It's your turn now."

Loretta pushed back against the wall with her head protruding low.

"No need to cry and sulk over spilled milk. It's time to get your life and your family back." Her mother comforted her. "On a lighter note, I've already signed you and the kids up for housing two years ago and your name is now in the top ten of the housing list. You can call tomorrow to find out your exact number on the list."

A slight smile formed on Loretta's face. "Thanks, Mom."

"Stop thanking me and work on building up your relationship with those kids. They can still be saved."

Francine walked in the house yelling Loretta's name, just in time.

"Where's that huzzy Loretta at, Mom?"

"I'm right here, Pancake."

"Well, come the hell on. I'm ready to go." Francine gave Loretta a welcoming hug and waved at Mom Flossy.

"Hey, Mom. How's it hangin'?" Francine asked walking out to the porch.

"What do you mean *how's it hangin*?" she fired back.

"Mom, you know you have more balls than a man," Francine responded, making them all laugh.

It was back to happier times. Francine rolled her eyes back and forth scanning over Loretta's gear.

"Yes, it's official. We need to go shopping, to get you out of that old-ass shit. I'ma make sure we put you in something cute and sexy."

Loretta studied Francine's body. There was an apparent change.

"Pancake, what happened to ya ass? It was *never* that plump."

"Ah ha, I got a strong back, beatin' it up!"

"Get out of here!" Loretta answered with a clueless look.

"Let me stop messing with you. Girl, I had cosmetic surgery to fatten up this pancake," she said shaking it in front of her. "It's phat to death, ain't it?"

"Damn sure is," she responded staring at it a bit too long. "You seeing other men?"

"I wasn't lying about that!"

"Hmm," Loretta hummed.

"Don't get carried away shopping, Francine!" Mom Flossy stressed.

"Awe, come on, Mom. It will do her some good. She'll be alright."

Loretta had picked up extra pounds, but she didn't look sloppy with the new weight. With the right outfits, she would be back on track.

Loretta and Francine enjoyed the day; like they were high school students once again. They shopped, ate and laughed like they'd never lost time with each other. Each time Loretta tried to pop a pill, Francine stopped her.

"You don't need that. You're home now. You have nothing to hide from. That stuff is not going to do nothing but create worse situations, coating all you feelings. The best way to readjust is to take it like a true champ. The Loretta I knew would never let a drug control her."

Francine's words were true. She had hoped she'd take heed to her words.

"I don't know how I'm going to deal with this shit, Francine. I found out today that Sheena is pregnant and Nasir is out there in the streets." Their eyes locked on one another's.

"That damn Sheena. At least she waited 'til she was twenty. Most of her little friends done had two and three kids by now. I knew when she started to develop that stank-ass attitude, she'd been sexed-up one good time. Or, at least she thought she was. These young folks don't know anything about real lovin'." Francine sneered, thinking about how she was the same way in her younger years. It wasn't until she met Stan that she found out what lovemaking was really about.

"Now Nasir, I'm not the least bit surprised with his fine ass. Most of the young boys go through the fad of hanging out in the streets with "the boys". This stage will soon be over, don't worry about it. My concern though is him hanging around Tawny's son, Chauncey. Now that's what you should be worrying about. Nasir drives Chauncey's car and everything. I know for sure that Chauncey's up to no good."

Loretta dug into her scalp, scratching her head, as she listened with alertness. They were stopped at a red traffic light, waiting for it to turn green. Two young ladies took their time walking across the street, when the light turned.

"Some of these young folks don't have any respect. Now if I run their cute asses over, then what?" Loretta turned in Francine's direction.

"Then, you'll be locked up like I was for years. They're not worth it—please believe me."

Loretta had opened the door for communication about her prison term. For Francine, that was an entry for her to ask her questions she'd been dying to.

"Since you brought it up, what was it really like in there? You know people say federal prison time is better than doing state time."

Loretta sniffed in some air through her nose, digging into her scalp again.

"Whoever told you that bullshit you should have smacked some damn sense into them. Jail is jail; neither federal nor state prisons are a place you can get comfortable in. And if you can get comfortable, something is without doubt wrong."

Francine shook her head in agreement. "That's a logical answer. What about that lesbian shit happening, getting turned out and all?"

Loretta shifted in her seat, fiddling with her seatbelt.

"I'm not going to say that it doesn't happen, 'cause it does, but I will say it's not against someone's will. Females don't rape other females. They are either down with it before they get to prison, or they were always curious and finally acted on it."

Francine was so into the conversation, she almost passed the mall.

"Did you . . ." Francine began to ask.

"I ain't ever been into biting the burger." Loretta argued against lesbianism before Francine let that thought linger any further in her mind.

"I don't know, bitch. . . . You were looking at my new ass a little *too* long!"

"Kiss my ass, Pancake!" she embarrassedly laughed.

"How you doin'?" Francine asked, mimicking the queen of radio, Wendy Williams' favorite punch line.

"To be straight up Francine, the only way I did my time was with the help from drugs. Other than that, I don't know how I would've survived."

Francine realized it was tough for Loretta spending that many years of her life behind drugs, a gun and a man. Loretta was now in the same boat she was.

"You remember Mitzy and Marie, right?" Francine asked switching the subject.

Loretta stopped her to say, "Who can forget those two?"

"I hate to be the one to spread gossip, but Nasir is messing with Marie's daughter, Sonya, and she's almost 4-years older than he is."

Loretta got out the parked car and slammed the door. "Oh, no he ain't messing with that tramp's daughter. That's one relationship I'm going to put a stop to and fast."

"You should," Francine said, co-signing that.

The memories Loretta had of Marie were all too clear. She sure in hell wasn't going to let a home wrecker's daughter, disrupt her son's life.

"Loretta, that's not all. Nasir is also messing with one of simple-ass Daisy's daughters."

Loretta cast doubt upon her on the last sentence. "Daisy?"

"Yeah, Daisy. You know her. She's the one Mitzy fought back in high school 'cause she was dipping off with Mitzy's old man. Do you remember her now?"

"Sort of."

"Anyways, her girls have really made a name for themselves. Girl, they're two of the hottest young girls moving around on your side of town. You better stop Nasir from messing around with both them girls. If not, you are soon to be a grandma."

Loretta respected Francine, but thought curiously how Francine knew all of that information.

"Francine, how did you find all of this out?"

Francine smiled. "Girl, I'm up on any and everything that's going on in my niece and nephew's lives."

She had a genuine interest.

"The first time I suspected Nasir of doing wrong down in the park, I pulled him up on his behavior. I caught him talking to Fat Al, exchanging hands. Girl, Fat Al gets high as a bird now. Nasir almost shit in his pants. He didn't lie to me though about what he was doing." Francine opened the heavy glass and steel entrance door to the mall.

"I don't want Nasir to fuck around with that fat nasty fucker!"

"Calm down, baby. It's gone be alright." Francine convinced her, knowing how she felt about Fat Al.

"Francine, when I told you earlier about Nasir, you acted like you didn't know," Loretta said walking in behind her.

"I never said I didn't know. What I said was, I wasn't surprised. Don't twist my words up now."

"But still!" Loretta interjected.

"But still what?" Francine responded right back. "The boy told me it was a temporary thing until you came home."

"And I guess that made it alright?" Loretta said in disbelief of her friend's justification.

"No, that doesn't make it right, but at least he was honest."

They let the conversation dwindle down and began their day of shopping and spa treatment. Time had gone by so fast that Francine almost forgot about the surprise party for Loretta. She hadn't a clue whom Mom Flossy had invited. Most of Loretta's friends were into other things. Eighteen years was a long time to try to regroup together some friends.

Pausing, Loretta used all her energy to ask Francine,

"Before you take me back home, can you please take me to Marv's gravesite?"

Francine knew that was soon to come up. "Sure sis, no problem."

Back at the house, Mom Flossy had prepared a buffet style dinner for those attending the party. Fried chicken, beef ribs, baked fish, collard greens, macaroni & cheese, corn on the cob, flavored rice and big chunks of fresh baked corn bread. She ordered a full sheet cake from the bakery, Sweets To You, with strawberry-cream filling on the inside of the cake. The house was decorated with welcome signs and many colorful balloons.

Nasir was already there with Nakea. Actually, he was going to rotate Nakea and Sonya on shifts. After he'd spend two or three hours with Nakea, he would drop her off and pick up Sonya, so she could meet everybody. He didn't want either one of them to feel left out, trying to be a lady's man.

Sheena did arrive, but with Eric lodged by her side. Ms. Anna was there in support of Loretta. She felt sorry for her; getting locked-up all those years, behind her son. She knew Loretta loved him as much as she did. Mom Flossy invited everybody she could think of, over. People who knew Loretta when she was a teen were there, as were some of her old schoolmates.

Francine pulled up in the Gracelawn Memorial Cemetery and led Loretta back to the section where Marv's body rested, since his spirit moved on. She gave Loretta time to herself as she watched her cry and sob for more than ten minutes. She wanted to go over there and hug her to conceal her from the hurt and pain, but she knew it was best that she let her release all the hurt and frustration she built inside all those years. Loretta knelt down on Marv's grave, kissing his tombstone. This was her final goodbye to Marvin Bundy and the start of her new life. She knew in order for her to move on, she had to put this behind her. Her love for Marv would never die; only remain as lasting memories.

"Okay," Francine said, watching her kiss the grave. "That's about enough. The girl is kissing the tombstone. It's time for big sis to intercede."

Francine walked out the car to Loretta's side and picked her up from the freshly cut grass. Once inside the car, she handed Loretta some tissue to wipe the falling tears and snot coming from her nose.

"Here. Take this tissue and wipe your face clean." Wiping her face, Loretta still had tears streaming softly after each wipe.

"I loved him so much Francine and he's gone—gone forever. I based my life around Marv. He taught me almost everything I know. How am I going to move on?"

Francine monitored the steady flow of traffic before pulling out the cemetery exit.

"You just live on, Loretta. Live on for your children. It's been eighteen years and you still haven't evolved from Marv's death. Let his death be the reason you chose life—a life surrounded with love for your children. Out of everyone, they were affected the most by both of your tragedies. You have to be strong for them."

Loretta reached over while Francine was still driving and partially hugged her.

"Girl, don't make us crash. I ain't trying to join them over there," she said pointing to the cemetery.

"I love you, Francine. Thanks for everything," Loretta contentedly said shedding tears.

"It's all love, little sis," Francine gracefully responded.

Loretta promised when she did come home, that she would continuously give praise for those that helped her and her children while she was down. Francine was one of them.

Francine took Loretta over to her new house for her to see that things had really changed for her by living positive. Loretta was surprised that Francine was now a homeowner.

"This is awfully nice, Francine."

"It's cute and cozy," Francine said turning on the television.

Since Francine didn't have kids, all she needed was a two-bedroom house. It had the precise dimensions of living space for her. Contrary to Loretta's beliefs, Francine was still lawfully married to Stan, and still went to see him—every now and then. Although, she had a steady fling on the side for years. Francine was not one of those women who wasted away their lives waiting for a man incarcerated. She loved Stan to death but she had to move on. She had other needs that had to be addressed and from where Stan was living, he couldn't meet the needs. Loretta noticed all the pictures on the walls of her, Francine, Marv, and also Stan. Francine rarely talked to anyone about her situation with Stan and she didn't want to talk with Loretta about it, fearing it would make her relapse in time.

"Francine, what's up with Stan?"

Francine came out of the kitchen with two wine glasses and passed a wine glass to Loretta, who stared inside the flute glass when she passed it to her. Francine popped the bottle and poured some wine into both glasses.

"Drink it. It's not going to hurt you, girl. If anything, it might calm you down." Francine insisted, sipping on her wine glass full of Merlot.

"Stan is Stan. He's doing his bid like a trooper. He's into his spirituality more than ever. He done converted himself to Islamic beliefs."

Loretta took a sip of the red wine. It had a very bitter taste from what she was use to drinking.

"This is bitter and *nasty*. You know I used to drink sweet drinks." Having that one drink reminded her of her past. "Remember when I was a barmaid?"

"Hell yeah. You used to serve up crunk juice before these young folks knew anything about it. By the time the night was up girl, we'd be drunk as a hooting canary."

They literally bent over in laughter.

"You still think you got the skill?" Francine asked.

"It wouldn't take long for me to find out. I need a job anyway. Flossy talking about I need to start looking for one tomorrow, already."

Francine and Loretta exchanged more laughs.

"Some people never change," Francine said of Mom Flossy, still amused.

After Loretta changed into her beautiful new garments, they proceeded to the party that was still a kept secret from Loretta. They arrived to the party and from the looks on the outside, with people loitering in front of the house, the party surprise should've been blown, but Loretta still hadn't figured it out. Francine helped Loretta pick out the red halter top, with the red and white Capri pants that it came with, drawn out by her cute little summer slides. Her hair was pulled up in an uppity do, with a few pieces of her tresses sweeping across her face. Francine wanted to really make her face up, but it was a little too much make up for Loretta; for a woman who was a plain Jane.

When they walked inside the house, she heard the music playing and everybody shouting, "Welcome Home Loretta!" Loretta started crying again. Nasir got up to wipe the tears from his mother's eyes. For the first time in all his years, he saw the sparkle in her eyes.

"She's back!" he hollered.

People were giving Loretta hugs from all over. Nasir had to break in to steal his hug.

"Mom, this is Nakea. Nakea, this is my mom, Loretta." Nakea intentionally avoided eye contact with Loretta. Her head was face down as she said hello.

"Hi, Ms. Loretta."

"Call me Loretta, honey. Ms. Loretta makes me feel old."

"Nah, she can call you Ms. Loretta out of respect, right, Nakea?" Nakea hit Nasir on the forearm.

"Yeah, boy." Nakea wasn't the least bit shy when it came down to Nasir though.

"What about me?" Francine asked.

"I'm sorry, baby," he said leaning into kiss her on the cheek. "Nakea, this is Francine."

Nakea curled her lip. "Hi," she said softly.

Loretta greeted the visitors and almost choked on her spit when she saw Mitzy laughing it up, with Mom Flossy.

"Hey Loretta, long time no see. It's been a long time, a very *looong time*," Mitzy stressed.

"It has been Mitzy. I'm still surprised that you lived this long. Your liver ain't gone bad yet?" Loretta declared fiercely.

"Please, not me. I'm doing great, as you can see." Mitzy twirled around in her little summer dress, revealing too much flab. "I have three kids and I'm in good health. I have a nice apartment and a damn, I mean a damn good man," she sarcastic remarked, pointing out that she at least had a man.

"How lucky you are," Loretta said walking away.

"Hey Loretta, before you skate away to relive the past, you didn't tell me your handsome ass son, looking just like his father, is dating my niece."

Loretta shot right back at Mitzy with a nasty stare. "Cause I didn't know. But, I don't think he's that sweet on her. Take a look over there. Do you see him with that young lady? That's Nakea, his *real* woman."

Mitzy picked up her beer bottle and gulped down some beer. "I see them. He's just like his father, ain't he? Running women just like he did before he died."

Loretta wanted to bust her directly in her right eye. "Well if you know that, you know his father had no problem with loving them and leaving them alone. I hope that's not the case for your niece, but knowing my son, he'll follow behind his father ways."

"Don't worry, my niece will be here in a few. I'm going to call her."

Loretta found her way to the porch in the blink of an eye; where Nasir was play-fighting with Nakea.

"Come here, Nasir. I need to talk to you!"

This conversation couldn't wait. Nasir lifted off the seat and walked off the closed-in porch with his mother.

"What's happening, baby doll?"

Loretta blasted on him. "First off, I know about your so-called, temporary drug dealing and I'm pissed about that. You know I did eighteen years behind drugs and your father was murdered behind that shit. So, why jeopardize yourself and your future?"

Nasir started dipping his leg in place. "It's in the blood mom, I can't help it. *I'ma pimp by blood, not relation,*" he rapped. "You were a hustla', my dad was an OG, original gangsta, what do you expect?" he popped his collar.

Loretta didn't find any amusement in his words.

"Boy, listen to me and listen to me closely, that OG shit is dead. It will land you in the cemetery where I just visited your father. Or, by the grace of God, you'll get three-hots-and-a-cot. So, whatever you doing out there, stop now. Don't ever think you have one last run in you. That one last run, may be your last!" she said, thinking back to Marv's occurrence. "That's exactly what happened to your father . . . one last run and that's all it took to end his life and mine too. Look at you with your white T-shirt and your jeans hanging off your ass, looking like you just came off the block."

Nasir's posture changed as he searched the area to see if people were paying attention to their intimate chat.

"Ain't nothing wrong with a white T-shirt. Maybe that's all a brotha' could afford. At least it's clean, ya know. *"I smoke trees with my white Tee, look clean with my white Tee, count change in my white Tee, forget a throwback I look clean in my white Tee,"* he joked, reciting Dem Franchize Boyz latest single.

"No, I don't know! And, what you call yaself doing? Sleeping around with a bunch of girls at the same time—that's trifling!"

"Who said?" he paused.

"I'm not joking boy. I'm serious. I don't know much

about Nakea or Sonya, but the little I do know, isn't good."

Nasir hadn't known his mom was told about Sonya.

"How do you know about Sonya?" he asked.

"I have my resources. Don't worry about that," she retaliated, waiting for him to say something slick. "What I do know is that Nakea's mother is crazy as hell and Sonya's mother has been a whore since I can remember. You know what they say, "the apple don't fall too far from the tree". I know for sure Marie, Sonya's mother ain't shit. I caught her in the bed with your father years ago."

"Word. I guess they love the Bundy di-di-uh, oh," he said bigheaded on the Bundy name.

"I know damn well you ain't bragging about that. You better make sure you're protecting yourself. You'll mess around and get a disease you won't be able to cure, playa."

"I've been keeping the jimmy extra tizz-ight. I'm extra cautious when I'm hitting these broads off," he sided with his mother.

That's not what Loretta wanted to hear. It was as if he was rebelling against her, as did his father, when she caught him and Marie at the motel together.

"No, just leave that damn girl, Sonya, alone!" she said with bitterness.

It wasn't about Sonya; it was about the fact Loretta couldn't stand Marie. Sonya had to go. Nakea could stay. If Loretta had to pretend like she cared for Nakea, she would for the sake of making Sonya disappear out of her son's life. She despised the ground that Marie walked on and since Sonya was apart of Marie, she couldn't stand her either.

Just as they were walking back toward the house,

Sonya came strolling up the street in her slices of cloth, that she considered an outfit.

"Shit, what is she doing here?" Nasir paused to himself.

"Tone that tongue," Loretta demanded with clarity, snickering at Sonya coming up the block.

"This is the shit I'm talking about. She ain't nothing but a troublemaker like her mother."

Mitzy had already given Sonya all the information she needed. She walked right up to Nasir without waving to Loretta and started questioning him about Nakea. This made Loretta even madder. Nasir tried to break the ice by introducing Sonya to her.

"Sonya, this is my mother, Loretta; and mom, this is . . ."

Before Nasir could finish, Loretta turned her back on them, walking away, not interested in being introduced to her.

"What's her problem?" Sonya asked him, disrespectfully.

"Yo, you better watch you mouth. That's my mother you're talking about." Nasir didn't appreciate that at all, regarding his mother. "What are you doing here anyway? I told you I'd be by later on to pick you up. You couldn't wait?"

"Stop playin' *Mind Games* with me, Nasir. My Aunt Mitzy told me it's another girl up in your grandmomma's house, now where is she? Don't make me turn this block the fuck out!" Sonya said twisting around, feisty as ever.

"I wish you would try to act stupid. This is a welcome home party for my moms. If you came here to get rowdy, go the fuck back home. This is my mom's day and I'm not going to let you spoil it. Do something dumb and you're going to force me to beat your ass, understood?" he warned her, pinning her against a neighbor's car.

Sonya loved how close he was to her. She was ignited by physical violence. That made her believe he wanted her even more. Nakea looked out the door.

"Uh, huh, what's going on Nasir? Who's that?" Nakea said coming off the porch.

Nasir at this point was mad at both of them trying to ruin the party.

"My mom was right. I need to leave both of you bitches alone," he said out loud. "I don't owe either one of you an explanation. Neither one of you are my girl, ya know. The best solution I can give is to deal with it," he said, sounding just like his father in the past.

Sonya was piping hot. "How you going to play me like that for some young girl?"

"Oh, I got your young girl. You that same chick that was fucking my sister's man, ain't you? You San-ya, right?" Nakea said pronouncing her name incorrectly on purpose.

"Bird, get the name right. It's Sonya and if that was your sister's man, what was he doing with me then? I'll tell you why young girl . . . 'cause, *Mmm,* my shit *is* good," she said holding her tongue to the tip of her upper lip.

Nasir was embarrassed by Sonya's bluntness about sleeping with someone else's man.

"You ain't nothing but a project-nympho," he told her, grabbing his member. His shit was getting hard looking at her juicy red lips.

"Whateva'! I wasn't a ho when I was sucking your lid dick, was I?" Sonya screamed out at him.

"Little? Bitch, I always give you a mouthful," he frowned.

Loretta was standing in the doorway and said, "I told you so." She turned her back and let her son handle his affairs on his own.

"Only a ho, would put her business out there like that. Get lost, tramp," said Nasir, wanting her to leave downplaying him, telling everybody what they did.

"Okay, I'm going to leave, but you'll always remember me," Sonya yelled.

"No, he won't. Because his focus is going to be on me and his baby, that I'm carrying," Nakea yelled back at her.

Hearing that, Loretta stepped outside and tried to prevent Nasir from punching the glass window out of the neighbor's car. It was too late, the glass shattered everywhere and Nasir's hand was bleeding. Loretta now had two grandbabies on the way and to make matters worse, her long lost brother Bucky showed up to the party to welcome her back home.

The scene got real ugly when Bucky appeared.

Nakea leaned back in the car not saying a word, listening to Nasir's conversation.

"Tonight is no good. I'm tied up."

The caller inhaled her cigarette, tapping the ashes in the ashtray. "Can't you get free? I got on something extra special for you," she said real seductive.

"Do you?" he asked.

"Yes, I do. I'll be waiting for you." "I'll see what I can do," he said before hanging up. He looked at Nakea thinking of a way to break free.

SAME SHIT
DIFFERENT DAY

After the events of last night, Loretta was in no condition to go out job seeking. When Bucky showed his face, all hell broke loose. Loretta searched the house for the biggest knife she could find and chased Bucky for blocks. Everybody around the park saw it go down. Bucky had the nerve to come to the party knowing he was part the reason why Marv got murdered.

To top things off, after an unsuccessful chase to catch Bucky, Loretta had to face Sheena with her bottled up feelings that she carried around with her, about *her*. Add that to her having to deal with two grandbabies coming, she was stressed on her first night home.

Sheena stayed out all night long and so did Nasir. Neither one of them were home when it all boiled over. Mom Flossy was up early fussing and cussing about last night and Loretta just couldn't handle it. She grabbed her pill bottle that she hid under the bed and popped two anti-depressants to help her sleep.

* * *

Nasir paid for a room so he could talk Nakea out of having the baby, but his plan didn't work. It backfired.

The night they spent together was different from the previous times they were together. Nasir didn't touch her or make any advances that suggested sex. She felt betrayed by his actions. He was acting like he didn't want to be there with her and his mind was somewhere else. She had to air her feelings.

"All that time I gave you the cold shoulder when you tried to kick game and when I finally give in, you treat me like this. How are you gon' dog me, Nasir?"

Nasir took their conversation to another level.

"Could it possibly be because all I wanted to do was fuck you?" he asked her, sitting on the couch in the suite, not lying in the bed as he usually did. "Anytime I came through the park, you were more than willing to leave with me. You knew the rules. Stop acting like you never knew what was up. Yo' ass only played hard to get 'cause your boyfriend was still home. When he went to jail, you let me hit that off. Cut the bullshit, would ya!"

Nakea eased up on the motel bed, propping up the pillows.

"So what, you gon' be a deadbeat father, like my daddy? Is that what you're saying to me? I don't need you to raise a child. My mother raised us by herself and I'll do the same for mine. We don't need you." she said doing the best she could to stop crying.

It was Nasir's non-caring attitude that caused him to go raw with both Nakea and Sonya. He knew damn well, he wasn't ready to be a father, but now he had to suffer the consequences of his actions.

"Your mother did a fucked job, might I add. You and Shonda are some ho-ass bitches. You think I didn't know you wanted me for my cash? Be the fuck real!"

"Nasir, you don't have to call me out my name like that."

"My nuts!" He grabbed his crotch and slumped deeper on the couch. He was hoping by being totally disrespectful, she would change her mind.

"We don't know shit about raising a child," he blasted her.

Nakea let his comments go in one ear and out the other. Any emotion from Nasir was better than receiving none from home. She was keeping this baby.

"Nasir, it's not your decision to make. This is my body."

"Well let me ask you this, how are you sure that the baby is even mine? I mean you had a man when I started hittin' that."

Nakea's body became rigid, "I can't believe you just said that. You are an ignorant mothafucka!"

Nasir's honesty usually offended everyone, and today, Nakea was suffering the repercussions of his honesty.

"Well, believe it, 'cause I'm not taking that back," Nasir stated to her. "Yo, I'm outta here. I'll pick you up in the morning."

Nakea immediately rose from the bed and got all up in his face. "You are going to be a deadbeat father, aren't you?"

Nasir thought about it. "I already told you, I wasn't ready to be a father. Since you are making the decision to keep it, bitch—do you!"

Nakea started crying without ceasing. "It's like that, huh?"

Nasir felt bamboozled. He really didn't mean that he

wouldn't be involved in his child's life. He knew he wasn't ready, that's all. He still had other females to chase and money to make. A child would slow him up.

"Nah, it ain't like that. If it's mine, I'll handle mines; but you better know it, I'm not with your decision to keep it."

He left her in the room to meet up with another one of his women.

Nasir was up early waking Nakea up to take her home. He'd paid Chauncey so much to rent his car that Chauncey decided to sell it to him. He had a new ride anyway. It was nothing to let Nasir shine (profile) in his old one. They pulled up to the park, the usual spot he let Nakea out at. Sonya was walking down the street with a clothesbasket on her way to the laundry mat. She posted up next to the car when she got of reach. Her attitude was much calmer than yesterday.

"Nasir, can I talk to you for a minute?" she politely asked him.

"Hell no," Nasir promptly responded to her question.

"Please, I'm not going to act out. I promise."

"What do you want Sonya?" he asked.

"I'm pregnant," she said unpersuasively.

Nasir instantly fired back, "Get the fuck outta here with that bullshit, girl. You're just saying that shit because Nakea told you that shit yesterday," he said unable to distinguish her genuineness from her falsehood—if she had a genuine side. "Bitches are so predictable."

"No really. I'm serious."

The sincere look on her face would make a judge believe she was telling the truth.

"I knew you were going to act this way, that's why I carried my pregnancy test with me, to show you."

Nasir looked at the positive blue mark on the EPT over-the-counter pregnancy test.

"I don't give a fuck what that test says, it's not mines and I'm sticking to that. You can go tell the next man your sad story."

No way did he believe that Sonya was pregnant by him. He thought to himself, what would his father do in this predicament? Most importantly, how would Loretta react when she found this out?

Sonya was itching to let everybody know, Nakea wasn't the only one carrying his baby.

NEXT IN LINE

It was on a Monday, four months after Loretta came home that her name came up on the housing list. Instead of the Housing Authority assigning Loretta to a Project house, they appointed her to a scattered site apartment. The down side of that was the home wasn't but eight blocks away from her mothers. That was closer than she wanted. Her kids would still be subject to the happenings in the park and soon, she would be too.

Sheena had already decided that she wasn't moving in with Loretta. She wanted to either remain with Mom Flossy or move in with Eric, at his father's expense. Sheena's little feelings were hurt when Eric flat out told her that his dad wasn't having her moving into his house. Then, she had no choice, but to remain cool and reside with Mom Flossy, but still spending everyday over Eric's.

Nasir however, moved in with his mother. Although, he noticed the change in her behavior since she'd been home. On the weekends, she'd hang out with Francine and during the week, she worked a part-time job cleaning offices to make ends meet. He was surprised when he seen his mother talking to a man or two, in front of the crib. That was a sure sign that Loretta was moving on with her life, finally.

They were settled in the new crib and things were going good for them. Nasir was sitting in his room when he heard Loretta scream up the stairs from the hallway for him. Nakea had shown up again—unannounced. Her pregnancy was visible to all with her stomach, getting nice and round. It wasn't that big, but it was starting to get pudgy. Loretta had taken a certain liking to Nakea, feeling sorry for her and the distant relationship she had with her own mother. Daisy started putting her out every other week since she found out Nakea was pregnant. Instead of trying to make amends with Daisy, Nakea used this to her advantage to stay with Loretta and Nasir. She knew they had an extra bedroom since Sheena was living with Mom Flossy. Nasir was less than thrilled that Nakea was at his house again. He'd just come in from staying out all night.

"What are you doing here?" he asked, giving her the screw face.

"You know what I'm doing here. I don't even know why you asked me that." Nakea snapped at him. "My mom put me out."

She'd hoped, Nasir would feel sympathetic to her like Loretta was. After all, she was carrying Nasir's only child.

"You mean she put you out again. This ain't the first time."

This was becoming redundant.

"You mind if I crash here tonight?"

"Actually, I do. I'm meeting my new honey later on and I may need my room to give her some of this good dick."

Nakea sat looking stupid, with a perplexed face. She was sure he was calling her bluff.

"You can sleep in the spare room, if my mom says it's okay."

He opened his bedroom door to get Loretta's attention. "Hey mom, Nakea got put out again. She wants to know if she can stay overnight."

Loretta yelled upstairs, "I don't care. The damage has been done. I keep telling y'all that."

Nasir pressed off his khaki pants and his button up shirt. He changed his clothes in front of Nakea, enticing her as he removed each piece of clothing.

"Word on the street is that slut Sonya is pregnant too. Is that true?"

She had been longing to ask him that question since she got there. Nasir continued to get dressed, dabbing Amber White oil for men on his neck.

"You believe everything you hear on the streets?"

"No."

"Okay then, that's your answer," sounding very testy, he said. "If you don't mind, I'm getting ready to leave. My mom already said you could stay, so do like you normally do and go talk her head off."

He knew both Nakea and his mother used each other for their own personal reasons, exchanging information about him. For Loretta, she could relive her memories of his father. For Nakea, she could live out her fantasy of being with him.

Nasir gathered up his wallet and made sure he had enough money to treat Farren, his newfound interest. He met Farren during Spoonie's Basketball Classic tournament out in the park during the summer league. She was a coach for one of the teams. At first, he thought she was dressed a little boyish with her hair pulled back in a ponytail, with a headband on and a pair of Air Force One mid's to match, but when he seen her off the court, she was a black man's princess. She possessed qualities that Nakea and Sonya didn't. However, that was easy because he knew neither one of them were working on a damn thing. Nakea never completed the 9th grade. Sonya was jobless with no formal job skills or training.

Farren was a college student and worked at the Greyhound administrative office, in the Associate Sales department. She took classes at the community college and she was trying to better herself, unlike either one of them. He was really digging Farren's style. She was original and had her own style, not following the trends—she set her own. She had her own place and a car. It was only a Toyota Corolla, but it beat not having a car at all. She was older than Nasir by three years. He was accustomed to messing with older women. His interest for older women stemmed from his molestation occurrences with Simone, when he was young. Tonight he was taking Farren to Hibachi's, a Japanese restaurant. Farren lived on the other side of town, away from the Nakea and Sonya drama. He felt at ease in the company of Farren. She came from a stable household with both parents, representing a positive lifestyle. Her mother Leslie worked as a Litigation Specialist for a prestigious law firm and her father was a union worker at the local port. They were homeowners and considered themselves good citizens in their community. Farren was an only child, but did not possess the "only child" syndrome. She was decent and compassionate toward others. They'd only been on three dates. Nasir hadn't kept from her the song and dance that Nakea and Sonya put on from time to time to pre-warn her. Farren frowned upon it when he originally spoke about it but that was about it. She had no reason to believe her decision to be with him would involve her in his twisted triangle.

Before the Mazda 929 pulled up in front of Farren's apartment, Nasir had a sixth sense that someone was following him. He disregarded it initially, thinking he was bugging out, but when he looked in the rear view mirror and saw the same red Mercury Tracer, he knew he was on point. An unfamiliar face sat behind the driver's seat.

Farren was sitting outside on the steps, waiting for him. Unsure of who was following him, Nasir kept going on to make a second trip around the block. The car kept following him. *I hope this isn't that dumb ass girl following me.* Dodging the car, he parked his car and greeted his new project. Farren's hair was out in a natural wet and wavy hairstyle. Her outfit matched with Nasir's khaki outfit perfectly. She had on a knee length Khaki skirt and a sheer off-white and brown symmetrical cut blouse, with a pair of brown slide on heels.

"Are you ready?" smiled Farren, with her even teeth.

Nasir graced her with a warm snuggly hug. They walked down the steps, arm to waist, waist to arm.

Most of the guys Farren dated in the past were older guys. Nasir was the youngest guy she'd ever messed with.

Nasir searched around to see if the driver of the Mercury Tracer wanted to make their presence known. They hadn't. When the coast was clear, he opened the passenger's side for Farren and proceeded to get in the car. They left without any interruption and made way to the restaurant. Tailing right behind them was the

Mercury. Farren and Nasir were so engulfed in their conversation, they never paid the car any attention.

Reservations were made in advance, which made the transition from waiting to being seated easier. They ordered drinks and both benefited from the time that they shared together.

"This is so sweet, Nasir," Farren commented, feeling very special.

"No, this is not special. You are," he macked. Getting a few brownie points.

They pulled closer together and Nasir leaned over to give her a nice suction kiss to her cheek. He never saw the conflict coming their way.

"So this is the bitch you left me for?"

Farren and Nasir quickly raised their eyes to see who the rude and ignorant person was. Sonya stood there with her hands on her hips with a pair of tight unbutton jeans to ease the pressure from her stomach. Indeed, she was pregnant and showing.

Nasir immediately tried to defuse the problem. "Excuse me Farren, but this is one of my many mistakes. Let me get rid of her please, and forgive her ignorance. This is all she knows how to be."

He went to get up and out the seat, and Sonya pushed him back down. Mom Flossy always informed him never to put his hands on a woman, but he never obliged. Sonya's false sincerity to portray that her and Nasir had an ongoing relationship, was all to disrupt this new relationship he was in with Farren.

"If you knew any better, you wouldn't do that again," Nasir angrily enforced to her.

"What you goon' do, hit the mother of your child?" she said turning to see Farren's reaction.

"That has yet to be determined girl, so don't start

telling people that's my baby. For all I know, you were pregnant when I fucked you."

Sonya continued to block the table. Farren had one hand over her face, embarrassed because of the scene Sonya was making and from the stares of the other patrons. Farren knew of Sonya from a mutual friend. Sonya was known for talking loud and saying nothing. Always hooking up with other female's men. When they got what they wanted and dumped her ass, she would stalk them. Fighting the girl was the only refuge that would give her peace of the ordeal.

"Why don't you have a seat and say what you came to say? It's obvious that you want to make a point, otherwise you wouldn't have come to cock block." Farren's hands were now sitting on the table folded together.

Sonya rolled her eyes. "Ain't this a bitch? He done went and got himself a well to do bitch that's sassy."

Farren was only trying to get her out the way to continue on with the evening. Nasir thought Farren's request was absurd.

"Move out the way, Sonya. You're not sitting over here with us. Your best bet is to get the fuck up outta here with that bullshit." Nasir didn't care if she was pregnant or not. He shoved her, not pushed her, out the way. Sonya fell back on another couples table and started to put on a grand performance.

"Call the ambulance! I'm pregnant and I might lose my baby," she sensationalized, watching people come to her aid.

Nasir grabbed for Farren's hands and they fled out the restaurant before the help arrived, if they were coming. Sadly, they didn't even have the chance to watch the Japanese chef cook up their food in front of them with shimmering flames.

"I can't believe this," Farren mused. "Mistakes we make." She never gave thought about Nasir shoving Sonya. She felt that she deserved it. She should have never pushed him to his limit. She should've gotten out of the way when he asked her nicely.

The night had been ruined and as an alternative to the night's events, Nasir took Farren home, not to another restaurant, as she thought he would. That fumed Farren more. He'd left to go see his other friend for a few hours.

Back at home, the only reason Nasir participated in Nakea living from house to house was, because he felt bad having her out on the streets pregnant with his child. Unlike Sonya, he knew he had a greater chance of Nakea's baby being his. In his heart, he could feel that he was the father. He wasn't that sure with Sonya. The way she forced herself upon him made his suspicions that much stronger.

"I'll see y'all in the morning. I'm going to bed." Nasir's comments weren't an open invite to Nakea who was sitting up waiting for him to come back in. But, she took it as such following him up to his bedroom.

Nakea pulled the covers back from the bed and slithered her body between the sheets, ignoring his demands earlier about her sleeping in the spare bedroom. He overlooked her coming out of his pants, grabbing a pillow to sleep in the unoccupied bedroom. Nakea sighed but didn't give up. She gave him about thirty good minutes alone and wobbled her way into the same bed he slept in. Nasir was a hard sleeper but when he felt his nature rise, he thought he was in a good dream getting ready to have sex with Farren for the first time. He moaned, feeling the warmness surrounding his groin, grinding Farren in his dream, in and out. He could feel her muscles tensing up, or was it his muscles, he couldn't tell. In his dream, he gripped Farren's bottom deeper into his groin. This dream was feeling more and more like reality. He knew it to be true when he let out a pleasuring moan. Thinking he'd masturbated on himself, he opened his eyes and there sat Nakea on top of him, smiling with mischievous coveting eyes.

Lightly he eased Nakea off of him mad that it wasn't Farren he was giving his loving to. His boxers were still on him. Nakea used the small opening of his boxers, exposing his personals, to ride him. It was pleasurable, but it was unwarranted coming from her. This was a night that Nakea would mention to Farren, once they'd encountered each other. He had to concentrate on a way to get rid of Nakea, pregnant and all, to be with Farren. That's who he really wanted as his main girl.

In the morning, Nasir woke to the absorbing smell of turkey bacon, scrambled eggs and cheese grits. Loretta was in the kitchen making plates for breakfast. Nasir walked into the kitchen with his wife beater tee, a pair of blue and grey, New Jersey Nets basketball shorts on and a pair of black flip-flops. It was Sunday morning and nobody in the house had any intentions on going to a Sunday church service or at least watching BET Inspirations. Instead, they gathered to eat breakfast. That was the worship of the day. The only praises to God that was going up was praises for the meal that was sitting before them.

"And good morning to you too, Nasir," Loretta spoke acknowledging his presence.

"Good morning, Mom," he replied sourly.

"What's the attitude about?" she asked, turning over three pieces of turkey bacon.

"Nakea has got to go. Seriously, I know I asked you yesterday if she could stay but I made a mistake in asking you that." He wouldn't dare tell his mother about the stunt that Nakea pulled last night. "I'm uncomfortable with her staying with us. She needs to work out her problems with her mom and go back home. When the baby comes I'll do my part . . . if it's mine, but if it's not . . ."

Loretta turned to face him. "You know that baby is yours. You weren't saying that when you was going in raw-dog, was you? How can you think about putting that girl back on the street? You know she has nowhere to go. I'm not going to see her on the street and she's carrying my grandbaby."

Nasir was confused. "How come you're not this concerned about Sonya? She's claiming to be pregnant too."

Loretta's reaction explained it all. "That damn girl ain't pregnant by you. All the men she's been with. Anybody could be the father of her child. I know Nakea's carrying my grandbaby for sure!"

Nasir paused. "How are you so sure mom? You weren't the bed or the bedpost." With that, he reached for his plate and almost dropped it, knocking into Nakea. "Make this your last night staying here," he said angrily, grazing her shoulder.

"She can stay here as long as she wants too. I pay the bills in this fucking house," Loretta answered in Nakea's defense.

"Yeah, with my help," Nasir mumbled.

The shakiness in his voice was a sign that he was

bothered by his mother's sudden concern about Nakea. He was now experiencing what Sheena had for years now.

"If she stays, then I go," he powered back, reckoning that his mom would ask Nakea to leave.

"Then you can get to going, negro!"

Loretta's words cut through Nasir with sharpness. His eyes turned to face her.

"So, it's like that, huh?" he stammered with his words.

Loretta stared at him directly without blinking. "Yeah, it's like that. You heard what the fuck I said!"

Nakea had a duped up smile on her face. Nasir had been hood-winked out his own house.

"I'm outta here then." Thinking one of them was going to convince him to change his mind, he slowly packed his things. Only no one came to intercede. The thought that his mother crossed him for a stranger smeared their relationship forever.

BITTER SWEET

"I thought it was over between us. That's what you said the last time we were together."

"Can we not talk about this?" Nasir begged, feeling remorsefully guilty. "I need my dick sucked. That's all I came for."

The soft French-tip manicured hands reached down to place her mouth on Nasir's hardened member pointing straight in her direction.

"Damn baby, your shit is much bigger than your father's," she professed, licking the veins on each side of Nasir's erection.

His eyes went to the back of his head. He pulled her head into him to deep throat her. She began to gag.

"Don't gag now, bitch—you a dick sucka' from way back. I know you can swallow this!"

He pulled her so close her head was no longer bobbing and weaving it was stuck from the pressure he applied to the back of her head. She tried to raise up. He grabbed her hair and yanked her head back.

"Stand up," he commanded. "Bend over. Lift one leg to the side." He stimulated the tip of his penis across her wetness.

"This pussy is so fuckin' wet and juicy. I can't keep doing this," he said penetrating her. Cream was all on his shaft.

"Damn," he moaned.

He stroked ten good times and nut went all in her.

After his sexcapade Nasir rested in a motel for a couple of days secluding himself from everyone, laying low at the stale scented burgundy and brown decor room. He purchased a new cell phone and a pager. The pager was for the use of deliveries only. His game was stepping up and his clientele was building.

Resting on the un-fluffed flat pillows, he tried his best to shake the life back into them by hitting them back and forth on each other. That didn't work, so he compromised and folded up the bedspread and propped it up behind the pillows. *I need to sort this shit out today.* He said on his nineteenth birthday. *What a birthday present!* He had three thousand dollars saved up. After that was gone, with his deliveries, he would still be able to eat for about a month. He thought about going hard to flip his money because Chauncey had messed up and left the number to his connect in the car. Now Nasir had access to the main supplier.

"What's up Farren?"

There were only selected individuals he had given his new cell number to. Farren was one of them. He received less than a hospitable reception from her.

"You, that's what's up. Where have you been?" Her heart fluttered by his raspy voice.

"I've been chill'n. What about you?" he said trying to find out if she'd heard the latest news about him.

"I'm alright; could be better. I stopped by your house when I hadn't heard from you."

"And?"

"And," she responded with many thoughts. "I was greeted by your other baby's momma, Nakea. What was she doing there? I thought it was over between you two."

"Easy with the questions. One at a time please," he said rubbing his forehead. "What did she say slick out her mouth? I know she said something dumb," he owned up, knowing how petty Nakea could be.

"She did. I asked her were you home and what was she doing there. She told me you and her were still together and that you asked her to move in that's why she was there."

"Was my mom there?"

"No, I guess she was at work."

"I hope you don't believe her."

"Well, it's hard for me not to. She was there wearing a shirt I seen you in before and, add to the fact she said you are still sexing her—it's hard not to believe her."

"Yo, a chick will tell you anything to make you mad. Especially throwback-broads!"

"You know what Nasir? I don't need this in my life. Honestly, I can't understand why older chicks date younger men. This shit is for the birds. It ain't working for me. You come with too much baggage."

"Damn, that's how you gone treat a nigga on his birthday?

Nasir had no point to argue, Farren had a legitimate gripe.

"You can't get a nigga back like that. I was just fucking them broads. I was gone get right back," he joked impersonating Jay Z.

The line went silent.

"Let me be straight up. Nakea was telling you the truth. She is living at the crib."

Farren's gut instinct was correct. "That's the bullshit I'm talking about, but you expect me to keep it real with you. Forget this."

"It wasn't my decision, baby I promise you. My mom made the call," he pressed.

"What the fuck Nasir? What do you expect me to do? Just sit back and let shit go down like that. Count me out!" she retaliated in frustration.

"Hold on, before you go jumpin' the gun. When my mom said she could stay, I chose to leave."

"Say word, nigga?" Farren was happy to hear that.

"My word is my bond baby," he expressed, pumping his fists in the air. He flipped the script on that ass.

"Where are you staying then?"

"I'm staying at the Days Inn. Why you coming to see me?" he asked, hoping she'd comply with the request.

"Give me the address."

He gave her the address and immediately started cleaning up the room before she'd arrive. He rambled through his bags to find the Blue Nile oil he packed away. With the oil tipped over, he dabbed drops on the bed and the vent for the scent to blow out hoping to over power any foul smell. He jumped into the shower to freshen up, wanting to be fresh and ready for her. Afterwards, slipping into his black jeans and a white t-shirt, he put on a black New York fitted.

Farren drove her Corolla like she owned the streets. Today was her day off and besides all the crazy encounters she had with Sonya and Nakea, she had fallen head over heels for Nasir. He had charm, finesse and he was always sweet to her. She was dressed very casually with her jeans that had a split midway on her legs that exposed her sexy, dripping, strawberry tattoo. That innocence she depicted was dismissed once people saw it. Her parents were the community role models, she wasn't. Had they seen the panther resting across her lower backside near the crack of her ass, their outlook of her would really change.

Farren never confessed to be the perfect girl people assumed her to be. She had her times, especially with her last boyfriend, Quinton. Three months in a relationship with Quinton would make any women fearful of being in another relationship. He had females claiming to be his mother figures, sisters, aunts, and cousins that he was boning. His baby momma even posed as a sister when Farren caught them together. That's why she was so skeptical about the "baby momma" ordeal. She knew they played games right along with their baby's father. Her bad relationship with Quinton helped her to appreciate herself more. This is what pushed her to focus on going back to school to obtain a degree. She had ambitions of becoming a General Manager at Greyhound, not just an Associate Sales person. Her goals were always set high. That's how she got down. Mediocrity would keep her at the entry-level position she was in. Her parents taught her early to maintain good credit, which she had. However, she had more credit cards than necessary. Once she paid off her credit card debt, she was sure to qualify for at least a $65,000 mortgage. With her demands, that low mortgage wouldn't suit her. Until then, she had to be content in her one bedroom apartment that she only paid $400 a month for. It was nothing fancy, but it suited her needs. Her mother and father picked out a floral loveseat and couch set with glass end tables and a huge overhung lamp to give it some pizzazz. She took the queen-size bed she had at her parent's home to sleep on. It had low mileage on it. There was no need for her to buy a new one.

Farren pulled up to the Arby's drive-through window to place her order.

"Five cheddar and roast beef sandwiches please."

The cashier spoke into the microphone, "Will that be all?" acting very impatiently.

"No, wait one moment. Let me get two orders of curly fries and two large sodas, one sprite and the other a coke. And, I have a coupon."

"Will that be it?" The gentleman asked her again.

"Um, no, let me get two Dutch apple pies and that will do it."

"Alright, that will be thirteen-fifty with your coupon at the second window. Please pull up."

"Thank you," Farren professionally responded this time.

Farren had a well-portioned size fourteen body. She was thick as the chick in Big Boi's video featuring Sleepy Brown, *I Like The Way You Move.*

After getting the food, she pulled into the Days Inn Motel to the room Nasir was in. She tapped lightly on the door, not wanting to draw any attention to herself.

"Who is it?" Nasir hollered, testing Farren's insecurities.

"Who else did you expect?" she instantly snapped.

"Who? I can't hear you," he continued to say.

"It's me Farren, now open the door." She was tired of playing mind games with him.

"Who?" he repeated.

By this time, Farren realized that Nasir was leading her on.

"Come on, stop playing and open the door. The food is getting cold."

When Nasir heard the word food, he hurried up and answered the door.

"Here, let me help you with that." He snatched up the food and tried to push the door shut on Farren.

"Stop playing so much," she laughed. "You are so stupid."

Nasir was licking his lips, ready to dig into the grub. "You thought about me, huh?" he smiled, kissing Farren on the cheek. "I love a tinselfish woman."

"I guess. I was hungry so I stopped to get myself something to eat. I just so happened to think it would be rude of me if I only bought food for myself. Plus, I knew I was on my way to see you."

Nasir pinched her on the arm.

"Oow! What you do that for?"

He spread the food on the table for them and responded after he took a bite of one of the sandwiches. "To bring you back to reality. Now come and eat. The food is not going to stay hot forever." Cheese sauce dropped from his mouth.

"Close your mouth when you eat, that's nasty."

"I know," he responded, showing his chewed up roast beef.

"That is so nasty. Hand me my food please."

They parlayed for the rest of the night. Farren was real comfortable, removing her shoes and flexing, laid - back on the bed. She didn't know how to pop the question or slide in her suggestion to Nasir about rooming with her, so she just blatantly asked. She'd encountered Nakea and Sonya. What else would she be up against?

"Do you want to room with me instead of living in the motel?"

Nasir looked at her surprised, wanting to immediately respond, yes, but he kept his cool. He was ready to bag Farren and make her wifey.

"What's wrong with living in the Mot?" he inquired.

Farren took that as an indication that he was saying no and felt terrible that she was so outspoken.

"Excuse me, Mr. Motel Man," she said, trying to play it off.

He reached across the bed and pulled her arms closer to his.

"Come here, girl."

Farren pulled away.

"Stop front'n, you know you want to be close to me," Nasir said, still tugging at her. Farren didn't resist him this time. He held her tight resting his groin on her behind, with the front side of his body facing the back of her head.

"If I move in with you, does that mean it's official?"

Farren turned around slightly. "What's official?"

"That you and I are lovers," he said, setting her up. She thought he was going to say a couple, not lovers.

"How can we be lovers and we've never made love?" she asked him, feeding right into him.

"My point to be exact. Before I can move in with you I need to make sure you got that bomb azz puzzy," he said cunningly. "If not, I'll take a rain check. I need a woman that will keep me in the house. Her shit has to be fire!"

"Baby, I can assure you of one thing—my lovin' ain't on fire, but like music, it can soothe the savage beast." She could feel Nasir's erection stiffen, poking her butt.

Turning to face him their eyes meet enticingly. His warm mouth reached hers and hers met his. It was that night, Nasir fell deeply for her. When they made love, it went beyond a hit and miss, every now and then. Their relationship was on another level than the others. For all the drama Nasir experienced with other chicks, he wouldn't dare let this one slip away. Everything would be gravy, a smooth ride from here on out.

LOVER'S QUARREL

Within a 72-hour turn around, Nasir had moved all his belongings into Farren's apartment.

"Are you going to help me with the bags?" Nasir asked, struggling to get up the stairs to the apartment. "You didn't tell me you lived on the fourth floor. I would have used my back brace to lighten the load on my back."

Farren chuckled to herself. This was the first time she'd seen Nasir break a sweat.

"I'll get the smaller bags if that will help you out, but first I need to open the door for you."

Nasir leaned against the hallway railing. "Ah, don't you think you should've done that first? Hand me the keys."

Farren stretched out her arm to hand him the keys. Nasir clutched them and at the same time one of the three bags he was carrying went tumbling down the flight of stairs, whipping pass Farren. She busted out laughing, while Nasir gritted his teeth.

"I'll get it," she told him. Nasir wiped the sweat that formed on his forehead.

"No, you just unlock the door. I'll get the bag." He lifted the other two bags he had and dropped them on the white and black tiled area right in front of the door.

"Let me get the bag, I'm closer," she said again offering her assistance. "Why don't you just open the door, Nasir?"

Using the keys, after trying three or four of them, he opened the door and kicked the bags inside glancing at the layout of the living room. This was a first for him— moving in with a woman. He'd hoped his decision was the right one. At least the living room was cleaned and the place smelled fresh. He was hoping the rest of the apartment was the same way. Had it not been, he'd have packed up his belongings and went for self. He sat down on the couch to take a little break going against his thoughts. No one made him feel wanted like Farren did except for his midnight creep. Farren had a deep concern for his well-being, but so did his fling. Farren wanted him to leave hustling alone. His side joint told him to *get that money*. He respected her for that.

Farren shut the trunk of Nasir's car, staggering with the last few bags.

"Here, let me get that," he said, back to work.

"Make up your mind, please. First, you said help with the bags, now you're saying let me get that. Which is it? Do you want my help or not?" she complained.

Nasir gave her a bear claw face by putting the palm of his hand over her entire face. "Be quiet girl, and hand me the bags." Farren let them go and followed him up the steps, wishing that another bag would fall down the steps, so she could tell him. *I told you so, you need my help,* but one didn't.

When inside Nasir sat down again on the couch from all of the physical labor.

"Can a nigga get somethin' to drink?" he asked Farren as she was walking back to the bedroom.

"It's some soda in the fridge."

"Soda?" He wasn't big on drinking soda. "You don't have any juice up in here?" he asked opening the refrigerator—not being ungrateful.

"You didn't say shit when I bought you a soda from Arby's the other day," she came back.

"And if you noticed I didn't drink it, did I? Come in here and stop yelling. I can't stand a chick that hoops and hollers all the time."

Farren joined him in the kitchen. Here he was seconds into moving in and already demanding changes.

"So you do have a sensitive side," she puckered for a kiss, waiting for him to reciprocate.

"Okay, whatever floats your boat. I'll stick to soda and you stick to juice. As for now, though, this is all there is to drink. Wait a minute. . . . I think I have a can of ice tea mix in the cabinet." She had the cabinet door ajar, searching for the tea mix until she located it. "Here you go." The panther on her backside stretched and her hips moved from side to side turning Nasir on.

"Damn, you sexy, girl."

He thanked her and began to make a pitcher of tea for him to drink. When he was through, they walked into the living room to remove the rest of his clothing.

"So where should I put my clothes?" he asked.

"Well, my bedroom closet is pretty much full. You can use the two hallway closets."

"That's cool, do you have any extra hangers?"

"Anything for you baby," she said straddling his neck with her soft hands, to massage his tight muscles.

"*Aah,*" he released. "I can learn to love this."

Farren playfully slapped him in the back of his dome. "That's nothing compared to the mean body massage I give."

"Is that right?" His eyes were cut sharp in the corner trying to read in between the lines.

Farren went into her bedroom to retrieve the sturdy gold-plated hangers with the rubber-ribbed tips. "Here, these are my good hangers, treat them with respect. They're not the typical hangers you get from the cleaners," she smiled.

"Thank you baby." His thick juicy lips made way to his favorite spot, her kissable cheeks.

"You like kissing me on the cheeks, don't you?" she said unable to hold back her glow.

"Yeah, I do. Do you have a problem with that?"

"Not at all, not at all!"

Once his clothes were hung up, Nasir excused himself from the apartment telling Farren that he had business to take care of. It was cool with Farren, because she had to be to work in two hours. He'd asked her before he left to make sure she had an extra key made just in case he came home before she did. The sound of Nasir saying home was music to her ears. She informed him that she would have a key made before she went to work, letting it be known that he would have to meet her on the job to get it.

She stood in front of the mirror holding two fingers on her mouth, reminding herself of the lasting tender kiss Nasir placed on her lips, this time. "*He is sooo fine,*" she reflected.

* * *

Nasir arrived at his mother's crib hoping that Nakea wasn't there. Nakea was posted up on the couch just lounging, covered with one of Nasir's blankets watching the new Christina Millian, "Dip It Low" video, praying that all she had to do was "Pop That Thang" to keep him home. She was comfy making herself right at home, eating a pint of butter almond ice cream.

"Hey Nasir, where you been?" Eagerly waiting for his response, her eyes roamed up and down his body. She dipped her spoon back into the ice cream bringing it back out with more than a spoonful of butter almond on it, licking the spoon slowly.

"None of ya business. Where's my mom at?" he asked, disregarding the attention she was screaming out for.

"She's back in her room. But um, I wouldn't go barging in there without knocking first if I were you."

Uncertain by her slick comment, he ignored her and kept walking toward Loretta's bedroom.

"She got company!" Nakea blurted out.

"Company?" Nasir repeated.

Loretta had never invited a man over to her house since she'd been home. This would be a new experience for him. He didn't expect his mother to turn cold toward men. However, he wasn't ready to deal with a street sucka that would never come close to the thoroughbred his father was.

He knocked hard on the locked bedroom door juggling at the knob at the same time to get it open. He heard faint voices talking and laughing like they were enjoying each other's company. The smell of marijuana seeped through the cracks of the door.

Loretta unlocked the door for him to enter. Nasir eased through the door as she was opening it disturbed by what he smelled. He'd smoked, but sparingly. He was a drinker but only dibbled with that.

"What now, you smoke weed and pop pills too?" His nose flared.

"What's up, lil nigga? I'm Tru." The strange man said greeting him. The glare in Nasir's eyes was full of disregard. *Who does this cat think he is?*

Loretta stood at the door holding it open for Nasir to go right back out. "Boy, don't come up in here like you running shit. Whatever I do in the confines of my own house is my *own* damn business! You need to be handling yours and stop being so concerned about me. I'ma grown ass woman, damn it. Worry about that hot-ass girl Sonya! She's running around telling everybody you made her miscarry."

Nasir snapped his head around to face his mother letting the serious grit he had on Tru go. "What? What you talking 'bout?"

"Yeah, thought I didn't know, didn't you? The night you pushed her in Hibachi's when you was out tricking with your new whore Farren, Sonya was out the hospital complaining about cramping and later that night, she miscarried." Loretta smirked mid-way, telling him verbatim what she'd heard. "God works in mysterious ways, don't he?"

Nasir didn't even address his mother's behaviors, for it was obvious of the hate she had in her heart for Sonya.

"That girl is crazy. I didn't have nothing to do with that," he pleaded. No longer was he concerned about what his mother was doing, but now he was focused on this newfound information Loretta dished out. "For all I know that girl probably did that shit to get back at me."

"Whatever! You better find out if she signed a warrant out for your arrest."

Nasir clinched his teeth tight. "That bit—better not have."

"Watch your mouth!" Loretta intervened.

"Have some respect for your mother, Jr." Tru said in her defense, sipping on his warm Budweiser.

"Yo, who is this bum ass nigga? Get the fu . . . outta here," he replied, stopping before he cursed again. He stormed past Loretta before he got into an argument. His eyes grazed at Nakea's feet propped up on the sofa still eating. She had devoured the ice cream. Now she was scarfing down a five-pound bag of Herr's sour cream and onion potato chips.

"I went to the doctor's yesterday. The baby is really growing."

He wanted her to shut the fuck up.

Even though he had the gut feeling the baby was his, he did not want a baby with her.

"My next appointment is in four weeks. Do you want to go with me this time?"

"No and stop asking me. I'm not going to any of the appointments. The only one I'll be at is the one when you deliver."

Nakea sucked her teeth. "Damn Nasir, you don't have to be like that. I didn't lay down and make this baby by my damn self!"

Nasir had to hold his tongue, given that, in his mind he was thinking, *I wish you had!*

"It's not that serious. Just make sure you're there when I deliver." she said, okay with his limited involvement. "Can you leave me a few dollars? My clothes are getting too small and I need some new ones. Look at how tight these pants are. They suffocating the baby."

As much as he hated to do it, he peeled off $200 and tossed it on the table. Like a vulture, she immediately grabbed it up, counting how much it was.

"That's it? What about food? I can't keep eating up your mom's food."

A bitter taste filled his mouth. "Get your lazy ass up and get a job!"

"Nasir, how can I do that with morning sickness everyday?"

He went back into his pockets and removed an additional $200. "You're not getting anymore, so don't ask," he stated firmly.

Nakea rubbed her belly wishing that Nasir would join in and show interest in her, like he had in the past. "Oh, I guess I should be saying, 'I'm sorry to hear about Sonya miscarrying'. But I would be faking the funk, cuz' I don't give a shit," she said, placing about four or five chips in her mouth with crumbs falling down her shirt.

Nasir pulled up his pant leg and grabbed his crotch. "Don't tell me, tell her. Oops, I forgot . . . she might put another whooping on dat' ass, if you do." he said, laughing in her face. This was the second brawl they were in.

Nakea didn't find that funny at all but as long as she was getting money from him and living in his mom's house, she still felt like she had the upper hand.

Nasir walked down the park to handle his affairs. His pager had gone off a number of times when he was at his mother's house. He spotted Chauncey and exchanged a few words with him. Once he did what he had to do, he went to relieve stress at Mom Flossy's. As usual, Mom Flossy was sitting on the porch paying attention to all movement on the block. Sheena was there basking in her grandmother's affection.

"There's my baby boy. Come here, suga'." Mom Flossy gripped the side of the chair, raising her wide hips to hug him.

"Hey, Grandmom. What's up, Sheena?"

"Look what the wind 'den blew in." Mom Flossy teased him. She only lived blocks away, yet Nasir was too busy to stop through most times.

"What you been up to, playa, playa?" Sheena asked.

"Not a thing. I just stopped by to see my family. Can't a brotha miss his family?"

"That's what your mouth says. I've been hearing a lot of shit. The streets are talking baby boy." Sheena replied. "I heard you moved out of mommy's."

"Did she tell you why?" he responded back.

"No," Mom Flossy arbitrated.

"She let Nakea move in. That's why I left. I told her it was either Nakea or me. She chose Nakea." His voice went very low and cracked a little when his last three words rolled off his tongue.

"Mmmm," Mom Flossy sang. "No that bitty didn't."

"Actually, she probably did," Sheena, agreed not the least bit surprised. "You know how mom gets down."

"Loretta ain't working on nothing," Mom Flossy tightened her fist, not caring if she hurt their feelings.

"Yes she is," Sheena, begged to differ. "She's working on a relationship with Nakea. Nasir now you know how I feel and been feeling all these years. Mom was always more concerned about you than she was about me. Now you're getting the cold shoulder. It's a bit nippy, ain't it? I've got plenty of blankets to cover you up, don't worry!"

Both of them knew she was telling the truth and cared not to really elaborate.

"Loretta ought to be shamed of herself, putting you out and letting the damn girl stay. You can always move back with me baby."

"Thank you Grandmom, but I moved in with my new woman." he expressed voluntarily.

"What!" They both screamed in unison.

"Who Farren?" Sheena inquired. "Or, is there someone else? I know how you do playa. With you, you never know. You keep a new girl."

"Just like his father," Mom Flossy chimed in.

"Cut that out, you know it's strictly about Farren."

"How is Nakea and Sonya taking this?" Sheena wanted to know.

"Neither one of them know about it yet. They'll find out soon enough."

"Oooh, the shit is about to hit the fan!" she sheared.

"Damn it, I done told y'all about cussin' and shit. Watch your mouth!"

Sheena and Nasir laughed watching the seriousness of their grandmother's face. How did she expect them to stop cussing when that's all she did was curse between every four or five words?

"Hey, Grandmom, guess what? Mom told me today that Sonya had a miscarriage."

"Well, baby, God knows best. It just wasn't meant to be that's all. If you had any goddamn sense, you'd leave her fatal attraction ass the hell alone."

"Speaking of the devil, look who it is?" Sheena said pointing.

"Damn," Nasir mumbled. "Shouldn't she be on bedrest or something?" he said trying to go inside of the house to hide from her.

"Come on outside, Nasir! I already seen you," Sonya screamed.

Mom Flossy turned to Nasir, "Go on outside and take that girl around the street somewhere with all that damn noise."

"Alright," he staggered off the porch down the cement steps.

"Yo, don't start trippin'. If you can't talk to me in a civil tone, step off."

Sonya started crying.

"Here we go," Nasir muttered.

They walked down the street and Sonya began with her sob story.

"I lost the baby, Nasir. All because of you and that uppity-bitch. How could you do this to us?" She wanted him to feel bad when really she didn't have a miscarriage. She injected the Methotrexate liquid abortion shot in her naval to terminate her pregnancy.

"Don't blame me for that shit, Sonya. That shit is on you."

"No mofo, it's your bitch's fault. If you hadn't been out with her, it would've never happened," she exploded.

"That's one too many times you done called my woman a bitch!"

"There you go taking up for her *stank-ass* again. Just know that bitch got it coming to her, trust and believe that."

"Look," Nasir snatched her up. . . . "The only thing you can give me is a good head shot, other than that, you have nothing more to say to me," he said trying hard not to blow his top.

"That's what you think!" she said pulling away from him. "It's not over, Nasir. You should've never stuck dick in me. I'll always be your baby's momma."

Nasir couldn't believe his ears. *This bitch is stone crazy. I thought my mom said Nakea's mother was the crazy one!*

"I know where your girl works at. She better watch her back."

As if he didn't have enough drama with Nakea, Sonya didn't want to fade away. She was like a reoccurring case of acne that kept haunting him.

They parted ways when they reached the park area. Nasir caught sight of Brian, relieved that his boy was out there to be a listening ear.

"What's up, B?" he asked opening the door for conversation.

"You the one."

Nasir leaned against the basketball court fence and pulled the hood of his coat over his head.

"These damn girls are driving me crazy."

"Yo, don't complain now. You should've let me win that bet we had on Sonya. Her ass would be in check by now."

Both of them had to laugh.

"I damn sure should've. You can have her fatal attraction. The chick is loco man. She's threatening my girl and everything. I haven't even hit that in months! Yo, that isn't even the half. Nakea is posted up in my mom's crib bugging me to death and check this out, I moved in with Farren."

"Word, man! Sounds like you need to get rid of some baggage, fo' real."

"Man it's cold as Alaska out this piece, let's take a ride," Nasir suggested.

They walked up the block to Loretta's to get Nasir's car. When they reached the car, Nasir noticed a note in between the windshield and the wiper blades. He opened it and read it. *I love you Nasir. When the baby comes we will be one happy family. Love, Nakea.*

Nasir balled up the note and threw it on the ground.

"See man, this is the type of shit I'm talking about leaving little love notes." His frustration was obvious as the wrinkles in his forehead appeared.

They pulled up to the red brick townhouse. Nasir made sure the coast was clear.

"Yo, who lives here?" Brian asked.

"Nobody man. I'm dropping off. Sit tight for a moment, I'll be right back."

Brian put his seat in recline cracking open a Dutch.

Nasir rang the bell three times giving her the cue.

"It's open," she purred to him. "I'm in here."

"Are you here alone?" he asked following her voice into the den.

"I wasn't expecting you," his knock-off stated. Her legs were oiled to perfection and the black v-shaped body suit hugged her mane between her legs. The lace robe draped from her shoulders. He stared at her print.

"What was you in here doing?"

She looked him directly in his eyes. "Playing with my pussy; thinking of you."

"Oh yeah? Lift your legs up for me ma," he said stroking himself.

She spread eagle. Nasir yanked the one piece to the side dropping his Polo boxers.

IT'S TIME

"Thank you for calling Greyhound for the lowest traveling fares, Farren speaking, how may I help you?" Farren had repeated this greeting so many times; she would say it in her sleep.

"You can help me alright," the caller responded.

"Excuse me?" Farren said in return.

"Just answer one question for me, Miss Priss."

"Sure, I'll do my best," Farren happily answered, extending her quest to help.

"Is Nasir living with you?"

The question came as a lightning bolt from the sky. The caller's voice didn't sound familiar to Farren.

"Who is this?" Farren asked slightly disturbed.

"It's Nasir's baby momma, that's who this is, bitch!"

Farren thought Nakea was tripping calling her on her job with this pettiness.

"If you want to talk to me, get with me after I get off work," she calmly stated.

"Do you think I care about you being at work? Just

answer the question, later for that *call me after work bull-shit*. It's either, yes or no."

Farren didn't know if she should feed into the child's play or address it at another time. What the hell, she might as well tell her. Where did she think Nasir was living for the past couple of months, at Mom Flossy's? What did she have to hide from her? She realized that Nakea was in her last trimester of her pregnancy. The closer she came to delivery the worse off she'd become.

Nakea was sitting on the other end vexed, waiting for Farren to respond.

"I'm waiting," she said impatiently tapping her swollen feet. She'd picked up over 40-pounds during her pregnancy and her face had broken out with a bad case of acne.

"Let's clear the smoke screen, Nakea. Of course, you don't have a problem with confronting me on my job. You don't respect that because you don't have one."

Nakea wasn't trying to hear that. "Bitch, fuck all that. Answer the question!"

"Where do you think he's been staying? Nasir is my man . . . and your baby daddy nothing more, nothing less—case closed."

"So what are you saying, Farren?"

Other calls started blinking on the line. "Hold, please." Farren professionally mimed. She answered about five other inquiring Greyhound customers and Nakea was still holding.

"Thank you for holding, Farren speaking."

"It's still me. I'm still waiting."

"What's sad is, you're still holding. What is it Nakea?" Farren didn't give her a chance to respond. "I know what your problem is . . . you can't accept rejection. I'm sorry to tell you dear, but Nasir don't want you. There's no other way to put it. And to answer your question, yes. Yes, we are living together. Any other questions? . . . because I need to get back to work!"

An instant feeling of rage mixed with feelings of depression came over Nakea. She wanted to kill Farren, literally. What did she mean Nasir didn't want her? How was that so? That couldn't be. If Nasir didn't want her, she would make it her number one priority to make his life a living hell. She was green with jealously over Farren but was intrigued by her poise. What did Farren have that she didn't? For starters, a job, an apartment, a loving family to support her and most importantly, Nasir. Nakea yearned for his acceptance but he seemed to keep ignoring her, sending her conflicting signals. He had to want her. Why else did he go against the code to take her from another man? She was happy in her relationship before he came along. Appending that, his mother repeatedly told her how Nasir was just like his father. His father ran women but he always kept home tight. All she had to do was keep being persistent; Nasir would come around, especially when the baby was born. Loretta fed Nakea's sickness, contaminating her mind. Nasir had to know that she was the one for him but it was taking him too long. He wasn't coming around quick enough. The script wasn't changing. But, why did he continue to give her money? Not only for clothes and food but also, change for her pockets? He even offered to help her get an apartment if she took the steps to get one. It couldn't have been because he wanted her out of his mother's crib. He was never there. It had to be that deep down inside he loved her and wanted her to get a place of her own for them to be together. Why did he move in with Farren then? Most importantly, why didn't her friend Loretta, tell her? She had to know he lived with Farren.

Loretta had crossed the friendship boundary line when she withheld this information from her. Nakea had to come out of this situation a winner, if she had to take everybody down that was climbing up.

Farren was on the phone less than a half a minute after she hung up the phone with Nakea. Her ear was pasted to the phone receiver while her mind traveled. Would this drama continue for the duration of her relationship?

"Nasir this has got to stop. You need to set this girl straight," she said frustrated. If it wasn't Nakea, it was Sonya she had to deal with even though Nasir hadn't messed around with either of them since he committed to Farren. They were becoming stalkers.

"Calm down, Farren. Which one are you talking about?" he exhaled noisily knowing the obvious answer.

"It was Nakea this time. These girls just don't give up do they? This is out of control. I feel like going against some heads—taking it to the streets on these chickens. They are trying my patience."

He understood how she felt. He'd felt like that a time or two himself, but he knew fighting would escalate the drama.

"Baby, Nakea and Sonya are forcing you to react on their moves. Stop feeding into their stupidity. You know I only want you. Start redirecting that negativity they keep pushing your way and let them be the ones that become frustrated about us being together, not you. You're doing exactly what they want you to do." His response was precise. "They are both setting traps for themselves. Learn how to control your emotions and play on theirs."

He toyed with the CD player in his car, rotating his Usher CD to Young Buck.

"Seriously, Farren. I don't care if the situation is eating you alive don't ever, *I mean ever,* let them know it. Never wear your worries on your shoulder." He hit play on Young Bucks' club banger, "Shorty Wanna Ride Wit' Me."

"Give it some thought. You look foolish wasting your time pleading your case to them birds. They don't want nothing out of life. You have too much going on for yourself." He rubbed his nose, sure that his pep talk helped. He was ready to zone out with his music. "Now get back to work. I'll talk to you when you get home."

Farren agreed. The conversation helped her release some stress.

Hours later, Nakea was on the phone stressing Nasir.

"Nasir, I need you to come and get me." Her voice was cracking, echoing through the phone.

"For what? Come get you and take you where?" He wasn't for any silly games.

"I'm cramping real bad. Farren just called me with some bullshit. *Oh, my God,*" she over dramatized in false pain.

"Are you alright?" he asked in concern.

"I think I need to go to the hospital. Can you come and get me please?"

Nasir contemplated on her request. "Why don't you call an ambulance? They will probably get there sooner than I would."

Nakea wasn't having that. "Oooh, ooh, the pains are

getting stronger. The baby might be coming. You have to get here fast!"

"Here I come," he said finally giving in. "This better not be no bullshit either."

She'd done it! He fell for her scheme. "Yeah, who's got the upper hand now, Farren?" she said with *Grimey* intentions. All she had to do now was drink a spoonful of castor oil. Her sister told her if she drank a spoonful of it, it would help her go into labor. She was 38 weeks, only 2 weeks shy of being full term. A little castor oil wouldn't hurt her.

Nasir called Farren back to tell her about his plans before she heard them from someone else. He was sure Nakea would get on the phone and blab her mouth to anyone willing to listen. He opposed Farren's request to join him, telling her, that wasn't a good idea.

BABY BE MINE

Nasir drove Nakea to the nearest hospital. She sat in the front seat of the car smiling on the inside. At least they were together even if it was under false pretenses. Being courteous, he helped her out of the car into a wheelchair that was sitting on the outside of the hospital. "Ugh," Nakea moaned, this time from actual contractions. The castor oil was kicking in. Sharp pains became steady, and her pelvic area felt like it was about to burst.

Nasir left his car parked in the emergency parking space until he wheeled her on the inside. Nakea screamed out to the nurses that the pressure was killing her. They hurried over to her and rolled her into a prep room to exam her.

Nasir went outside to move his car and use his phone. The first person he called was Brian. "Man, I think tonight's the night. It's official, I'm going to be a father." Despite his feeling towards Nakea, if the baby were his, he would be a loving father, as his father was to him.

"I don't' know dog, I thought you weren't sure." Brian probed.

"Man, I'm not, but until I get that stamp that it's not, I'm going to do right by my seed. I'd rather be there physically and financially, in case it is mine. Back support is a bitch, ya heard me?"

Brian agreed, "That's the right decision to make, homey. Big Marv would be proud."

"Thanks man, I'll call you later on to let you know what's really popping."

"If you need me, call. I'll come out there to keep you company."

Nasir appreciated the offer. "That's okay. I can handle it." He called Loretta on her job, who immediately said she was on her way. He called Mom Flossy as well. She didn't take the news too lightly.

"Now grandson, don't be no fool. You know that girl was whore hopping around the neighborhood when you met her. I could tell she was a whoremonger by that ankle bracelet she always wears." Nasir was on the other end gassed up—laughing at his grandmother's remarks. "If the child don't look like you and looks like your best friend Brian, chances are, the baby is not yours son."

Nasir busted out with laughter. "Alright, Grandmom. How's Sheena coming along with her pregnancy?"

"Boy, she's big as a house eating everything in the house from the bread crumbs to the table."

Mom Flossy sure knew how to make Nasir smile.

"You know her and that boy Eric be arguing everyday now."

Nasir had enough drama to deal with. He wasn't trying to add more. "Okay, Grandmom, I'll talk to you later." He knew if he didn't hang up the phone just then, he'd have been on there much longer. Shonda, Nakea's sister came running past Nasir like a bat flying out of hell going to her sister's aide. It was apparent that Nakea called her because Nasir couldn't stand Shonda. They were both in for a long night. He figured he'd wait to call Farren until after he learned more about the delivery. It was no need to bother her if Nakea's labor hadn't progressed.

"Only two visitors at a time," The nurse reaffirmed. Shonda wasn't about to leave her sister's side. They had taken Nakea away from her family long enough. It was Nasir and Loretta that would rotate.

Finally, Nakea felt love. Everyone was fighting on who would be there to help her, though she was quite embarrassed with her loose bowels. The after effects of taking castor oil was long hours in the bathroom. Beyond her control, bowels eased out cleaning her digestive system. Shonda had to keep cleaning her up. The room was filled with stink.

Nasir tried reading the latest issue of *4 Front Magazine,* featuring a story on the latest buzz—"Hip-Hop Fiction." His thoughts were running fanatically. He still hadn't called Farren and it was after two in the morning. They'd been in the hospital for hours. Loretta finally came out to the waiting room and called out to Nasir.

"It's time. She's fully dilated."

One man waiting to hear the same news about his daughter wished him good luck.

"I'm staying out here mom," he responded with nervousness.

"Are you sure son?"

"Yes, I'm sure."

Loretta rushed back into the delivery room excited to become a grandmother for the first time. Nakea was pushing hard. Shonda wiped away the dripping sweat as it formed on her forehead.

"It's going to be all right," she coached her on.

Nakea was delighted her sister showed up, but disappointed that her mother hadn't.

"I see the head," Loretta said all giddy.

Nakea grunted hard and low and behold a son was born. When Loretta seen the cracked up skin on the baby boy looking like a fresh plucked chicken, as did Nasir, she knew that was her grandbaby. Nasir would've been a fool to request a blood test.

Nasir waited patiently on the results of his fate to be a father. When his mother came busting through the labor and delivery room waiting room doors, he knew from her facial expression that the baby was his. She hugged Nasir tight. This night made her flash back to the day he was born, only a key person was missing— Marv.

"It's a boy, and baby, don't worry, he's ours! You can go and see him now. Nakea is asking for you."

Normally, that would've upset him, but tonight was different. Inside the delivery room, he washed his hands and put on a hospital gown to hold the baby. Nakea was exhausted but longed for Nasir's reaction to the baby. The birth of their baby had to bring them closer.

"Daddy's here, Li'l Marv." Little Marv harmonized out her mouth. Nasir reached out to hold him. For a brief second, he gazed at Nakea in an admiring way. She placed the baby into his arms. Shonda left out the room in repulsion. Loretta came back in. She'd seen the sparkle in both their eyes. It was the same radiance Marv and her once shared. What time but the present, when they were both at peace, to give them her thoughts raw and uncut.

"You two are going to have to cut all this foolishness out. This baby gives both of you someone else to think about," she pointed in their direction. "Nasir I don't care who you are shacking up with, your son always comes first. That's how your father was and that's how you need to be. He never let anything stop him from being a father to you. Don't you ever let anyone come between that! When Nakea needs you, you need to be there for her . . . for both of them. After all, she is the mother of your child. Nobody else holds that title but her," she boldly announced.

Her words didn't impress Nasir at all, but for Nakea that was all she desired to hear. Regardless to how his mother felt, he would be a father to his son but not at Nakea's dispense. She wasn't dictating his moves. He let his mom continue with her words of wisdom, never making direct eye contact with Nakea, who was steady trying to get his attention.

Nakea had constructed a smoke screen so Loretta couldn't fully understand her spiteful behaviors. Tonight, Nakea felt another one up on Farren. She was winning in her own eyes.

"Are you staying with us 'til the sun comes up, Nasir?"

"What for? What can I do here? The baby is born. I'm going home to my woman."

Actually, he was thankful that she reminded him it was so late.

"Thanks, Nakea."

"For what?"

"Thanks for reminding me to call my woman and tell her I'm on my way home. I was a little caught up with this baby shit."

The frown on her face didn't form fast enough.

"I don't want my son around that bitch!"

Here the baby wasn't even twenty-four hours old, and she was already starting that dumbness.

"Anyway," Nasir disregarded her. "What are you naming him?"

"What do you think she's naming him?" Loretta blurted barging back into the room after giving the new parents time alone.

"I don't know mom, that's why I'm asking."

"Tell him Nakea!" Loretta said forcing her to spread the news.

Nakea smiled, "I'm naming him Marv Bundy III."

Nasir didn't smile. As a matter of fact, he thought that was ridiculous. He was already a Jr. and now a third?

"What are we going to call him?" he asked nonchalantly.

Loretta couldn't wait to answer. "We'll call him Li'l Marv since you never took the name on."

"Whatever." Nasir admired his son one more time, looking over his features. "I guess he favors me," he said with hesitation.

Loretta punched him hard in the back after he passed Li'l Marv back to his mother, who sat with her mouth open.

"I'm out. I'll check back with you later on this evening." He stood in a moment of silence. "Oh yeah, and I'm bringing Farren back out here with me."

Loretta folded her arms. She had met Farren but wasn't too warmhearted of her little goodie-two-shoe ways, not even giving herself the chance to find out what Farren was really about.

Someone needed Loretta for once, since she'd been home. That someone was Nakea. Nasir was independent. Sheena was independent and now, she had someone under her wing that depended on her. She loved the feeling of control. Nakea listened to everything Loretta said, and valued her input like she was a mother figure to her. She felt comfortable telling Loretta her problems than she never did tell her mother, Daisy. All doubts of Loretta betraying her were washed away after this night.

If there was a chance to salvage the relationship with Sheena, Loretta now had the chance. But would she seize the moment? Sheena was due to deliver any day now. If Loretta stood by her side during her delivery, that would create a window of opportunity for their failing relationship.

SPLIT DECISION

Nasir called his jump-off and told her the news. Her only reply was, "I'm here if you need me."

Just reaching home he moved quietly in the house praying that Farren was asleep. He wanted to avoid the shower but being gone all day, he couldn't. Farren's eyes slowly opened smelling the freshness of the Lever soap. She still was wondering why Nasir hadn't called her over the course of the night. Not knowing she was awake, Nasir called himself gently lying down on his side of the bed like he'd been there for hours but Farren was unlikely to let that slide.

"Well? Did she have a boy or a girl?"

Nasir's body jerked. "Hey, boo, I didn't know you were up."

Farren swallowed hard. "I wasn't until I smelled the soap from the shower," she lied. She was up much longer than that, waiting for him to come home.

"I had to get fresh for my baby," he said trying to butter her up.

Farren's eyes rolled up to the top of her head. "Did she have a boy or a girl?"

"She had a boy," he said vaguely. "His name is Marvin Bundy III."

"It figures," Farren said under her breath.

That comment went over Nasir's head.

"What happened to all that talk about you being uncertain?" she mouthed, coming clear out the blue.

"I used to feel that way Farren, but after seeing my son and getting my moms seal of approval, I know that's my seed." Nasir stressed feeling uncomfortable where the conversation was going.

"You know what they say," she said with hatred.

Nasir's lower body tightened from his tenseness. "No, Farren, I don't. Why don't you share with me, what the fuck they say?"

"The longer you feed 'em, the greater the possibility that the child will look like you." She pulled the cover tight and snug under her body, leaving him in the cold.

Nasir flinched inside. "Farren, I've been straight up with you about Nakea. I'm sorry if you can't handle that we have a child together. That's something you need to work out by yourself. If I say that's my son, then that's what the fuck it is, point blank!" he said snatching the cover from her over to his side. "And to feed your insecurities, I'm not getting a blood test if that's what you are insinuating."

Farren's feelings were hurt not because the baby was born but that she felt Nasir hadn't included her in the birth of his child. He felt like he didn't have to—she wasn't the child's mother—why did it matter? They were only boyfriend and girlfriend. They weren't a married couple. He didn't have to involve her if he didn't want to.

Nasir drifted off to sleep, leaving Farren angrier than she was before he came home. He made up his mind after that conversation to go back to the hospital by himself. Farren wasn't ready to accept the new addition to his family, why take her out there to create more drama?

The next day Loretta called everyone to inform them about the birth of her first grandbaby. She believed it was her duty to call Nakea's mother since she never showed up. After all, this was her grandchild as well, even if this was her second one.

"Hello, may I speak with Daisy?"

Daisy wiped her wet hands on her blue housekeeping uniform to dry the excess water from washing dishes. The house was a junky mess. Dishes were piled up everywhere and Shonda's daughter's toys were all over. Consequently, Daisy almost injured herself when she tripped over a Barbie car. That was frustrating enough and when she looked over the bills next to the telephone, she wanted to throw the towel in.

"This is Daisy, who's speaking?"

"Loretta"

"Loretta who?"

"Loretta. Nasir's mother."

"Nasir's mother. Ooh! I never knew your name," she mimicked. "What can I help you with, Loretta?"

"You know you're a grandmother all over again!" she said with delight, warranting the same response from Daisy.

"This I know," Daisy calmly indicated, looking at the $500 electric bill that was overdue.

"So you've already been out the hospital?" Loretta

questioned, dabbing a little perfume on her palms to rub on her clothes.

"No, I haven't." Daisy lifted her legs up on another chair in the kitchen after sitting down.

Loretta sensed her disregard. "Why not? Aren't you excited to see your grandchild?"

"This must be your first grandchild. I can tell from the enthusiasm in your voice, but for me this is my second, which means another mouth to feed, more money out of my pocket when your son forgets all about her and the baby. Nakea knew how I felt when she got pregnant the first time I put her out and you let her in. Since you wanted to help save the day . . . you make sure they're alright. That's one less problem on my hands."

"How in the hell can you say that about your child? She's just eighteen years old. You shouldn't be throwing that girl out in the streets no-how with nowhere to go."

Daisy crossed her feet and shifted in her chair. "Oh I get it. She's worn out her welcome, like she always does. That's why Sean's family put her out. You can send her back. Shoot, come to think about it, welfare will give me extra food stamps if I add the baby to my case. Yeah, send her back home."

"That's real ugly of you to say that, Daisy."

Daisy was offended. "Clean around your own front-door before you start sweeping in front of mine!" Her voice rose.

Loretta was taken aback. "I didn't call to start bickering. I want the best for Nakea and my grandbaby. It's not that she's worn out her welcome. That's not it. Don't you feel you need to be with your daughter during this time? Why let her stay with us and give them another opportunity of making another baby? I think it's best that she come back to live with you. Maybe this time, you can try to develop a relationship with your daughter instead of throwing her out to the wolves!" Loretta scolded her as if she had room to talk.

"Nakea is grown. When she turned eighteen, she was less one responsibility. If she wants to sit up and have baby after baby, let her! She's the one that will be trapped in the system years on end from making all those babies. Your son ain't going do nothing different than these other deadbeat fathers. He's going to leave her high and dry like they all do."

Loretta lips puckered and her cheeks puffed up. "That's where you're wrong, *Ms. "I* don't give a damn". He has his father's blood. He'll always take care of his children. Too bad, you can't say the same thing for your other daughter!"

As much as Loretta adored Nakea, she knew it was best that she went back home. Besides, her body was too fertile. In the event that Nasir backtracked, Loretta didn't want them to experience back-to-back pregnancies.

"Send her home then, Loretta. I can use some help cleaning this damn house anyway!" Daisy was finished with talking.

Loretta heard the dial tone. "No she didn't hang up on me." She started to redial her number but felt it would be a waste of time. She knew Daisy's position about Nakea.

When Nasir finally woke up it was mid afternoon. He was so tired from being out the hospital that he needed the rest. Farren was already gone off to work. He picked up his cell phone and pager. He had twenty-four missed calls and twelve pages. It wasn't anybody but Nakea or

Chauncey needing him to make a run. That was money he missed out on, but it was for a good cause. He couldn't decide if he would spend the day at the hospital or take care of business to make the almighty dollar. The thought of his baby boy quickly evaded his other thoughts. He was on his way to pick up Mom Flossy and Sheena to visit with the baby. That was his agenda.

"Grandmom," he yelled from the front porch. The inside door was locked and he forgot his keys.

"Are you crazy? Yelling like that, boy!" Mom Flossy asked agitated, pulling her feathered wig down tight on her dome.

"I had to yell so you could hear me, Grandmom. Where's Sheena?" he said easing his way in while planting a kiss on her cheek.

"She had a doctor's appointment to attend. Her and Eric left here about fifteen minutes ago."

Nasir sighed, "I came to take both of you to the hospital to see the baby."

"Don't start getting all mush-mush. Loretta called me already and told me he made way out of the sack. By the way, does he look like Brian?"

"Grandmom, you say anything."

"I'm going to speak my mind. I'm ready when you are to see this crumb snatcher."

"Let's go."

They talked in the car as always when they drove together, chalking up old times. Loretta was already at the hospital when they arrived, sitting inside Nakea's room in the maternity ward. She had purchased balloons and a vase full of fresh flowers to make her feel upspirited before she dropped the news about her going back home.

"Looka, looka who's here," Loretta screamed referring to Mom Flossy. "You're a great-grandmother now. How does that feel old lady?" she kidded her.

"Blessed, that I'm alive to see this day. You better hope you can say the same, when you get my age."

Nakea had primped and prepared herself to look presentable when Nasir came to visit. She was sitting pretty, lips shined up. "What happened to bringing your girl, Nasir?"

Perhaps he should have responded differently but he didn't and this fed Nakea's ego.

"This is my girlfriend," he responded hugging Mom Flossy tight.

Because he was angry with Farren, he inadvertently disowned her as his woman. That's how Nakea took it.

Loretta and Mom Flossy were looking through the glass window observing Li'l Marv at peace in the nursery.

"How precious," Mom Flossy cooed. "Sheena should be delivering soon." she reminded Loretta.

"I know. Is Eric's family going to be around?"

"Does it matter? As long as you're around, that is what's important." Mom Flossy remarked knowing Loretta's intent.

Nasir and Mom Flossy hung around the hospital long enough for Daisy and Shonda to arrive. Daisy eyed everyone in the room, as did Shonda.

"So, where's this baby everybody seems to be over-protective of?" Daisy asked Nakea.

She smiled, happy to see her mother, despite of how she treated her. "Hi, mommy. He's right in there," she said pointing in the nursery's direction.

"Time for me to go," said Nasir. "Come on, Grand-mom."

Loretta stayed behind seated in the reclined leather chair watching the interaction between Nakea and Daisy.

"And how are you Daisy? I'm Loretta."

"I'm great and you?" she asked arrogantly. "I suppose you told Nakea the plans already haven't you?"

Shonda looked at Nakea to see if she knew already. She was pre-informed before coming there. The look on Nakea's face gave her the answer.

"Tell me what Loretta?" Nakea asked.

"I see you didn't, otherwise she wouldn't be asking what."

"You didn't give me a chance too," Loretta fired back going to Nakea's bedside. "When you get released from the hospital, you are moving back home with your mother."

"But why?" Nakea asked confused, scrutinizing the question.

"Risks, that's why!" Daisy blurted out.

Nakea wanted to cry but didn't want her mother to see how upset she was about going back home. Loretta held her hand knowing that Nakea was trying to be strong.

"It's best that you move back with Daisy. You just had a baby. You understand, don't you?"

Nakea didn't understand but shook her head yes, anyway.

After the visit, Nakea was left alone, holding Li'l Marv. Tomorrow morning she was being released. Daisy was coming to pick her up but no way did she want that to happen. Nasir was going to be their ride home. She had his baby, now she had control over him. That's what she seemed to think anyway.

TIME TO MOVE ON

Nasir had handled some business for Chauncey and made some extra cash. He was chilling in the car, kicking it with Brian, smoking herbs.

"You want some of this?" Brian asked passing the weed Nasir's way."

"Naah," he answered and then reached out for it. "Let me hit it a few times."

"You knew you wanted to hit in the first place," Brian laughed.

With addiction running in the family, Nasir had no business even taking a few pulls. On his last inhale his cell phone rang. The number was unfamiliar.

"Yo," he responded choking inhaling the thick smoke.

"Nasir, it's me. The baby and I are getting released from the hospital in the morning. Can you pick us up?"

"What time?" he coughed.

"Around nine-thirty—ten."

She knew Daisy was coming at eleven, which meant he had to beat her there.

"What are you doing and why you coughing like that?" she asked prying.

"I'm chillin', why?" He discerned where the conversation was going and quickly put an end to it. "Yo, because we have a son together don't mean we're going to be together, so get that out ya head. On the strength of my seed I'm coming to get you—nothing else. Word up! Don't think I'm going to play your childish games. I'll do anything for my son, but you are cut off. I offered to help you only if you helped yourself, but you're too damn lazy to get a job. How do you expect to keep an apartment up if you don't have no money coming in?" The weed was kicking as he started to analyze Nakea's situation.

Brian was trying to cue Nasir, who was lost in the conversation with Nakea. Farren could hear him going back and forth on the phone with Nakea outside of the car.

"Here we go," she said to herself knocking on the window. "Hey, baby," she said interrupting him.

He turned around surprised to see her. "Hold on Nakea. Matter of fact, let me call you back," he insisted wanting to give Farren his attention.

"Is that Farren?" Her faced was grilled with animosity. "You'll hang up with me and forget about your son for that no-name bitch?"

Nasir tried his best not to cuss her out. "I'll call you back." He gritted to avoid the confrontation with either of them. "What are you doing off of work so early?" he asked Farren.

She shrugged as the tension built on the inside. "In case you forgot, I was scheduled 'til seven p.m., it's now eight p.m.," she stressed. "When I got home you weren't there and I was questioned where you were, cold as it is." Her attitude was heard in her boisterous tone.

Brian excused himself so they could talk privately. He felt the friction between the two lovebirds.

"Why didn't you call me on my cell? You didn't have to come out here. What's up with that? You checkin' on me 'n shit?"

Lately, Farren had been on edge worrying if Nasir was backtracking in his steps with other women. She had nothing to worry about, but instead of trusting and believing in him, she let her idol thoughts divert her mind. It was situations like these that made her have skepticism.

Sonya's nose could smell beef a hundred miles away. She came out of nowhere, on cue, approaching the both of them. Nasir was standing near the basketball court fence looking in Sonya's direction; Farren's back was turned facing Nasir. With total disrespect for Farren, Sonya advanced toward Nasir.

"Congratulations, daddy." Sonya teased. She had on a short, butter-soft winter-white leather coat and a winter-white Kangol, overtop of her two Pocahontas plats with her knee-length winter-white boots, just barely touching her winter-white skirt, to dazzle prospects.

Nasir blew hot steam her way. "Get outta here, girl, with ya deranged ass." Sonya stood there wanting more conversation, still not acknowledging Farren.

"Didn't you hear what my man said?" Farren was ready to release the hostility that was brewing within.

Sonya waved her long, cultivated-air-brushed finger-nails, snapping them in Farren's face. "You don't want it, Farren. So, beat it bitch!"

Nasir went to grab Sonya; Farren caught his hand

mid-way. "That street-thumb hooker is not worth a charge baby!"

"Like I said," repeated Sonya, turning her back without fear on them, "You don't want it."

Farren watched her cross over to the opposite side of the street while Nasir's heartbeat raced with fury. "I'll see you when I get home, Farren."

Farren took that as though he were brushing her off and left dismayed.

Nasir spent another hour or so in the park before heading home. The night chill was the only reason. He flipped open his Nextel phone and twirked his creep.

"What time do you need me to come through?" he asked.

She sat back watching porn movies bringing together her words. "It's that time for me."

"Which means what?" he said unconcerned.

"That means only two openings are working. You want them both?"

"Since when haven't I? Is the coast clear?"

"Always for you," she responded.

"I'm on my way."

Farren was in the kitchen making a hot turkey, ham and cheese sandwich, sitting down at the table not knowing what to think. The keys rattling the door interrupted her silent meditation.

"Smells good, what did you cook?" Nasir asked. The empty air pockets whizzed around in his stomach.

Farren bit down into the sandwich licking the melted cheese, teasing his hunger. "I only made enough for me."

That was not the response Nasir wanted to hear. "You didn't think your man would be hungry?"

"It's not that, but lately you've been eating out. Why waste food?" she said, placing the last bite of her sandwich in her mouth. Nasir pulled out the dining room chair waiting for Farren to get up and rattle the pans. After ten minutes, the pans still weren't rattling and Nasir's air pockets caused him to burp up air.

"Ain't this is a bitch? . . . A man can't get a meal now?" He had the refrigerator door open, placing the fruit punch container to his lips.

Farren rose from the table. "Don't do that!"

"Why not?" he said in between gulps. "Every little thing is bothering you nowadays," he said, striking a nerve with her.

Farren had one hand on her hips snubbing his comment. "Not everything," she threw his way. "Just some things," she guaranteed him. She didn't mind expressing her views to clear up any confusion. Nasir leaned back on the refrigerator taking all this in.

"Let's talk about it, then. You first." he demanded, not knowing she was a time bomb ticking, ready to explode.

"Why talk about it when you're not open to what I have to say, Nasir?"

Nasir flapped his ears in her direction giving her the cue that he was, all ears.

"You don't even see what's happening. Me, I'm on the outside, looking in." she proclaimed.

"What is it that I don't see?" he asked indifferently.

Farren sat back down at the table with her hand in tee-pee position over her face, smothering her words. "Nakea is going to use the baby as an excuse for you two to get back together."

Nasir sat down in the chair next to hers scooting it closely to hear her clearly. "Is that what this is all about? What would make you think that already? The girl hasn't even come home from the hospital yet."

Farren let out a grieving sigh. "You can't see it, but I can. I know her kind. I've been through this before. Watch what I tell you! She is going to take you on a roller coaster ride."

Nasir's vein muscles formed in his temples. "That's what this is all about," he nodded. "Another man? You could've kept your dealings with old niggas."

Farren tried to convince him it wasn't about that. "This is not about me, or my past. I know how some females get when they have kids. More than a handful of them use their kids as pawns to keep a man around. That's all I'm saying."

Nasir was tired of going back and forth with her. No matter what she said, he was going to do for his son and if that meant having an open relationship with Nakea, then so be it. If Farren had a problem with that—he would leave.

"Can I get some head?"

"What! You know I don't do that nasty shit. I don't put nothing in my mouth that can shoot back at me."

"So does that mean no?"

"Yes it does!"

"I ain't going beg for it, but know what you won't do—another female will!"

"What kind of response was that, Nasir?"

"Maybe I should give you some space, Farren. Time to think about how childish you are being."

"Space?" Farren said panicky. "What are you saying, Nasir? Are you leaving me over this?"

His response raped her mentally. "That's exactly what I'm saying. I'm going back to live with my mom."

That was a tough comeback to swallow. As much as she wanted to beg him to stay, her pride wouldn't let her. In the back of her mind, all she could think about was Nasir and Nakea lay up in that tight-ass bedroom all cozy. She didn't have an inkling that Nakea wasn't there. How dare him leave her to go back to Nakea's hood rat ass! She sulked.

"Wait, Nasir," she tempted to plead. "Don't you think this is going a bit too far?" She didn't want to bare the thought of their relationship ending for good.

Nasir paced lax in movement to the closet to retrieve his clothing. He was leaving with what he came with. Farren pushed her hand to shut the front door when he tried to open it.

"You ain't going nowhere!"

Nasir pushed her hand. "Yes, I am. Now get out of my way."

"Just like that," she nodded in rhythm, blood boiling.

"Yo, just like that. Nobody, not even you is going to come in between me and my seed. Now move!"

Farren felt the rage building. She wasn't accepting what he was saying. The voice inside her told her to bug the hell out, but the positive energy was telling her to let him go—why waste time on a grown man, living up in his momma's crib, without a legitimate job?

"You know what, Nasir? Fuck you, Nakea and . . ."

Nasir didn't let her finish her sentence before he dropped his clothes and slapped the taste out or her mouth leaving her stunned, holding her stinging face. She threw a combination at him, tapping his jaw. She was a fighter; she wasn't going out like some fucking wimp.

Nasir's thoughts were contaminated by his personal feelings. He wanted to live righteous but the streets kept calling him. He would take the steps to change— but he had a hidden agenda.

HIDDEN AGENDAS

Six months had past since Li'l Marv was born. It was early June, and after a gruesome winter, the weather, compared to the snowstorms was beautiful, even with scattered raindrops. Nasir was back living with Loretta and had managed to keep Nakea from sneaking her way back into the crib.

The morning when Nasir picked up Nakea and Li'l Marv from the hospital, he found out that Daisy was all ready set to pick her up, but by the time she arrived, they were headed to his mother's house. He didn't find out until they reach the house that Nakea was supposed to go back home. After Loretta asked Nakea what was she doing unpacking her bags there, it was then he knew Nakea was still playing games.

Farren hadn't called him at all and he'd left her hundreds of messages. Every time he went past her job, they told him she was never there. He was at the point of giving up on trying to get her back. He tried to cut back sexing his undercover chick. They'd been keeping their affair on the low for some time. Lately she'd begun demanding more attention that he couldn't give her. His guilty pleasures started to backfire. He went hard the last six months hustling. Chauncey's connection cut out the middleman and dealt solely with him. Nasir had to wean himself away from Chauncey telling him that school and women were taking up most of his time. He had enrolled in the GED program at the community college that Farren pressed him about. That wasn't a lie. The classes were going well and the Instructor, Ms. Hurdle was a tremendous help to him in class and in times of duress. She had a spiritual presence that drew him in. He looked to her as a mentor. His concentration became his son, schooling, tending to Mom Flossy who withstood two mini strokes during this time and getting money. Sheena and Francine were the only two he could turn to. Although, there were times he would get agitated because Sheena decided to move out to live with Eric and the son that she finally gave birth to, into an apartment of their own. He was happy for her, but her timing was off. Mom Flossy needed attention majority of the day. It was difficult for her to get around due to one side of her body being paralyzed. She stayed in and out of the hospital given that her blood pressure would not regulate. Loretta recommended to the family that Mom Flossy be placed in an assisted living environment. That infuriated everyone, not to mention she kept the pot brewing stirring Nakea up with old stories and false hope of getting back with Nasir.

The fire was still lit in Nakea's eyes. Nasir had gone against his word by dipping back in the pudding, only this time he was smart enough to wear protection. He wasn't suffering a second round knockout. He was cautious. That throwback pussy was too tempting for him not to run back up in. He proved the theory right. *The door is always left open to sex-up your baby's momma if she still has feelings—even after you've moved on.*

By doing this, he set a double standard, but it made his life easier—drama free when dealing with his son. The more he dipped—the worse she became. He felt humiliated as man that she would use their son to manipulate him. He prayed that the wind of news didn't blow in Farren's direction. It would affect all probability of them reconnecting. He was stressing big time. His GED test was coming up and he hadn't done an hour of studying. More than ever, he was hustling for the big pay-off. Every other day, Nakea was calling him for pampers, baby formula and money. It was ridiculous. Daisy was beefing with him about coming around the house too much to see Nakea and Li'l Marv. Sheena was still pissed about Loretta not rushing to her side as she did Nakea when her baby was born. Loretta was more concerned about reshaping her love life from missing time than she was rebuilding a family foundation.

Seemed like everybody had his or her own agendas. Things had to get back in order. The only place Nasir found solace was at the place where he began with his father at the cemetery. This was one time he went alone without someone to comfort him. He got himself into the rut he was in and he would somehow get himself out of it. He knelt down pulling the excess grass from around the face of the marker. "Why did you have to leave me?" he cried, invoking his pain out in the open. He loathed the emptiness of being alone without a father or a father figure, present in his life.

Even with Loretta pressing forward, she hadn't fully recuperated from the substantial loss, so the men she befriended were only hit-and-misses. When she felt the urge she would hit them up with a call, when she didn't, they'd miss out.

Dad, please help me get my life in order. Help me to get Farren back and help me straighten out Nakea. I'm trying to do right by my son, but this girl is driving me crazy. Mom Flossy, she's not the same. Her health is failing her. You know she's going downhill when she won't fuss with mom anymore. I can't take losing another loved one. I'm fucked up real bad. I don't know who to talk to about this. . . . I'm knocking off one of your old joints. I can't even begin to explain how it started. All I know is I can't stop fucking her. Was it good to you like that? I think I'm pussy whipped by an old head! If mom finds out she will never talk to me again. I want to leave her alone. I know she's a dirty playa. She even told me she couldn't wait until I turned sixteen. She was plotting on me the whole time. How could I betray y'all like this? I know you don't really give a fuck, but what about mom? Do you think the old head has any remorse for what's she's done? I'ma stop fuckin' with her. I'm trying to make Farren, wifey. I'ma get this money and parlay, watch me! My shit is tight. Dad, I'm dealing with too much shit. Can you help a nigga out?"

He cried silent tears, fighting back the flow that hid behind his weary eyes. In a passive posture, he remained until the distraction of a phone call poised his body to stand erect. Not even noticing, this was the fifth time Nakea tried to get through in less than a half an hour.

"What the fuck do you want?" Nasir asked her agitated, viewing other mourners exit their cars to visit loved ones.

"Li'l Marv needs some new clothes. He's outgrown the ones he has." She held the baby in one arm bouncing him up and down on her hip. "Our son is getting bigger and bigger by the day." She sang praises. "And,

he's favoring you more and more, with his handsome
self. You can just bring me the money and I can do the
shopping or we can go together. Whatever you want."

If giving her money were going to get her off the
phone, he would say, "yes".

"I'll be by there," he said to make her happy.

"What time?" she pressed.

"I said I would be there. Peace."

He flipped the receiver of the phone, closing it.

*See what I'm talking about, Dad, unnecessary bullshit.
Everybody is trying to control my actions when their shit is
fucked up!*

He left the cemetery thankful to release a bit of pressure heading straight to Nakea's to appease her request
for cash.

When he knocked on the door, Daisy had a foreign
look about her, like she objected his arrival.

"What are you doing here?" she asked sourly, holding the screen close to her body, barely opening it.

"I'm here to see my son and to give Nakea something." he responded, not making trouble.

"I told Nakea you weren't to come around here no
mo'. Don't you think you've been creeping around
here enough? You do live with your woman, don't you?"
she threw that in. "That's what I thought. Why do you
keep chasing behind my daughter then?

Nasir wasn't shocked by her candor. Daisy always had
a cunning remark.

"If Nakea wants to see you, she can go around to
your mother's. I told that girl I don't want no drug deal-
ers making my house hot with the po-lice."

"I don't know what you're talking about, Ms. Daisy.
You got me mixed up with Nakea's last boyfriend, Sean.
I'm not a drug dealer," he said earnestly.

She still hadn't summoned Nakea to the door. "How do you afford all these expensive things if you have no job? Where are you getting the money to give to Nakea every time she calls?"

He could have fed her curiosity, but he didn't. "Ms. Daisy, is Nakea home?" he asked as pleasant as he could before getting rude with her. He was trying to be respectful to his elders.

Instead of her answering, she turned around and shut the screen door in his face. Nakea ran to the door from the third floor, catching her breath. "Nasir," she called.

"Here, take this money. I have things to do." He pushed the money in her hands.

"Don't you want to come in and see your son?" she asked hoping to get a quickie.

"Nah, bring him around the house later. He can spend the night."

"Okay," she smiled. "I'll pack our overnight bag."

"Nah, I said bring *him* around to stay. Not you."

She didn't care what he said. She was going to stay regardless. They came as a package. A red car came zooming down the street, blasting "Dangerously In Love" by Beyonce.

"Nasir, baby, *I'm dangerously in love with you.*" Sonya sang. *"I'll never leave, you set me free,"* she continued. "Come to the crib later on."

"Her ass is whack! Some chicks don't give up!" Nakea cursed Nasir as they watched the car turn the corner.

Nasir doubled back. "You're absolutely right, some chicks don't give up," he reinstated, pointing his finger firmly in her direction and went about his way.

"Nasir," Nakea shouted. "I love you. Those other

bitches only want your money. Where were they when yo' ass was broke?"

His discontentment showed when he failed to acknowledge her insincerity. His mind was on getting Farren back and today he was determined to talk to her. Too much time had lapsed and before she got serious with another man, he had to make his move. She was avoiding the hell out of him—the flowers he sent, the notes he left on her car, the notes on her apartment door, telephone calls and all. If she didn't respond to him today, he was going to sit inside her apartment building stairwell until she came home. He'd given Nakea money that made her content, at least for the rest of the evening.

He positioned his body on the hard stucco wall of the Greyhound building waiting for Farren to get off of work. All the days he was told she wasn't at work, they were all lies. She was there, but she didn't want any bother. He grinned seeing Farren strut outside the office wearing a peach colored pant set. Nasir leaped out at her, scaring her. From the exit door it was impossible to see if someone were lurking on the side of the wall. That's why for security reasons, employees were informed to use the front entrance. After each shift, she'd used the back exit to avoid bumping into him. This was a gambit to get him out of her system. Her ploy was hard to follow. She still felt deeply about him. Had the security guard never put him on, he would still be waiting at the front entrance.

"What's up Farren?"

"Why are you doing this, Nasir? It's been over with us for six months. Why do you keep stalking me?" It was obvious her reason for evading him. His presence made her weak. Her words were not convincing.

"It was never over. We took a break from each other, that's all."

"Not true," she scrutinized.

"You snapped. I snapped. The situation got out of control. I'll be the bigger person and apologize." His act was straightforward. "I didn't mean to hit you and I know you didn't mean to hit me. Those were knock-out blows, you threw though."

Farren sent out a radiant smile his way. "I was trying my best to knock your ass out."

"Come on, you have to admit—you said some foul shit. Who cares how you feel about Nakea? Not me, but dissin' my seed, that's going overboard."

"And how do you know I was dissin' your seed?" Her body sullen without movement.

"That's where it was headed," he said certain.

"You didn't let me finish to find out if I was going to say that. Why would I disrespect your son like that? Think logically. All of a sudden, you became so protective and secretive about him. I told you before, I don't need this in my life." She wiped the oil that shined from her nose. "Why are you hard pressed with me?"

Nasir could feel her anger as the words formed from her lips. He listened closely as Farren shared her inner thoughts.

"If you would excuse me, I have class to attend. Don't you?" she asked.

Nasir was surprised she knew, since he hadn't been the one to tell her that he finally enrolled. He grabbed her without pre-warning, embracing her very tight, whispering in her ear.

"I love you girl. *I need you in my life. I want you in my life.* I promise, I'll change. *Baby, baby, give me one more chance, baby, baby, give me one more chance.*" he rhymed.

Farren had been waiting for this day. She wanted to say no, but her heart wouldn't allow the words to surface. "You promise?" she replied softly.

"Yes, baby. I promise," he said as he released her, gently kissing her neck. "Do you mind if I ride with you to school? How did you know about my enrollment? We're not scheduled on the same days. I be seeing you though; looking all sharp."

"That's what you think! Besides, I find out every thing," she said followed by a wink of the eye. "What about your car?"

Uh-oh, he thought. How much did she know?

"What about it?" he asked with a delayed reaction. "You can swing me to get it when class let's out."

"Cool." Farren was still upset with him and she planned to talk it out with him later, when the fog thinned out, right now the fog was still thick.

"Hold tight for a minute. I need to get my book bag out of the trunk."

Even with all the drama going on, he still found the time to go to his classes. He may not of been studying but damn if he was going to miss a class and suffer the consequences of failing due to an unexcused absence. This was his last class before the big test.

TESTING, TESTING

Opening the door to the GED Prep class, Nasir hurried. He was the last student to make it in. His instructor, Ms. Hurdle was a stickler for being on time. If you were 15 minutes early, you were on time. If you were there at the requested time, you were late. No if's, and's, or but's. That was her rule.

Ms. Hurdle's reading glasses were almost sliding off the tip of her nose, as she took role call. "Nice to see you made it Mr. Bundy. Have a seat quickly, please," she commented, in the midst of greeting other students. After roll call, she picked up a piece of chalk and proceeded to guide the class into the lesson.

There were fourteen students still hanging in there. In the beginning, there were thirty-two students. Most of the adult students dropped out when the demand of learning was presented. Good notion on Nasir's behalf to stick with it. He hadn't befriended any of the classmates. He was there to learn and earn, his GED. Too much socializing would cause him to miss out on important test data. The class lasted two hours each week.

On Saturdays, Ms. Hurdle held a study group for those who needed extra help. Nasir had been to the study group only once. He was more advanced than most of the remaining students. His pre-GED test revealed that. That's why Ms. Hurdle was so hard on him. She saw his full potential.

"Students, this is the last class before the final GED test next week. It's been with great pleasure working with each and every one of you. You've proven to your families, friends, significant others and most importantly, to yourselves that when an obstacle is placed before you, you're up for the challenge! All of you should feel at ease. Only the strong have survived and the strong individuals . . . mean you! No need to stress and worry about what's to come. Claim victory now and all of you will be victorious. For the remainder of the week, get some rest and study hard. Until then, I'll see you next week, God willing. Have a good night!" Ms. Hurdle gave them one last pep talk before the anticipated day.

"Mr. Bundy, I need you to stay after for a few moments," she required, having a seat behind her grey metal desk, removing her reading glasses, before he walked out the door.

"Sit down, son."

Nasir took a seat.

"My sources tell me that you became a father recently, true?" She looked to him for confession.

"Yes, Ms. Hurdle, that's about right."

Three thick wrinkles formed on her forehead. "I don't normally congratulate young folks on becoming parents, for most haven't a clue what they have gotten themselves into. Don't take this as a lecture of should've, would've, could've . . . take this as a word of advice from someone that truly cares. Raising a child is hard work and if you haven't been properly raised, chances are you will raise your child the same way you were brought up. The easy part of making a baby is over. The hard part came when the baby arrived. Don't be fooled by thinking purchasing materialistic items for your child means you're a good parent. It's your duty as a father to raise that child with love and affection. Teach and instill in them morals, values, loyalty, honesty, with account-ability and with jewels—with every action, there's a re-action. Make sure their reaction is a positive one. You have to teach them and test them at the same time. Teach him or her to respect themselves, in that, they will learn to respect others. Understand, son?"

Nasir placed his hands lightly on the desk, taking in her words of wisdom.

"May I ask, if you and the mother of your child are still together?"

"No, Ms. Hurdle, we're not." His guard was let down.

"Do you plan on getting back together?"

"No, but I think she believes so. I've moved on, sort of." he said hesitantly.

"Listen, son, if you're not going to be with the young lady, don't lead her on. That's the worse impression you can make. It's best to establish a mutual understanding early on. I've seen many men get caught up in that baby-momma nonsense. Remember . . . it's always about the child. The moment it stops being about the child, you need to let the family court system handle it. You know you have rights as a father, don't you?" She could tell no one ever had this conversation with him by the way he attentively listened. "What I mean is, recognize the signs, before it gets too late. Don't let the small stuff slide. Begin with a line of open communication. Be straight with her and don't dibble in the cookie jar if it's over."

Nasir nodded.

"And, if she's weak in some areas, you step right in as a man and balance it out. Don't dog her out. Help her with the process. As a father, you are viable, just as the mother in that child's life. Always, be there for your child." Ms. Hurdle stated, patting down on Nasir's hands. "This may help both of you. There's a parenting class held at the college once a month. It might be a good idea for both of you to take advantage of the service. It's free of charge. Alright, you have a good night, Mr. Bundy," she said wishing him farewell.

Nasir wasn't sure who told Ms. Hurdle about his situation, but it sure sounded like she knew about it from a familiar source. The advice she unveiled to him was needed. He'd have to thank the person who informed her when he found out. That was the best advice he'd heard yet. It made him take another outlook on becoming a father. From this day forward, things were going to change. Not for Farren, Nakea, nor Loretta—but for himself.

Sitting on the hood of the car satisfying the lust of an old flame, Farren flinched, watching Nasir exit the college, keeping her composure. *This will teach his ass a lesson.* She thought. The scene was unpleasant to Nasir, but he wasn't going to let that spoil his joy. The road to recovery is a selfish process, and on that course, there are some internal feelings that need to be addressed. For Nasir, one of his internal behaviors was insecurity.

He would nurse that wound first, then tackle the others.

Farren acted as though she was really having a pleasurable time talking to Quinton. This was the same guy who dogged her out before, continuously cheating with his baby's momma. He really wasn't worth shit, but here she was winning the Stellar Award for the Best Actress of The Year fronting like "it was all good". All the pain he put her through, she wanted to Mike Tyson his ass, but played the game trying to figure out, where Nasir's mentality was. At times, she found herself comparing the relationship she had with Quinton to the one she shared with Nasir. That had proved to be one of the problems they had in the past. She hadn't completely gotten over him. That pain was still haunting her. Quinton's conversation was straight up bull. He was hoping that Farren would meet him on a late night creep. However, this time, he'd be inclined to cheat on his baby's momma, not Farren. She giggled to make it appear that she was into him, to make Nasir realize what he'd been missing out on. Nasir compressed his feelings, examining the way Quinton played Farren too close. When he reached the car, Nasir bonded a kiss on Farren's cheeks, like glue to paper, taking seconds longer than he normally did, without letting up. Had Farren been a redbone, her face, no doubt would've turned fire engine red.

"Are you ready, baby?" he asked, not addressing the fact Quinton was there trying to parking-lot-pimp on his woman. Farren placed her feet on the ground, scanning other vehicles zoom down the divided byway.

"Yes, I'm ready," she responded to Nasir, forgetting all about Quinton, not even saying goodbye. The weight of the air was heavy.

"I'll hit you up later on, Farren." Quinton said disturbed from the arrival of Nasir.

Farren tossed Nasir the keys to the car. "That's not a good idea, Quinton. I have a man."

Nasir threw his hands up in the air to Quinton. "What can I say, bro? You had your chance."

Farren reclined back in the passenger's seat, twiddling her fingers goodbye to Quinton. That was satisfying enough. Nasir wanted to drill her about him, but played his cards. This was the hand he dealt.

"Are you free for the rest of the evening?" he asked, watching her and the road simultaneously.

"It depends," she said, opening the door for invitation.

"It depends on what?"

"It depends on whether or not you are willing to focus specifically on me. No cell phone, no pager, no park action, no baby momma drama . . ."

"Okay, I get it, knuckle head," his smooth hands traced the steering wheel, as his body gangsta leaned.

The night was soon to end and the transformation of a good relationship gone badly hadn't reserved itself back to being peaches and cream, yet. Nasir knew Farren wasn't finish reading him, although she pretended to be tolerant with him to this point.

"I have a suggestion, why don't I follow you back to your apartment and we catch a movie on television? I know how much you enjoy those Lifetime movies. Help me figure out why though?" He gave her a second to think.

Farren stuck her head out the window yelling to know one in particular. "Earth to Nasir, earth to Nasir."

He tugged at her blouse pulling her back inside the car. "What are you doing girl?" he asked, watching her burst out into laughter. He couldn't help but to join in with her.

"Nasir, we ain't never sit-back and watch a sitcom together, let alone, a damn Lifetime movie—the movies you call "male bashers".

"Most are. That's not my concern. My concern is a lot of black women are dedicated to that broadcast and majority of the stories are about white families. Am I lying?"

"Humph, I never gave that any thought. They have black actors and actresses on there, every now and then," she shrugged.

"Count on your fingers the number of times the lead person was black."

Farren tapped her head, trying to recall if she remembered any.

"That's what I thought. To hear you, my mom, and Francine tell it, Lifetime is a woman's refuge. I'm open to find out instead of speculate. So what do you say? Is it on tonight or what?"

Why did he have to mess up the good vibe mentioning his mother?

"I'm with it. Since you brought your mother up, how are things between you two?" She bit down on the tip of her index fingernail.

"Mom is going to be who she is regardless. She is who she is. I'll never be able to change that."

"How come she doesn't like me?"

"She never said that."

"She never had to. Her actions always speak loud and clear."

"Don't worry about that. It's about us. *Just me and my bitch. Me and my bitch*," he replied. "Nah, seriously the last six months have taught me much. Trust!" His words were heartfelt. "My mom is holding tight to Nakea and if she gets close to you, she'll feel like she betraying her. You have to understand, my mom is trying to relive her memories of my father. Nakea gives her that undivided attention and listens to her old stories, over and over again. She allows my mom to live out those happier times in her life. In return, my mom gives Nakea hope that one day, she and I will be together. My father is deceased. It's no coming back for him, but I'm alive and as long as I'm here—she believes the possibility for a reunion is there. My mom doesn't realize that Nakea and I were never a couple. It was strictly about sex. The only time we spent together was in a motel. I've never taken her to the movies, out to dinner or for a walk in the park, feel me?" Nasir put the car in park. "Regrettably, I got caught out there thinking with my second head, not using protection. And now, I have a son the system calls a bastard child because we're not married."

Farren was shaken by how candid he'd become. "The last six months have done you good. I've never heard you speak this way before."

Nasir had changed. His eyes were opened after reading *Soledad Brother* by George Jackson, and *The Spirit of a Man* by Italia Vanzant. He still had a way to go but that was a start.

"Can we continue vibin' at the crib?" he asked seriously.

"If I said no, would you be upset?" Farren pondered, getting out the passenger's side going over to the driver's side thinking if all this came about because of her encounter with Quinton.

Here he was pouring out his inner emotions and she

was going to shut him down. It's hard enough getting a black man to admit his wrongdoings and she had this man willing to give her all of him.

"I am not going to lie. Yes, it would bother me. I'm giving you my heart, girl." Nasir wondered if she could feel how he was feeling on the inside.

Farren sat in the driver's seat. "Pour it out then, but when you do—don't leave a drop inside—I want all of it!"

She pulled out from the parking spot leaving him standing there. That was an open invite for him to meet her at the crib. Like an obedient puppy following behind his master, Nasir trailed Farren to her apartment. The anticipated night of relaxation and movie watching turned into in-depth conversation. Farren gave her word to trust him and not to get jealous or feel insecure about his dealings with Nakea. They both agreed taking it slow was best and that for now, Nasir should remain at his mom's.

The following week, Nasir spent preparing for his GED test right up to the testing day. With his drive and willpower, he knew he aced the test. Ms. Hurdle gave him the nod of approval that day, before he left the class. Never had he felt so delightful about an Instructor or Teacher. His GED certificate would arrive in the mail. Instead of sending it home, he had it addressed to Farren's. She was the one who stressed to him about going back to school, to at least obtain a GED.

A WOMAN SCORNED

"**H**and me my great grandson," Mom Flossy demanded. She already had Li'l Marv in one arm and now wanted Li'l Eric in the other.

"But Grandmom, you're holding Li'l Marv. You can't hold them both with one arm paralyzed." Sheena was frightful, scared that she'd drop one of the babies.

"Give her the baby. She's not going to drop neither one of them. I'll be sitting right here to help her." Nasir assured, easing Sheena's doubt. He sat next to her paralyzed side putting his arm around her neck, using his body for support. This made Mom Flossy's day.

"How's everything going over at your mother's?" She slurred in speech, sensing that something was wrong. She wished the time Loretta spent in prison helped her change, but it didn't. In fact, Loretta had become worse off than she was before going in. Hanging around young girls, soaking up all the gossip of the hood, that was her favorite past time. All thanks to Nakea who kept the logs burning. Loretta acted as if Nakea was her best friend. She barely went places with Francine anymore because

Francine was solo. The excitement they used to share died down.

"Grandmom, I don't know where to start." he stressed, exasperated. "I wish my dad were here to straighten her out. If dad were here, things would be different."

"Mm, hem, as much as I didn't agree with your father's behaviors, it's unlikely that this would be happening. Outsiders weren't allowed in when your father was living. Hell, he didn't want me in their business!"

Nasir sat unsteady, receiving his grandmother's comments.

"Do you think mom is going to come around?"

"I don't know. Your mother did a lot of time in prison—time away from you, Sheena and from reality. She lost time while there. Now she's trying to play catch up. When your mom got locked up, she was 18-years-old, a young woman. I hate to say this but them drugs she was on while in there, only coated her mind from being depressed. They didn't help her deal with reality. They relieved her mind to forget about what was really going on. That's why when she came home she latched on to anything or anybody that would aid in her recollecting her younger days. Your momma is stuck baby. That's all that is. Prison's don't do people good. They are designed to kill the will to survive, make prisoner's give up on life." Mom Flossy kept rocking the babies, who were both asleep.

Nasir rested his head on her shoulders. "What are you saying, Grandmom?" he asked, fearing the reality of the conversation.

"I'm saying, your momma is like so many others that are stuck in time and haven't moved on. She's moved on physically, but mentally, she is stuck and will be until she faces herself in the mirror."

Nasir didn't know how to internalize his pain. He got up from the seat, picking up Li'l Eric, placing him in his stroller and did the same with Li'l Marv. He kissed his grandmother on the forehead, saddened by her words, but also, her health conditions.

"I love you, Grandmom."

"I know you do, baby. Have faith that everything will work out."

Nasir reached for the inside entrance door to the house. "I'm trying to keep the faith, Grandmom, but it's hard," he said in despair.

Sheena had already left the porch, leaving Mom Flossy and Nasir to chat. She was now on the telephone having a heated discussion with Loretta. Internal feelings from both siblings were left unresolved. Sheena held dear to the negative feelings she had stemming from her mother. Nasir walked in when the conversation was at a head.

"I'm sorry you didn't love my father like you did Nasir's. Why does it seem like I have to compete for your love? Huh, mom? I used to compete against Nasir for it but now, against Nakea? . . . A damn outsider that's going to stab you in the back. And when she does, I'm going to be there to say, 'I told you so'! She don't care about you. She's using you to get closer to Nasir. The writing is bold on the wall!" Sheena carried on.

If only Nasir was a fly on his mother's wall, he would have seen how unconcerned she was for Sheena's feelings. Her body language told it all. The only comment she gave Sheena was, "That's your shit, Sheena, not mine!"

Tears streamed down Sheena's face. "This is my shit. That's all you can say. This is how you respond to me?

You will never have to worry about me doing this ever again, Loretta. I'll never talk to you again!"

As Sheena hung up the phone, Nasir immediately grabbed onto his jaded sister, who cried into his firm chest for over fifteen minutes.

"I'm sorry it has to be this way Sheena. I'm here for you always."

She knew it wasn't his fault; that she was dealt a raw deal leaving her with issues from her mother and father.

Grandmom Flossy had been sitting on the porch attentively listing, holding back the tears that she wanted to shed for her grandchildren's hurt and pain. She felt it was her fault, raising Loretta. It was her imperfection as a mother that Loretta turned out so bad. As God was her witness, her grandchildren were going to survive from this hurt and pain. She would guide them differently so they wouldn't make the same mistakes with their children.

"Nasir! Sheena! Come out here," she called to them.

Sheena blew her nose and cleaned up her face, straggling behind Nasir.

"You see these two beautiful babies right here? Don't you ever allow the problems that scarred your lives, to scar them. They are blessings from above. It's your job as a parent to guide these babies in the right direction. It's your duty to see fit they are taken care of. Do you hear me? Nasir, I don't care if the dizzy-ass girl is trying her best to use Li'l Marv, you endure and ignore. Continue to be a father to your son, no matter what. Ain't gon' be no deadbeat fathers originating from this household. Sheena, as for you, if you and Eric decide its not working for you two, don't you use Li'l Eric as a tool against him. These babies are not items or play-toys that you use as pawns." Mom Flossy was serious.

On cue both babies awoke, probably feeling the intensity of their great-grandmother's feelings.

"Well, Grandmom, I've got to get going. Eric is waiting for me and Li'l Eric to get home." Sheena gathered the baby bag and Nasir assisted her with the taking the stroller down the steps.

"Me too, Grandmom. Nakea is most likely losing her mind, thinking Li'l Marv is over Farren's house." Nasir stated knowing he was telling the truth.

"Don't let that girl dictate where you take your son. She should know you're not going to take him any place you don't feel safe at."

"Grandmom, I agree with that one-hundred percent." Nasir and Li'l Marv left out, on their way home.

When they arrived, Nakea and Loretta were sitting on the steps, outside of the apartment building. Nakea looked like she had been roughed up from her frugally hair and fresh scratch marks on her face. She immediately began to attack Nasir before he could get a word in edge wise.

"Give me my baby you no good motha . . ."

Loretta jumped up from the steps, pulling Nakea back. "Calm down girl, and watch your mouth in front of all these kids," referring to all the little kids playing, riding bikes and enjoying the summer-like day.

"I told you. Don't have my son around your trifling whores!" Nakea hollered in anger.

Nasir hated to be embarrassed and Nakea was doing an excellent job at that. He walked past Loretta and Nakea into the apartment, placing Li'l Marv inside the swing, winding him up, so he could deal with her hyped up ass. Nakea was behind him step by step, hitting his soles of Timberlands, as he walked.

"Yo, back the fuck up off of me!" He demanded his space.

Nakea used her index finger to point all in his face. "Nigga, don't act like you stupid. It is what it is. I just got into a fight with that trick bitch!"

If she got into a fight with Farren, it was because Nakea incited it, he was sure.

"You told me you left that whore alone. And now, you back with her, taking my son over to her crib?" she fumed. "Oh hell, naw! Nigga, it ain't going down like that!"

Nasir had no indication what she was talking about. Li'l Marv hadn't been to Farren's.

"What are you talking 'bout, girl? And stop saying my son, Li'l Marv is our son!" he stressed. "I don't have to explain a mothafuckin' thing to you. You're not my woman. Wherever I take my son, when he's with me—it's my business. Be a'ight with it! I ain't gone take him nowhere I wouldn't go." Nasir fueled Nakea's tantrum.

Nakea raised her balled up fist to hit him, but he snatched her arm away in mid-air.

"You better keep you hands to yourself, girl. If you try that shit again, I'm a deal with you like a man, since you want to act like one!" he said with a forcible grip on her inner arm.

"Fuck you, punk. You don't move me. You better tell your bitch, Sonya. It ain't over!"

Nasir was relieved when she said Sonya. He wasn't the least bit interested in her. Her didn't understand why Sonya kept hounding him.

"Sonya?"

"Yeah, Sonya. We were rumblin' over your stank ass," Nakea said crying from her intense resentment.

"Well from the looks of it, she must have gotten the best of you." Nasir laughed in her face, fading out the lies Sonya told her.

Nakea started swinging wildly at Nasir who in self-defensive threw her against the hallway partition, knocking out a hunk of hallow drywall.

"I warned you to keep your hands off of me, tramp! You are so dumb. A woman will tell you anything to get up in your head. That's how devious yell are," he added. "You so caught up, you can't recognize her lame game—stupid-ass girl," he mumbled.

With his strong force, Nakea couldn't move. Every word that came out of Nasir's mouth was accompanied by forceful air.

"Here are some words for ya ass to think about. *I DON'T WANT YOU OR THAT SLUT SONYA.* Both of you ho's were just a fuck . . . got that?" he screamed on her. "Get a life. Do something else instead of try'na kiss my ass all the time. Be a mother to your son. Use the same persistence you have trying to get me back and get some shit fa ya self. You can't get far with a 9th grade education girl!"

Nasir's strong hold loosened, letting her free to go inside his bedroom. Nakea hadn't gotten enough.

"Nasir, who the fuck do you think you are? Huh? You are no better than I am. You're a high school dropout. You're a grown-ass man living up in your momma's crib and ya so-called job is drug dealing. Oh, I'm sorry, *delivery boy.* You ain't no damn pizza man, mail carrier or no shit like that. You ain't nothing but a hustle'—and you ain't even the *Big Man, so* don't toot your own horn, nigga!"

Nasir searched in his closet for a hanger to whelp up her face.

"For the record punk-ass, you need to be a father to your son and stop chasing behind a piece of fucking ass!" she steamed, humiliated.

Nasir contemplated gripping the wire hanger tightly to pimp-slap her with it a couple of times. He knew it would be wrong. He stared at her, unmoved by her words.

"Nakea, that's where you're wrong! I may have been a high school dropout but I did obtain a GED. I may live with my mother but as of today, I'm out of here. I was peddling, nothing heavy, just enough to get me by. Only because, I was tryin' to keep up with your beggin' demands, always wantin' and needin' somethin' for Li'l Marv. But, again, as of today—that shit is dead. I'm gon' try my hand at a real job so I can be a good father and role model for our son." He threw the hanger on the bed, clearing his belongings from the room. "If I don't take the steps to change, it will never happen. If I weren't with Farren, we wouldn't be together. What could you offer me? You living like a crab. If I needed you to meet me halfway, you couldn't even do that." Nasir gathered everything not even knowing if Farren would approve of his request to move back in, but he knew from Sheena's conversation earlier with his mom and from the severe argument, they were in, drama would continue to happen. He lied to her about him hustling fearing she might snitch on him.

"Fuck you, Nasir. You ain't shit. This will be the last time you ever see my son again!" she said, slamming the door in his face, obviously hurt from his bluntness.

Nasir ran behind her, ripping out a weave track from

her head. "If you ever try to keep my son away from, I will hurt you girl!"

Loretta heard the commotion from the outside and hurried inside. "Marvin Bundy, Jr.! Get your hands off that girl. Your father never disrespected me like that!" she admitted, pushing him off Nakea.

Li'l Marv started to cry. The swing stopped swinging and was still.

"See what you're doing to my son." Nasir said, going over to get him out the swing. Nakea pounded on his back screaming, "Get off my son! Get off my son!"

Nasir knocked her down grabbing Li'l Marv's baby bag, with his son in his arms, going where, he didn't know.

Loretta and Nakea tried to pry Li'l Marv from Nasir arms without hurting him in the process. The commotion for onlookers was a site everyone would gossip about. Nasir maneuvered both of them off of him putting Li'l Marv in the car seat and speedily locking the door once inside. He never thought he would have to fight against his mother about his son.

"Nasir, give that girl her baby back!" she screamed in front of everyone.

Nakea pounded on the hood of the car jumping on it to stop him from pulling off, but that didn't stop him. Nasir pulled off with her sliding off the car into the street, just missing hitting her. The car tires shrieked. He sped with Loretta hollering, "Call the cops. My son just kidnapped this girl's baby!" Loretta's actions were uncalled for. Good thing no one adhered to her demand. Nakea lay in the street crying with a beat up face and oil spots all over her jeans.

Nasir quickly made way to Farren's house, not know-

ing why he put on a dreadful act like that. He reacted
without really thinking. His thoughts raced against one
another. *This is not going to last,* he contemplated. He
didn't have a full week's worth of supplies for the baby,
though he believed he would do what was necessary to
take care of him. He hadn't used his key to Farren's
apartment. He wondered if she changed the locks. If
she did, he'd be up shit's creek. Luckily, the locks hadn't
been changed.

The door opening scared Farren half to death,
thinking it was an intruder. She was in the middle of a
great conversation with her mother and father when
Nasir came busting in with the baby and bags. He greeted
them with a short hello and rushed his way into
Farren's bedroom.

Farren excused herself from the company of her parents who had a look of confusion of their faces. From
what Farren informed them, Nasir didn't live there anymore, but from what they bare witness to—that seemed
to be a lie. However, they weren't going to sit there to
find out. If Farren wanted to share with them, she would,
if not—it was her business. She was grown. Besides, they
had an event to attend to. When Farren exited the living room, so did they.

Nasir paced back and forth in the room wearing the
floor out with his hands on top of his head, jumpy and
worried.

"Nasir, what's the matter?" Farren asked, stopping
him from pacing. Li'l Marv was lying on the bed sucking his bottle with his eyes following them.

"Farren everything happened so fast. . . . Sheena,
the fight, Nakea . . . bottom line, I took my son and ran.
This stupid girl is going to try to keep my son away from
me. I'm not going to let her do this."

Nasir was enraged and the signs were apparent by his body motions. Farren tried to dissect his broken sentences.

"Calm down baby and tell me what really happened."

She wasn't ready to hear what he had to say. When he finished explaining, Farren grumbled thinking of a conflict resolution. She had to make him reason logically.

"There's a sure way to deal with seeing your son and kidnapping is not the way. Before things get out of hand, let's take Li'l Marv back to his mother and handle this the mature way." Her suggestion was appropriate. Somebody had to intervene positively. "I understand you are his father, but until you file for joint or full custody, Nakea still has the upper hand because they live in the same residence. Which means . . . she has residential custody until a judge decides differently."

"That's some bullshit," he disagreed.

Farren had Li'l Marv in her arms holding him tight. "Hey, lil guy . . . all this fuss over you." Li'l Marv lit up the room with his wide smile. "Aww, aren't you the cutest."

Any feeling Farren had about Nasir having a baby by another woman was thrown out by Li'l Marv's warm reception of her. She kissed his little hands. It felt good to hold the baby and be a part of him for the first time.

Nasir took a few hours to regain his sanity. He planned with Farren to take Li'l Marv back to Loretta's together. With Farren there, he would act more rational than he would than if he went alone. He called over to his mother's house to see if Nakea was still there.

"Bring that baby back, Nasir." Those were the first words parted from Loretta's mouth.

"Mom I'm on my way there, but I need to ask you— why are you in the middle of all this?"

"I don't have to answer that. Just bring him back, or else," she cautioned, sounding irate.

Vital as it was to stand by her child, Loretta went against the grain. This was not a one-time plot on Nasir. It was a lifetime plot to destroy his very being because he didn't want Nakea. Loretta didn't understand she'd joined in on the plot to destroy another black man— her son, at that.

"Okay, let's go over the plan one more time," Farren instructed.

"No need, I have it down," Nasir declared.

The plan was simple: take Li'l Marv back to Loretta's, call Nakea to tell he's there, convince her not to press charges even if that meant buttering her up.

"We're taking my car," Farren recommended.

"Are you sure you want me to go through with this? Your plot might backfire. Are you willing to accept the consequences, if they do?" he stressed, half gesturing that Nakea would take his kindness the wrong way. "Before we go, let's stop past the cemetery. It will be quick, I promise."

They lined the car in the narrow cemetery road. Nasir invited Farren to accompany him. Usually, the moments spent was time spent with his father, but today he wanted to share the emptiness that he felt from his father passing with Farren.

"Hey, Pop. Guess who I brought to see you? Your second namesake, Marvin Bundy, III and my girl, Farren. She has to be special for me to bring her here. You know that."

Farren wasn't sure how she should feel. It was an awkward moment for her.

"Say hello to my Pops, girl," he bumped her.

She didn't want to offend him by not saying hello, but thought *he can't hear me, if I do say it.* "Hello, Mr. Marvin, I'm Farren. I don't know if that's fitting, but whatever. I hope you are watching over and protecting your son from the evil that surrounds him."

Nasir put his arms around Farren's waistline, leaning his head on the side of hers. For a moment, she thought she felt a tear drop down on her shoulder, but she was too sensitive to Nasir's feelings to turn her head around to check.

"Let's go Farren and get this over with," he pleaded. "Thank you for riding this out with me baby."

Loretta was in a heated discussion with Francine, who was steady explaining to her that she was wrong by what she said, and for the role she played in this drama. Francine knew that Nakea was full of it; the first time she met her.

Nasir and Farren walked up with Li'l Marv. Loretta gave Farren an odd, uncomfortable stare.

"Did you bring her to start some more trouble?" Loretta seethed.

Nasir didn't feed into her child's play.

"I come in peace," Farren waved.

Francine stepped up to Farren's defense. "Loretta, leave that girl alone. She's backing her man, like you used to do." She introduced herself to Farren. "What's your name? Are you Farren?"

"Yes, I'm Farren," she answered proudly.

"Nice to meet you P.Y.T.—Pretty Young Thang. You are such a pretty girl."

Loretta held her hands out to Nasir to take Li'l Marv inside. While there, she made a call to Nakea.

"If you come now both of them are here, so hurry." she instigated. Nakea responded with, "I'm on my way with Shonda. Don't let them leave!"

"Where's your family from, Farren?" Francine inquired.

"They live on the north side of town, but I live near northeast."

Francine smiled, "I live on the north side too. What's your mother and father's name?"

"Leslie and Raymond Giles." Francine swatted her hand in the air. "Chile, I've known Raymond and Leslie for years. Those high school sweethearts still together? Isn't that somethin'! Come to think of it, you do favor your mother. I remember when you were this high," she reflected, making an invisible height chart.

Farren was content with Francine's personality.

"Francine, we'd love to talk with you, but we have to get going. Maybe we'll invite you over to dinner," Nasir willingly suggested.

Farren looked at him like *stop front'n.*

Francine hugged him and whispered in his ear, "I thought you were living back at your mom's." Nasir shook his head no.

Shonda's car came plummeting around the corner on two wheels. Nakea and Shonda both jumped out with the car and parked smack dab in the middle of the street. Nasir motioned for Farren to go, but chaos had already claimed its victory. Loretta peered from the living room window holding Li'l Marv, and eyeing the scene at the same time. Francine glanced up at her, mad as hell, because she knew Loretta had a hand in this.

"Bitch! *What* did I tell you?" Nakea snapped. "Didn't I tell you to steer clear from my man?" She had the heart of a lion.

Shonda had a baseball bat in her hands. Francine placed herself in front of them.

"Take that ghetto-fabulous mentality back around the corner, acting like crazy Daisy. This girl don't have anything to do with you and Nasir."

"Who dat trick is?" Shonda had the bat in her hands ready to swing.

"Chill, Shonda. That's his Aunt," Nakea acknowledged. She knew better than to disrespect her.

"She betta' mind her business."

Nasir pushed Farren behind him. "Get from in front of this house with that bullshit."

"Naw, you wanted to play dirty, and I'm game," Nakea owned up.

"Don't hold me back!" Farren warranted. "I don't need your protection. I can handle my own. I'm good with mines."

Nasir continued to push her behind him. "Don't stoop to her level, baby."

Nakea flew off the top. "Did he just call that bitch, *baby?*"

"Indeed, he did." Shonda added.

Nasir, you hounded me to be your girl. It took me some time, but I finally gave in—dropping the man I was with—for you. Now with the weight of a finger you think you can turn the switch off and on. I don't think so. I had a baby for you. Fuck that bitch you with! It's about us—me, you and Li'l Marv."

Farren freed herself from behind Nasir. "He don't

want you Nakea. Weren't you informed of that hours ago?"

"Bitch, you jealous because my sister got it going on and Nasir still want her. If he didn't, why he be creeping late night at the crib?"

Francine stayed in between the war zone.

"Shut up and find a father for your son, ho!" Nasir was under pressure. Shonda let the cat out the bag.

"I got your ho right here, Nasir!" Shonda stated, flexing the bat. "Ya girl don't know, do she?" Shonda watched for any body language from Farren. When Farren showed none Shonda knew she was in the dark about them creepin'.

"Miss Prissy, it's true. Your man is still dippin' in my sister's puddin'."

"Grow up!" Nasir said annoyed.

"Tell your girl that. She's the one mad because my sister has your only child and my nephew is cute."

Farren came back sharply. "That sounds real young and petty. How old are you?"

"No it don't, bitch. Stop hatin', cause I'll forever be in Nasir's life. The question is—will you? You ain't the first female he messed around with on me *and* you won't be the last. All you are is fresh meat. He'll get tired of you and come back to momma! One time up high, Shonda." They slapped each other five, swinging their arms rowdily.

Nasir glanced over to Farren and said, "I told you not to stoop to this girl's level. She's petty man."

A long line of cars was backed up behind Shonda's putt mobile. One driver yelled out, "Move that shit!"

"I'll be back to get my son. I'd advise you to be gone, bitch, before you meet your maker early." Nakea and

Shonda departed from the pandemonium that they started.

Francine tried to calm Farren down. "Don't worry about that girl, she's immature."

When Shonda passed by Farren's car, Nakea motioned for her to stop. "Hand me that bat." Nakea got out the car looking back down the street with "payback's a bitch on her mind". Approaching the Toyota Corolla, Nakea bashed the back window in until the glass cracked and the frame bent. She jumped back into her sister's car. "A bitch!" she said spitefully.

Nasir and Farren heard the sound of glass shattering, praying that Nakea didn't do what they thought she did. They sprinted to the car. Glass was trodden all over the back seat.

"No, she didn't! That whore created an enemy for life. I put that on my everything!" Farren let out.

They rode back to the apartment in silence. The drama had just begun. Nakea wasn't fading out that easily.

WHO KNEW?

"**H**ave you lost your natural born mind Loretta?" Francine scolded her harshly. "Suppose one of the girls got hurt. Did that ever cross your mind? You're too old to be in the midst of that young girl stuff. How come you can't be happy for Nasir?" Her comment hit where it hurt.

"Kiss my ass, Francine. You done insulted me one too many times," she snapped back.

"Don't get all huffy with me, sista girl. I'm the only one still in your corner; the only one who put up with your shit for years."

Nakea and Sonya started a war against Farren, and in no way was she going to let them win. Hopefully, it didn't destine her future with Nasir. Both of them were much like an unseen virus. They entered into Nasir's life without warning, and spread his very existence with poison, without him being aware of it, catching him off guard.

Farren was his anti-bacterium serum that helped to eliminate his disease. She wasn't spending a lifetime watching their actions without Nasir fully understanding the situation. She was going to prove to both of them, she was the captain and they were the servants. They were envious of her and she knew that. With her in the picture, neither one of them had a shot at getting-back with Nasir. Farren was poles apart from them. They had to step up their game if they even thought they had a second chance, because Farren raised the stakes. Nasir's expectations for women had increased ten times since his relationship with her. Nakea didn't become conscious that she was the one who pulled Nasir and Farren closer together by the turmoil she derived.

Instead of Farren taking her frustration out on Nasir, she made peace not remarking about Shonda's accusations. They sat in the living room contemplating on how to retaliate.

"I can't believe that girl had the guts to bust my car window out."

Nasir wasn't stressing about that, he would have the window replaced in the morning.

"Man, don't dwell on that. She got that and some coming to her."

Farren moved from the living room to the bedroom, removing her clothes.

I'm getting ready to shower," she panted with a distant response.

Nasir sat inside the bathroom on the toilet while Farren showered. "I'm sorry, once again," he pleaded.

"I want to kill that girl, you don't know. I'm dead-ass serious, Nasir."

"Don't kill her. She's evil, but she's still my son's mother."

"And?"

Nasir cleared the air. "Nah, not like that. It's Li'l Marv who would suffer. And, come on ma, she's still my baby momma."

"I didn't mean that literally," she said, soaping up real good.

"Why didn't I have a baby by you and not that crazy broad?"

Farren closed her eyes. She never shared with Nasir that she miscarried twice before in her relationship with Quinton. She was informed that her cervix had trouble carrying babies. She had yet to find the reason why.

Despite all of the day's actions, that night they made love. It may have lasted all of five minutes because they were both mental exhausted, but in that five minutes, Nasir openly confessed to Farren that he wanted her to bear his next seed.

Nasir's cell phone vibrated all night. Loretta had given Nakea his new number. She called and left nasty messages throughout the night. In the morning, Nasir and Farren listened to all of them.

Message # 1: *Ah, that's what your bitch gets. I told her not to fuck wit' me.*
Message #2: *I know you're laid-up with the tramp because you're feeling sorry for her.*
Message #3: *When I see her again, tell her, I'm going to beat 'dat ass.*
Message #4: *I can't believe you are choosing her over me. What about your son?*

Message #5: *Why don't you just leave her alone? What can she do for you, I can't?*
Message #6: *Nasir, how come you won't answer my calls?*

By the time message nineteen played, Nakea was crying, begging Nasir to talk to her. The last message played.

Message #20: *When are you going to learn? I told you to leave those young girls alone.*

Hearing her voice, Nasir hit the pound button trying to play it off.

"See what I have to go through?"

Farren was certain Nakea wasn't working with a full deck.

"That last message didn't sound like her," she said Questioningly.

"It was," he lied.

"Why would she call me a young girl and I'm older than her?"

"Farren, you are looking too deep into this. Don't you think I've gone through enough tonight?"

"Whatever!" she said not believing him.

FAMILY COURT

Family Court was mobbed with people going to court proceedings or filing court cases. They had to take a number to be seen. Waiting patiently to be called, Nasir and Farren sat listening to a couple argue over child support.

"I wouldn't need to bring you in front of the white man if you paid your child support," the young woman reasoned to her child's father.

"You can't get what I don't have. It's like trying to get blood from a rock," he countered.

"If you don't have the money, fine, but what about spending time with her? How about starting with an hour or two a week? That's not asking too much. Our daughter hardly ever sees you, but yet and still, you spend time with your new woman and her five kids and ain't nary one of them, yours!"

"Why you always got to bring her up?"

"Because I do. She's the reason we can't get no child

support. You're giving her the little bit that you have to feed her kids."

"How do you know?"

They argued back and forth.

Nasir tapped Farren. "This is what I don't want to happen."

"If you plan on supporting your son financially, it won't, but you need a real job first," she hinted, wanting him to adhere.

"Don't worry, that's second on my agenda." He was getting a job, but still going to do his thing.

"Praise God," she clapped loudly.

The small waiting-area was filling up with people. The elevator music was non-stop. *"Second-floor, Family Court."* It soon would be standing room only. Nasir took his time filling out his petition for visitation. This impending petition would piss Nakea off when she received it. He requested visitation every Wednesday and Thursday rotating every other weekend. He thought, what mother would oppose of this visitation schedule? He filed an emergency hearing based upon Nakea's displacement and neglectful behaviors.

After waiting four hours for the judge to rule, Nasir was granted an emergency hearing. In less than 48-hours, Nasir and Nakea would be in front of a Commissioner.

A court order had to stop this madness. Nasir was sure.

CRUSHED

Loretta had been assisting Nakea get her life together. Helping her fill out subsidized housing applications and teaching her how to move up on the list—telling her, all she had to do was move into a shelter for 30-days. When the 30-days were up, they'd have housing for her.

Nakea believed that things were working in her favor. Amazon warehouse called her in for an interview and they hired her the same day. She took Loretta's advice and went to the Home Life Management temporary residential shelter. They had a full facility of women waiting for permanent housing. Nakea joined that line. This was only for a limited amount of time. She could work through 30-days to get housing.

Daisy was glad to have her finally out the house. This time, she told her never to return. She promised her mother that she wouldn't. Shonda accompanied her little sister. They intended to weather the storm together.

It was whoever got housing first; the other would live with them.

Nakea coveted seeing another woman succeed with natural talents. It stirred a manifestation of insecurities. The way Farren shined made Nakea less attractive—day by day. Farren was a threat to her that had to be ousted from the picture. Nakea's mission became to outshine Farren whatever way she could. Her mind was set that when the thirty days were up, so was Nasir and Farren's love affair. He was coming home to momma. That was the initial plan.

SQUAD UP

In less than 24-hours, they would be in front of a Commissioner. Nasir exhaled. Farren had gone to work, leaving Nasir home alone. He wanted to check on his son though he didn't want the drama. He knew Li'l Marv was at his moms, but didn't want to face her either, but that changed when he missed the presence of his son.

Loretta was asleep with Li'l Marv by her side. His eyes were open and his little hands were stretching back and forth, as were his legs. Nasir picked his son up, kissing him.

"Hey, li'l man, daddy's here."

Li'l Marv smiled showing all gums. Nasir could smell the baby formula on his breath, snuggling him, in his arms. Loretta's eyeballs widened, like she'd taken a good hit of crack. "What are you doing here?"

"I came to see my son."

"How did you know he was here?"

"Mom, he's always here. Nakea has a habit of drop-ping him off to do her thing."

"There you go with that shit. That girl has a job. She's at work," she said wanting to change his opinion about her.

"Yeah? When did this happen? Overnight?"

"Maybe. I'll never tell."

"In some strange way, I believe that you wouldn't tell on her too, mom. That's the reason I don't tell you shit. I'm taking Li'l Marv with me," he said, teed off.

"No you're not. I'm babysitting for Nakea. She gets off from work at 7:00 p.m. and she has to be at the shel-ter by curfew, which is 8:00 p.m. Which means, Li'l Marv needs to be here when she comes. You don't know how to bring him home on time."

If Nasir heard his mother right, Nakea was now living in a shelter. He needed to contact Family Court imme-diately of the change. In order for them to have an emergency hearing, the court summons had to be de-livered to Nakea personally.

"I'll make sure he gets to the shelter. Which one are they staying at?" he asked deceiving her.

"They're staying at Home Life Management. You know where that's at, don't you?"

"I sure do," he nodded.

He wasn't thinking about taking Li'l Marv to a shel-ter when he had a place for him to live. He couldn't wait to call Family Court with this news.

When Nakea got off work, her arm muscles ached from stacking and shipping books in the warehouse. It was her first day. The hard labor wore her down. She had a backpack full of books that her supervisor had given her. Most of them were self-help books. The others were for mere entertainment, *Dime Piece* by Tracy Brown, *Sincerely Yours* by Al Saadiq Banks, *Hittin' Numbers* by Unique J. Shannon, *Street Dreams* by K'wan and one that really caught her eyes was, *Stiletto 101: Don't Let The Stiletto's Fool You* by Lenaise Meyeil. In her spare time, she had plenty to read.

The bus was quiet for it to be rush hour. Maybe everyone felt the same way she did—tired as hell.

"Kee?" Sean called out.

Nakea turned to see who was calling her. It could only be one person. He was the only one who called her that. Sean moved from his seat next to the empty seat by Nakea. Sean was Nakea's first love before she fell for Nasir. He was fresh out the penitentiary. From the looks of him, prison time did the body good. His oversized shirt was a give away that he had gain extra pounds of muscle. With his doobie skillfully tied around his head, he half smiled seeing her for the first time since he'd been home. If he hadn't picked up an additional charge in Juvenile Hall, he would have been home but unfortunately, the new charge sent him to an adult prison facility.

"Kee, what's crack-a-lacking?"

Nakea grinned so hard, her brown gums showed. "You. When did you get home?"

It didn't matter that she cut him off while he was incarcerated. When he was home, he did right by her. He didn't start to worry until he was faced with a prison bid.

"I've been home for two weeks. I was checking for you 'round the way. Yo, I heard some foul shit. You still with that older cat?"

"Hell no!" she blazed back like she wasn't the least bit interested in Nasir.

"Yo, I heard you had a baby with this dude. How could you do that when you killed ours?"

Nakea knew exactly what he was referring to. When they were together, she made the choice of aborting a baby they made together.

"I wasn't ready to be a mother then."

"Is that right? But for old boy, I guess you were." Sean stared out the tinted windows on the bus.

"Where are you headed?" Nakea tapped Sean on his leg to break his concentration. "Did you hear me? I asked where were you headed."

His mind was still stuck on her aborting his baby. When he was in prison all he thought about was Nakea. He knew that she was involved with Nasir, but he didn't care. His forward was to gain her back. No other man loved Nakea like he did.

"I'm on my way to the half-way house. I got like 30 days left before I'm free. Why? What's up? Are you waiting for me this time, or are you going to dis' me like you did before?"

Nakea knew that Sean still had love for her regardless of what she'd done to him, but she didn't know how strong. Her thoughts had to clear before she committed to him.

"Sean, before I answer that, tell me two things. One, can you accept me having a baby by Nasir? Two, will you be able to trust me again, being that I left you high and dry?"

Nakea lusted at Sean's small lips outlined by his thin black mustache. In jail, he let his hair grow wearing braids. People that didn't know him swore he was kin to

Young Buck from the group G-Unit. They resembled each other in appearance and with confidence.

Sean had developed that rude boy Cashville attitude. He was on a mission—ride or die—to get his woman back. That would gain him another notch on his belt. She was his to begin with, Nasir had to be straight with that.

"Come on Kee, you know how I get down. Word to life, I wouldn't front on you. If I weren't accepting, I would've never approached you. You should never question a man about accepting yours, that's on the real. If a man can't accept your kid, he ain't a real man. Word up!"

"I'm feeling you on that." Her head went down low and her eyes peered to the floor. Her situation was almost as bad as his. She had a curfew. He had a curfew. She had 30 days. He had 30 days. Maybe it wasn't that bad when she thought about it. The 30 days would give them time to rekindle their old flame.

"I need to tell you Sean—I'm living at a shelter temporarily."

"*Word*? That dude can't even provide a crib for you and you got his kid?"

"We're not together. He lives with his girl." A sullen pain went through her heart. The words hurt cutting through her.

"So what! I would neva have the mother of my child living in a shelter with my kid, that's foul. Yo, what type of cat is he?"

"A cat sprung over new putty-cat and not his son," she lied.

Sean put his arm around her neck. "I bet that putty-cat is juicer than before. I can't wait to tear that up."

Nakea agreed, "It's been a long time . . . bring it on."

EMERGENCY HEARING

"**Y**our honor, my baby momma . . ."

The pale older Caucasian man swept over his thin hair covering his receding hairline. "Address the court with her government name, please."

"My bad. Your honor, Nakea Perkins has not provided a positive environment for the welfare of our son's upbringing. She lives from house to house. Mostly in drug infested neighborhoods."

Nakea was boiling, ready to explode, but if she did, she knew it would work against her. Her eyes were pinpoints of fire.

"Your honor, Ms. Perkins has violent outbursts and on many occasions she's attacked me in the presence of our son," Nasir said trying to build his case.

Loretta sat in the courtroom in no one's defense. She couldn't believe that Nasir conned her out of the information to get Nakea to family court. She never fathomed her son would stoop so low and take his baby's momma to court. Big Marv would oppose this action. His philosophy was, what could the white man do that they couldn't settle outside the courtroom? She was stuck on that belief. She sympathized with Nakea going through these changes, but on another note she wondered who the young man was that came in support of her during the hearing.

Sean had that thug persona, but switched his style up for the court hearing. He had on a white dress shirt, a nice tie and black slacks. These were his interview clothes. They worked out perfectly.

Nasir was glad to see that Nakea finally had another man. Maybe now she would back up off him and Farren.

Farren was sitting pretty as Vivica A. Fox at the MTV Grammy's. Her corporate dress style was everyday for her. Someone should've informed Nakea about the dress code, wearing a little mini skirt with a sleeveless top to court. The outfit was cute, but it was fit for the go-go club.

Presuming he had the same rights as a mother would in court, Nasir was sure to have a say in the courtroom to win custody of his son. He pleaded his case to the judge who called Loretta to the witness stand. Her angry disposition stirred by a woman scorned, held true inside of her. With her unreadable face, she entered the witness chair. The rules were laid out: as much as she loved her son, she felt for another woman losing a child.

"Ms. Armstead, can you corroborate with Mr. Bundy's story that Ms. Perkins is an unfit parent?"

Nasir hoped that his mother was on his side. What mother wouldn't be? This was granted.

Her head went from side to side looking at Nasir and at Nakea. She read into Nakea's desperation for help.

"No, I can't say that I do."

Nakea sighed heavily enough for everyone to hear her. *That's my girl,* she thought.

Nasir stood up from his seat. Farren pulled him back down quickly.

"On many occasions, I've witnessed the both of them screaming and fighting in front of my grandbaby."

That was somewhat true, but the incidents were always inspired by Nakea's jealous rages. The Family Court Interventionist that worked with Nasir was confused. Nasir told him, his mother was the key witness. He had to come at her with another line of questioning for the position to be favorable on Nasir's behalf.

"Ms. Armstead, is it true that Ms. Perkins has been living periodically with you as well as other residences?"

Loretta knew he had her in a corner. "She's lived with me, yes."

"That's not what I asked you. Please answer the full question."

"Yes, she has."

"Now we're getting somewhere," his lips parted. "Do you know where the defendant currently resides?"

Loretta turned to face Nakea. It appeared to Nakea that Loretta had set her up. The only reason she was living at the shelter was to get emergency housing. Loretta was placed in a box without a ladder to bail her out.

"She resides at the Home Life Management shelter." Her heart pounced between her breasts.

Nakea eyes filled with tears. The interventionist thought he had Loretta on his side now.

"Lastly, Ms. Armstead, do you feel it's in the best interest of Marvin Bundy III to be placed with Marvin Bundy, Jr. or with Nakea Perkins?"

Loretta stared insolently at the dull white walls. "I

don't know how to answer that. Marvin Jr., is my son and Nakea is my friend."

That was the straw that broke the camel's back. Nasir would never think of his mother the same and Nakea wouldn't trust her—ever again. Nasir sat shocked and astonished that his mother had gone against him. *But why?*

Nakea was given a chance to rebut her side, but without witnesses or a strong case, the favor was on Nasir's side.

The judge left the courtroom recessing for an hour. Court commenced as scheduled.

"All rise please," the bailiff mouthed.

The judge didn't waste anytime with his decision. "Please be seated. In the case, Bundy versus Perkins, I do hereby find it in the best interest of Marvin Bundy III to be placed in the custody of . . ."

All parties were quiet; you could hear a pin drop. Sean stroked Nakea's shoulders. Farren held Nasir's hand tight.

". . . Be placed in the custody of Marvin Bundy, Jr." The words came out loudly, echoing in everyone's ears.

Emotional wealth grew inside of Nasir. This was one time Nakea would not win—for he had longed for this day. Finally, she was feeling the wrath of pain—not him. Nakea felt stripped as a mother. It was then she understood never to give your enemy an option. She gave Nasir and Farren an option, and now she was being punished for it.

Sean held tight to Nakea's shoulder trying to wrestle out the anxiety and qualms of temporary loss.

"Order in the courtroom," the judge demanded. "Marvin Bundy, Jr. will have residential custody and the respondent, Ms. Perkins, will have visitation every other weekend. To commence on Friday, returning the child on Sunday, by six p.m., until Ms. Perkins can prove to the court that she has a stable place of residence. Case closed."

The knocking sound of the gavel was all Nasir desired to hear. He grabbed Farren and held her tight. "You got him, baby," she squeezed him.

Loretta stormed out the courtroom. Nakea cried on Sean's chest. He did his best to comfort her. With her dreary, red eyes, Nakea's demonic being graced Nasir and Farren. "Be careful what you pray for. It may not be worth the consequences." They brushed her off and left the courtroom in route to pick up Li'l Marv from Sheena's.

FOR THE LOVE OF MY SON

Winning the court case for Nasir was the blessing he'd been praying for. By some means, he knew his father had a hand in the decision. The ruling made him change immediately instead of gradually. It wasn't the same as when Li'l Marv lived with his mother—he could get away with living the street life. But now with the baby in his custody, he had to be a real man and take care of his responsibilities. He was against taking the role as a father for his girlfriend to raise his child while he stayed on the go.

There were many conclusions he had to make. The most important was getting a legit job. He'd made snide remarks to Chauncey on the slide, but this time he was serious. No longer would he dip in the pot. He had his last bowl from it and while the combination was sweet, it would be a limited amount of time before it got sour.

"Farren, are you going into work this morning?" he'd hoped she say no.

Farren was in the kitchen prepping bottles for the

baby. Nasir was amazed how Farren lived up to her word. The only complaint she had was that they needed a bigger place.

"I took off for the day." The hot water poured down into the steel double-sided sink. One side was stacked with bottles and the other side, bottle tops. She was sterilizing them with boiled faucet water. The tap water was used to rid-away lingering particles.

"Baby, do you mind sitting with Li'l Marv for a few? I need to tie up some loose ends. I won't be long."

Farren studied Li'l Marv who was sleeping peacefully. This wasn't going to become a habit. She was willing to help in every arena, but wasn't willing to step in and take the place of being Li'l Marv's mother—he already had one. Farren thought the situation might slightly change, but it was unlikely. What kind of mother would give up the fight?

"I don't mind occasionally watching over the baby, but the buck stops there. This is what you wanted, and now that you have it . . . take care of your business." Farren's right hand was on her curvy hips. "Don't you agree?"

Nasir knew what she meant. That's why he had to cut his loose threads. "Don't worry. I understand you fully, baby. Just let me, do me. I shall return." He kissed Farren on the cheek sucking up some of her skin with the forceful pull. "You know I love you girl, don't you?"

"I love you too, handsome," she said all buttered up.

Nasir quickly removed himself from the house while he had Farren in the palms of his hands.

Chauncey was in the same spot, as usual. Nasir was taken aback as he watched Sonya holding Chauncey from the back. That's why he hadn't heard from her in awhile. She had finally moved on. Chauncey smelled the curiosity that possessed Nasir and before he said hello, he confronted it.

"Yo, I hope you don't mind."

Sonya laughed.

"Nah, man. Do you? You can have that crazy broad. She's only good for one thing anyway," Nasir stated explicitly.

Chauncey seconded that. "I know. That's why she's in my corner—for that one thing—this chick is the meanest, when she's suckin' on dis' penis."

Sonya hit him on the back and stormed away.

"What's good my man?" Chauncey asked.

"My time has come to say goodbye. I'm going cold turkey. I want out of the game."

The spite that filled Chauncey's heart caused him to cough. He didn't know how Nasir was going to make it without dwelling in the game. They came from the same background and poverty conditions. Most hustlers never made it out. What made Nasir think he was going to? Chauncey began to think that Nasir copped a better connect and was trying to cut him off. He needed to find out the truth behind him wanting to leave.

"I've been good to you all this time. Why now, when the game is air tight, do you want to give it up?"

Nasir didn't want to get into the particulars but at the same time, he respected Chauncey for looking out for him.

"I want to live clean—clear my life of negative things. Ya know?"

Chauncey wasn't buying that. What would he do for money from now on? How was he going to support his son? How was he going to support that pretty woman of his? No woman wanted a broke man. Instead of asking him the questions—his pride didn't allow it. He faked as though he was cool with Nasir's decision, lying to him.

"Yo, I understand. I've been thinking the same way lately." His eyes stayed keen to the streets. "Remember though, the game never changes, only the players. This opportunity will never be open for you again. If you're finished—that's it—you're done and so am I." Chauncey's tone had changed, perhaps from the rising feeling of betrayal. Nasir was holding out and he thought *how could he bite the hand that feeds him?*

Nakea lay on the twin size lower bunk bed and Shonda on the top bunk. Shonda's daughter was in the small bed across from them. Nakea had placed a pillow over her head to conceal the sounds of her cries. Her sister felt the pain with her.

"Don't cry, Nakea. We'll get him back."

"You don't know how bad it hurts. My insides are rotten. I feel the acid eating away my stomach lining. They took my baby from me. He's all I had to live for."

"Listen to ya words, sis. If he's all that you have to live for—then live," she shouted. "Get your shit together. If you hadn't of been chasing behind Nasir . . ."

Nakea took the pillow off her face. "This is not the time to drill me. Your daughter is right there, my son gone," she said somberly. Her eyes were puffy and red. She'd been crying all day. Sean tried his best to hold her down, but his comfort wasn't enough. She needed more—her son, to make it better.

"Nakea, please stop crying! You're stronger than this. This is what they want you to do—crack and fold.

Take it like a soldier. I promise you, we are going to get Li'l Marv back," she said with determined assurance. "Let's play this out. Our time will come. We're going to complete our 30 days, get a place and afterwards, do us! While we are in here, let's enroll in the free training and educational classes." Shonda jumped down off the top bunk to sit with Nakea. "Don't you know we have the upper hand? We can milk dis'! All we have to do is follow through. They guarantee us housing and a job, not a minimum wage job either. A job, that pays like $10 to $14 per hour. How you love that? We are going to be on top soon, baby sis. To hell with Nasir and Farren, we will get the last laugh. Now straighten yourself up, acting all guppy and shit. I believe you have one more courtesy call before the phone is shutdown. Let's call and find out how my nephew is doing. The court said you have visitation on weekends, right?"

"Every other weekend," Nakea corrected.

"Whatever, but they didn't say you couldn't call the house."

Nakea smiled.

"That's what's up. Smile, baby girl. This shit is not over. Grab your balls and let's handle this shit our way—fuck the courts!"

Nasir was on his way back to the apartment feeling good that he severed all ties with Chauncey. He was able to save up some money, opening a savings account to put the money in. Though he only had $8,000, it was a start. He had more money coming.

Ms. Hurdle his former Instructor told him if he wanted a job, to call her. Her husband was the Principal at Charter Elementary. All he had to do was fill out an application and her husband would guarantee him an entry-level job. Since he had no prior employment history, entry level was appreciated. In the morning, he would place the call to her.

At home, Nasir sat on the couch, yanking his Timberland boots off, wiggling his toes to circulate the blood. Farren came from the room holding Li'l Marv in her bosom. He was such a happy baby—all he did was smile. She had given him a bath and put on him a one-piece nightie.

"Let me hold him," Nasir requested.

Farren sat opposite of Nasir on the love seat, turning on the lamp to give the dark room some light.

"Did you handle your business?"

"Of course, I did." he said, very shortly.

"Mmm, okay," she hummed. "Are you happy now that you have custody of Li'l Marv?"

"Can't you see the permanent smile on my face?"

"Do you think Nakea will come around?"

"I can only pray that she will."

"Do you think the drama will end?"

"Now that, I don't know."

Loretta stood staring into the dark of the night. She felt 95% at fault for Nakea losing residential custody of her grandson. Though she knew he was in good hands, it felt wrong for it to go down that way. Her problem wasn't her son. Her problem was that another woman: that woman being Farren, who had taken her son away from her, and now, her grandson too. Farren was also the cause of her friend losing custody of her child. Why would another woman do that? The question didn't measure up. Farren didn't have any children and was secure without Nasir. Why did she need him to add to her "already full" life? Nakea needed him more than she did. Farren came from a two-parent household— the love and nurture was there. How come she had to reap the benefits of having a good man also? It wasn't possible to have the best of both worlds. Loretta, hadn't she missed out on both—Nakea, hadn't she missed out on both? What made Farren so special? This was not just a battle Nakea had to fight. Loretta was ready to tag team. But how would she get Nakea to trust her again?

Farren was already cozy in bed, with her mini silk turquoise pajama nightshirt on. Nasir had placed Li'l Marv in the bassinet.

"We need to buy a crib. This little bassinet is not working. Li'l Marv is just as big as it is."

"We can take care of that tomorrow. It's our time now," she winked.

Nasir slid under the covers, removing his pajama short. Just when he began pushing Farren's buttons the ringer of the phone sounded, interrupting them.

"Damn, I'll get it." Farren panted, since she was the closest.

"Hello."

"Hello, my ass. Bitch, put my son's ear to the phone so I can hear him coo-coo, gurgling or making some noises. Nasir may have custody, but that was the worst thing he could've done. You gone wish the mothafucka never did that."

Shonda was asking in the background, "Who's dat' . . . *his bitch?*"

Farren fell back on the pillow, handing Nasir the phone.

"Here, it's for you."

"Who is it?" he asked mad. "I told you not to answer the phone anyway, when we're in the mix," he argued at her.

"Yo."

"Don't yo me! I didn't ask to speak to your punk-ass. I called to talk to my son. Like I told ya girl—you may have custody, but that will never stop me. I'm going to be that thorn in your side that never comes out. You asked for it, now you got it. Be prepared to go to war 'cause I'm getting my son back!" Nakea banged the phone on him.

Shonda high-fived her. "That's what I meant by grabbing your balls. You have to treat them the same way they treat you!" Nakea nodded her head. Round two was about to begin.

Nasir tried to doze off to sleep. The doorbell sounded. "Who the fuck can that be?" he angrily shifted. He grabbed his robe from the back of the door and slid into his shower shoes.

"Who is it?" he asked looking through the peephole seeing nothing more than a beige trench coat. He opened the door cautiously. He damn near panicked.

"What are you doing here?"

"You haven't been to see me, so I'm coming to you."

He tried his best to whisper. "Farren is in the bedroom."

"She can watch if she want to!" Her trench coat hit the floor and she pushed her way in. Nasir heard Farren's slippers skating on the floor. She was getting near.

"Nasir, *who's* that?"

Nasir pushed his jump-off out the door begging her to leave. She picked up her coat and walked down the steps slowly.

Farren met his hand that gripped the door tightly trying to pull it open, but his strong hold wouldn't let her.

"What are you doin', Nasir? Let the door go!"

"They had the wrong apartment; now go back to bed," he said, mashing her face.

Farren went over to the window anyway, suspiciously pulling the Venetian blinds open. She rubbed her eyes focusing on the woman that was walking outside down the steps.

"Is that? . . . What's she doin' over here this time of night?"

"At The Courts Mercy"
By KaShamba Williams
December 2005!
Don't hate me for this ☺

AT THE COURTS MERCY

SNEAK PREVIEW

PROLOGUE
SOME SHIT ON MY MIND

NAKEA

I don't know why Nasir thought I'd fade out the mothafuckin' picture so fast. He thought he'd get my son and ride off into the sunset with his fake-ass princess Farren—*that Bitch*—afraid the fuck not! I hate both of them with every muscle that you can think of. Farren stole my life and Nasir allowed her too. For that, she'll be sorry she did. I'm going to make her life so fuckin' miserable she's going to be calling me cryin' to take Nasir and Li'l Marv back. This time, the shit I'm going to carry them through is some unthought-of shit compared to the stunts I pulled before. Time waits for no man and neither does Nakea, you got that! They ain't seen shit yet! This goes out to all my baby mamas holding it the fuck down! Fantasia couldn'a said it better, but I will uphold the song out in the streets. I'm that baby mama you never want to meet.

My teenage love, Sean, was released from the halfway house and we are ready to wreck some shit. When our thirty days ended in the shelter, I was receiving the keys to my project income-based apartment as they promised.

Shonda moved in with me and so did Sean. All those feelings I had for him, had been poured into Nasir and I had to find a way to take them back and give them to the rightful owner . . . Sean. Nasir had stolen my heart from him and I had to deal with the humiliating fact that I was just a temporary broad in his life. Boy, did that shit bruise my ego. Its cool though. I'ma show all you niggas out there how *not* to fuck with a chick on a temporary basis. You might end up in a fucked-up position like those muthafuckas!

THE JUMP-OFF

As I bend over in my magnificently sewn polyester nightie, exposing my hind side, watering my roses that my young boy Nasir sent me, I'm tasting the last bit of juices he left inside my mouth, on my tongue, and *how* tasty it is. With my bottom-lip pulled inside of my mouth, and my index finger tracing my deep-berry-painted lips to match my nightie, on my upper-lip, I can recall how Big Marv would talk dirty to me, calling me names like: home-wrecker, dick-pleaser, deep-cock, nasty-tramp and the one that made me especially cum minutes after he said it with his powerful voice . . . *"Slut for a nut."* Thinking about it is making me touch myself in my most sacred place; mmm . . . Big Marv can still take me to paradise even in his death. Although some-times, I dream of feeling his manhood deep inside, penetrating me like he were alive and well. That's why I had to make his son, Nasir, the closest replica of him, do me like his father used to, call me the same names and treat me like the slut I was for him.

You think I give a fuck about Loretta? That whore

can go back on the ho-stroll for all I care. That's where Big Marv picked her up. Had Loretta never told him I straight disrespected her ass when she was pregnant with Nasir, Big Marv might not had ever given me that ass kickin' and cut me off like he did. I believe had he not cut me off, my son Quinton would also have the Bundy name. Yeah, that's right paybacks are a motha-fucka! I'm sorry that my son's old flame, Farren, had to get hurt in the process. It's not her I'm try'na destroy. My vendetta is against that bitch Loretta! She should have known Lena wasn't a bitch to take lightly. Nasir is the only way I can keep my memories of Big Marv fresh. and also my only way to cut Loretta straight in the heart, like Freeze did the day he killed Big Marv. Too bad, Nasir had to be "forever the victim".